DARE YOU TO LOVE

A MCCORD FAMILY NOVEL

AMANDA SIEGRIST

Cover Designer: Amanda Siegrist
Photo Provided by: Nikkolia/Sundar/Shutterstock.com
Edited by: Editing Done Write

ALSO BY AMANDA SIEGRIST

A happy ending is all I need.

McCord Family Novel

Protecting You

Trust in Love

Deserving You

Always Kind of Love

Finding You

Holiday Romance Novel

Merry Me

Mistletoe Magic

Christmas Wish

Snowed in Love

Snowflakes and Shots

Holiday Hope

Sleigh All the Way

Perfect For You Novel

The Wrong Brother

The Right Time

The Easy Part

The Hard Choice

Conquering Fear Novel

1

_____

When the world starts going to shit, there's nothing to do except pull up a lawn chair, grab a beer, and enjoy the show. At least, that was something his dad had said a time or two.

But he wasn't his dad.

Far from it. Some days, very rare days, he wished he was a bit more like his old man. Carefree. Lackadaisical. Didn't give a shit about anyone but himself. If he could be more like that, life wouldn't be so hard.

Leaving wouldn't be so hard.

It was time for Dare to leave. To hit the road and find... Shit. He had no idea. That was the problem.

"Knock, knock. I brought pie."

Dare chuckled at his sister's cheerful voice filtering from the living room. Served him right for not locking the door, something he was terrible at most of the time. More so because he hated the feeling of being confined, and locking the door signified no way out to him. Now he'd have to deal with his sister, and he wasn't in the mood. Right now, he wasn't sure what he was feeling, and that made it iffy to be around him. He'd either be cordial and the happy, loving brother he could be. Or the macho asshole who pretended he didn't care about anything or anyone, Deja included. The part of his dad that lived inside him.

The only credit he'd give his dad was he had always loved his mom. Those two had been inseparable. Which was nice to think about—except they loved each other so much, they forgot about their kids. Or maybe they didn't know how to share their love. Maybe having kids was something they did and then decided, eh, we shouldn't have done that.

In the end, it didn't matter. They were gone. It was his fault, and there was nothing he could do to change that. If he could change things, he would in a heartbeat. He'd rather have a deadbeat mom and dad around than not at all.

Before Deja could invade his bedroom—and see his empty duffle bag sitting on the bed—he met her in the living room. She'd ask questions about why the duffle bag was out, and he wasn't prepared to answer them. Or how to answer them. He wasn't even sure why he pulled the thing out of his closet. He had no plan where to go—yet.

She smiled and threw her head in the direction of the kitchen and didn't wait to see if he would follow. She assumed he would, and of course, he did. The apple pie she set on the counter smelled divine. He wasn't in the mood for pie, but he wasn't going to say no to a piece either.

Deja pulled out a knife and sliced right into it, cutting a large piece. Then she grabbed a plate and fork, scooped the piece onto the plate, and handed it to him.

"So?"

So the pie was either to cheer him up from potential bad news or celebrate the good news. Either way, she was covered. Now he had to fess up which one it was.

He took the pie, forked off a huge piece, and bit into the deliciousness. His sister had come a long way in her baking skills. It helped her husband, Emmett, loved pie—as did his brothers and cousins—so pie was a huge staple in the family. She had to improve her skills quickly if she wanted to impress the McCord men. Not that she was ever about impressing anyone. They either liked her or didn't; she didn't care either way. So she said. He was the same way. But deep down inside, he wanted to be liked. He wanted people to see the real him and not turn away, disgusted by what they saw.

"Do you enjoy torturing me? Spit it out already," Deja said exasperatingly.

He took another bite, savoring the tart flavor before offering a half-smile. "I'm off parole. I'm a free man."

And I plan to leave town as soon as possible.

Though, he didn't have the nerve to confess that yet. His sister would hate it. It would crush her. She'd never understand why he had to leave. She'd run down the list of how great it was for him here.

He had a job—thanks to Emmett. Mowed lawns and made a decent wage.

He had a place to live—thanks to Ethan, Emmett's brother. Low rent that made it easier to save money on the side.

He had friends—thanks to his sister. She married into a good family, who were good to him, even when he felt like he didn't deserve it.

He had it made in this small town—for a felon.

And he still wanted to leave. He felt trapped for some reason. Hell, he couldn't even explain it to himself. Trying to explain it to his sister would be an epic failure. She'd end up with hurt feelings, and he'd have Emmett on his doorstep, hollering in his face for upsetting her. And rightly so. Because the last thing he wanted to do was hurt his sister. All he ever did was hurt her.

She stared at him for the longest time before whooping with joy and flinging her arms around him. He managed to hold onto the plate while wrapping an arm around her.

"I had hoped your last meeting would go well..."

Her words trailed off, leaving off what she truly wanted to say. *I would've gone with you.*

When she had asked if she could, and he denied her, he had seen the fight in her eyes. But Deja had come to learn since he'd been released over a year ago that once he made up his mind, it was hard to budge.

He hadn't anticipated anything going wrong today when he met with his parole officer for the last time. He followed the rules. He didn't break the law. He stayed away from his old life. He had a steady job and a good place to live. He'd acclimated back into society better than most did, he figured. His parole officer had never given him an infraction for anything. All good marks to confirm he'd served his time. But one could never predict the future. Anything could've happened. He'd learned early in life things could change on a dime.

Look at what one drive in the rain did to him.

He killed his parents.

"Hey." Deja tapped his shoulder. "You okay?"

He nodded, shaking off the memories he tried hard to forget. No matter how hard he tried, it never worked. They lived with him daily, night and day. Every hour. Every minute. Every second.

"Enjoying this pie. I'm shocked Emmett didn't come with you."

Or Ethan. While Emmett was a decent guy and perfect

for his sister, Dare got along with Ethan a lot more. The dude was as close to a best friend he'd ever had. It'd be hard to leave Ethan, too.

So why in the hell was he planning on leaving?

"Trust me, he wanted to, but you know." She shrugged, fiddling with the edge of the pie pan. "He doesn't want to crowd you. We even talked about having dinner at our house. With everybody."

"That's okay. I'm cool. I don't need all this. The pie is fine. Don't do a big thing for me. I hate parties."

She chuckled. "Which is what I told him. He's happy for you. We all are."

It still felt weird to hear. That someone other than Deja cared about him. That a whole family that didn't have to care worried about him and how he was feeling. Sometimes, the McCords could be too smothering. Always in each other's business. Constantly getting together and hanging out. They definitely weren't like his family. Not that he would even consider his parents much of parents. They hadn't cared about anyone but themselves.

And what did he do? Instead of being there for his sister —because his parents never had any intention of doing so— he not only screwed up his life, but he made Deja's life hell, too. Leaving her alone at sixteen to fend for herself. Making life more difficult than it had to be.

Now he was thinking about upending her life once more. Except the big difference this time: she wouldn't be alone. She'd have Emmett and the rest of the McCord family to lean on. As much as they pretended he was a part of that family, too, he wasn't. He never would be.

"You don't like the pie?"

He shook his head, as if clearing the rest of the melancholy feelings that teetered on driving him over the edge. He cracked a grin and took another bite.

"Na, it's delicious."

"You seem...not as happy as I thought you'd be."

"It's just another day, D. I don't know what you want me to say."

Because he sure in the hell wasn't going to part with the truth—not yet, anyway. He might've pulled his duffle bag out of the closet, but he hadn't packed it. Not yet.

Maybe he wouldn't leave.

Though his skin was crawling with unease. Like he had to leave. As if, if he didn't burn rubber out of town soon, he'd burn in hell or some crazy shit.

"Right. Okay." Her lips arched up as if she could hide her trepidation from him. She knew he was holding back but didn't want to press. He was grateful she understood him and his erratic moods.

"So, no dinner tonight. I get it if you don't want that."

"I don't. I have two jobs I need to do today, and then I'll veg out on the couch and watch baseball."

Typical day in his life. Work, eat, sleep, repeat. There wasn't much else for him to do. Besides hanging out with Deja and the McCords on occasion. Ethan tried to get him to date, setting him up with a few women. It never went very far. As soon as they learned he was a felon, they retreated. He learned to confess right up front so he could avoid all the awkwardness. Why set himself up for heartbreak down the road? If they didn't like him—all the nasty parts of him—then they weren't worth his time. He eventually told Ethan to knock it off. Even Deja stopped trying to set him up. Because she'd been worse than Ethan, thinking the sweet, charming ladies around the neighborhood would be dying to get in his arms. Not every woman liked a bad boy. He couldn't consider himself anything other than that.

"I'm sure Emmett—"

"Knows that I will do my job like I always do. I don't need the whole day off, D. Thanks for the pie. Tyrone should be here soon to pick me up."

Which translated into 'Get out. I'm done.' Of course, he wouldn't say that to her. He could control his temper, his annoyance when he tried. When it came to his sister, he tried hard not to lose control. Hurting her was the last thing he ever wanted to do.

"Okay, I'll leave you alone." She held her hands up in surrender, laughing. "Ava and Zane are having a small get-together tomorrow at the farm. It has nothing to do with you. So I expect you there."

"Why?"

It's as if his sister sensed his need to flee. That if he wasn't close to her at all times, he'd slip away without a word. While he wanted to leave town, he'd never do it without saying good-bye first. It was a dumb question he asked, but he wanted to hear why it was so important he show up. She didn't like Ava's get-togethers half the time— just like him. Ava worked for the crime scene unit, so she was friends with a lot of cops. Neither of them was comfortable around law enforcement.

"Because I feel like a fish out of water, and I need you there. It makes her parties easier."

He groaned. "You said get-together, not party."

Parties were worse. He hated large crowds. People introducing themselves, wanting to know every aspect of your life. "Hi, I'm so and so. Who are you? What do you do? How long have you lived here? Oh, I hear you were in prison? How was that?"

Maybe the last few questions were never brought out in the open so forthright, but pretty damn close. It was a small town, and news tended to travel fast, especially in certain circles. A small get-together meant he'd know most of the people and wouldn't have to deal with those dumb-ass questions. A party meant the opposite. And he'd have to deal with all of that. It wasn't any of their damn business, yet they made him feel like it was and he had to confess every nasty part himself. More times than not, he did it simply to get them away from him. It always worked. No one wanted to be around a felon—one that killed his parents.

"It's in-between."

Dare scooped a piece of apple pie to stop himself from expressing the anger he could feel bubbling to the surface. What the hell did in-between mean? Why should he have to go? Deja could handle these parties better than him. He always stayed in his own little corner and felt like an outsider every single time.

"Ava has a few friends visiting from New York. Not quite a party, but a bit more than a get-together. Please, Dare, come. For me."

As much as he wanted to, he could never deny his sister.

"Yeah. Fine. For you."

The smile that spread across her face made the anger simmer down inside. But it didn't hamper the desire to leave. If anything, this entire interaction made him want to leave faster.

THE DELICIOUS AROMA swirled in the air, making it impossible for her to resist. Another cookie disappeared from the plate and into her mouth, and she didn't feel an ounce of guilt about it.

"Do I need Eleanor to make another batch?" Ava said, chuckling as she joined Julie in the kitchen, catching her in the act of stealing another cookie.

Julie pulled the decorative plate filled with green vines and purple roses entwined on it closer to her. "You might. If I had known how awesome of a baker Eleanor was, I would've visited much sooner."

Ava put a hand to her heart as if wounded by her words, her mouth round in shock. "Loving cookies more than me. That guts me."

Julie rolled her eyes, giggled, then took another bite, chewing and swallowing before responding. "Girl, you know my love of sweets outweighs about..." She tossed her head back and forth as if pondering it. "Everything. Literally, everything."

Ava snatched a cookie. "I know, which is why I told Eleanor to be prepared for your arrival."

"This is why you're my favorite friend."

"After me, of course." Ashley swept into the kitchen, grabbing a cookie from the plate and chomping with delight.

Julie inclined her head, laughing with both of them. "Oh, of course. You didn't ditch me to move to Minnesota."

"Hey!" Ava's brows rose. "You can't help what the heart wants."

Julie sighed happily, ignoring the slight jealous pang that hit her. "I would've moved in a heartbeat, too. Zane is wonderful." Julie put a tender hand on Ashley's shoulder for a moment. "Just as wonderful as Markus. You both are so lucky."

Unlike her who was currently single and would remain

that way for the foreseeable future. It wasn't as if she didn't want to date, or hadn't dated a few good men in her life. She didn't have the time to date. Well, if she wanted to be completely honest with herself, she didn't *make* the time. Work was her life, and she was fine with that.

Most days, she was fine with it. She shouldn't lie to herself. Some days, she ached to have what her best friends had it hurt to the point she wanted to cry. And crying wasn't something she did often. The last time she cried had been when Ava was shot, fighting for her life, and realizing they could lose her like they had lost Jimmy.

Ava and Ashley shared a look, and Julie wanted to roll her eyes at what they were most likely thinking. But she didn't because then it would bring up the conversation she didn't want to have. Which, if it happened, would be her fault for commenting about their respective husbands.

Being the last single friend in their group had its ups and downs. Most days, more downs than ups. They'd been best friends for as long as Julie could remember. She, Ava, and Ashley conquering high school with chaotic fun. Rolling through college like they were on a mission. Getting jobs that proved women were as smart and capable as men. Ava, of course, as a crime scene investigator—not only investigating, but running the department, too, in one of the biggest cities in the country. Ashley was one of the best prosecuting attorneys in New York working for the District Attorney's office. Julie was equally proud of herself for getting into the FBI and working with some of the best agents there was. There wasn't a case that scared her. Then in popped Markus and Mahone, two good detectives that fit well into their group. Then Ashley fell in love with Markus and got married. Of course, Jimmy, Zane's brother, had been a part of their group, too, before he tragically died. That's when everything changed. The dynamics in their friendship morphed into something that she wished she could turn back time. Go back to the old ways. Not that she blamed Jimmy. He had died saving Ava's life, for which everyone was grateful. Sad, but grateful.

Ashley and Markus had a sweet, adorable baby girl, Cora, who was around twenty-two months old or something. She could never keep up with the milestones, although she always nodded and smiled when Ashley prattled on about her daughter. Julie was happy for her. Even though sometimes those stories killed her deep inside, she would never let it show. She wasn't jealous that Ashley had a child because she wasn't even sure she wanted kids. It wasn't a feeling that hit her often, and she was to the point in her life where it should hit her. She wasn't getting any younger, and the older she got, the harder it would be to have kids. What affected her most was the fact Ashley had someone to spend her life with and she didn't. That's what she wanted. That's what she craved so much that some days she thought she'd go crazy.

Ava and Zane had their little boy, Jimmy, who was fifteen or sixteen months old. Again, she couldn't remember all the things her friends told her. He was walking and talking and getting into everything like Cora. That's all Julie knew.

Mahone, who had been her partner in crime when Ava left New York to move to Minnesota, finally found a decent woman who could put up with his annoying ways. That left her the lone wolf in the group. All alone. Unattached. Lonely.

But jealousy was an ugly creature, and she never allowed it to emerge. She was happy for her friends, and no nasty beast inside would change her mind.

"You two need to stop looking at me like I'm going to

start crying or something." She hid her wince but hated how that sounded more snappish than she intended.

"Well, you aren't, right?" Ava asked in a soft tone.

"Why would I?"

Geez, she made one comment about how happy she was for the both of them and it had to turn into something that it wasn't.

That she was jealous.

"I tried to set her up with the new cute attorney that recently started and she refused," Ashley said, grabbing another cookie.

"I don't have time to date." And if she decided to start dating, it wasn't going to be with a lawyer. No, thanks.

Ava scoffed. "You never have time. You need to start making time."

"Maybe I don't want what you two have."

Liar!

Ava and Ashley stared at her as if she had lost her mind. They knew she was lying to them as much as she was lying to herself. Silence stretched for a long time before Julie started laughing. Slowly, the other two joined her.

"That was the dumbest thing I've said today. Of course, I want what you two have." Julie shoved the plate away, not liking the thought that she wasn't eating because the cookies were so delicious. More like she was eating to keep the pity party at bay. "How did we veer on this depressing topic? I didn't come to visit you to talk about my love life."

Ava walked around the island that stood between them and pulled her in for a hug. "I know, but it doesn't mean we can't talk about it while you're here. Maybe you'll meet someone, fall in love, and move closer to me. I miss you two way too much."

"So if this happens, can we talk Ashley into moving

then?" she asked, hopeful, although she knew that would never happen.

For one. She didn't fall in love that quickly. In fact, she couldn't recall a time she had ever fallen in love. In lust, sure. Infatuation, yeah. But love? No man had ever captured her heart that way—and probably never would. She was a realist, not someone who lived in the clouds. For two, Ashley would never upend her family for her friends. And Julie would never ask her to. Nor would Ava. She had only been joking.

"If Julie falls in love and moves here, you damn well know I will, too," Ashley said before Julie could reply to Ava.

Then they all started giggling.

"You would never," Julie said.

Ashley smirked and shrugged. "You never know. So keep your eyes peeled."

For a man? Here, in this small town? Yeah, sure, okay. She'd keep her eyes peeled. She couldn't even find a man to love in New York, and it had way more men to choose from.

She was here to enjoy herself. A well-needed vacation that she hadn't had in a long time. Over two years, if she had to guess. When Ava called asking if she, Ashley and Markus, and Mahone and his girlfriend wanted to come spend some time on the farm, she couldn't resist. Of course, it didn't mean she didn't bring work with her. She didn't know how not to work.

The back door suddenly opened, sending in a rush of hot air. Although Julie knew Minnesota wasn't cold all year round, it was surprisingly hotter than she anticipated it would be in early June.

The man that stepped in had her sucking in a sharp, inaudible breath.

He had short, buzzed hair, a strong jawline—which she

always loved—a nice dose of scruff that made him look more enticing rather than him needing to shave, and the most piercing blue eyes she'd ever seen. His gaze hit hers, and she swore if there hadn't been a counter behind her, she would've fallen to the floor in a heap of goo.

Then, just as quickly, his gaze left her and hit Ava, leaving her feeling a weird, aching loss. She didn't even know this man to be feeling this way. But what could she say? It was hard to look away from such a sexy guy. Her eyes were definitely peeled open right now.

She jumped when he set a large case of water on the island counter.

"Deja asked me to bring this. Where would you like it? Is there a cooler or something somewhere?"

Her heart pitter-pattered at his smooth, yet with a hint of roughness, voice. Solid and strong.

What the hell was wrong with her?

She never got this goo-goo-eyed over a man. This was what happened when her friends wanted to talk about dating. Her imagination went overboard at the first sight of a guy she didn't know.

"Yeah, there's a bunch of coolers in the backyard. The green one is filled with some water. Add it to that one. I appreciate it." Then Ava pointed at them. "These are my friends from New York. Julie," Ava said as she tossed a finger at her. "And Ashley," redirecting her finger. "Ladies, this is Dare, Deja's brother, who is married to Emmett, Zane's cousin."

Julie knew all the names of everyone because Ava talked about her family often when they chatted on the phone. She didn't know faces, though.

So this was Dare. The guy who served time for a crime that was sadder than anything.

Ashley said hello first. He responded in kind. Julie realized she was staring instead of doing the polite thing and greeting him.

"Nice to meet you."

Although his look hadn't been friendly when he walked in. It had been indifferent more than anything. He now looked at her with disgust. Perhaps she hadn't hidden her surprise as well as she thought. But she hadn't expected him to be so...well, she didn't know what she expected him to be. She didn't know him well, only knew so much based on the few things Ava had shared.

He nodded in her direction but didn't say anything.

"I'll take this outside."

Then he picked up the water and walked out.

"Whew." Ashley blew out a breath, laughing. "He's sort of intense."

A short chuckle left Ava's lips as a tiny smile appeared. "He's been through a lot. Deja told us yesterday he's officially off parole. I'm sure that's a huge relief for him. He can now focus on the future and not his past."

"He didn't seem overly joyed about that." Or about anything. Julie figured with news like that, he'd be walking around with a smile permanently on his face. She would. Not that she'd ever get arrested for something in her life. Of course, when she thought about it, he probably hadn't expected to get into a car accident that night while driving high.

"Oh, Dare doesn't express his emotions much. I'm not surprised. It takes a lot to get him to smile. He's nice, though. Quiet and keeps to himself, but he's a good guy. Everyone makes mistakes," Ava said, as if pointing out Julie's mistakes to her face.

Yeah, but big ones like killing his parents while high?

No, definitely not. While she wouldn't refute that she'd made mistakes in life, she'd never made any with so large of a price. Though, Julie didn't like to judge a person until she knew them, so she'd keep her thoughts to herself.

And she'd keep her distance. His glare at her before he walked out said she should.

2

The bench bounced as weight hit it, and then a beer appeared in front of his face.

"It looked like you could use another one," Ethan said, taking a gulp of the beer he held.

Dare polished off his old beer that was nearly empty, picked up the new one, and tilted it in Ethan's direction in thanks.

"I don't plan to get shit-faced here, but thanks."

"You seem like you're in a mood. I figured with the good news yesterday, you'd be a little more cheerful."

Yeah, well, so did he. But with the thoughts about leaving plaguing his mind night and day, it was hard to be cheerful. His sister would be crushed when he told her.

Not to mention, while Ava's friends seemed nice enough, they didn't like him. He could tell by their expressions when he was introduced.

Especially that Julie chick. The way her eyes flared with recognition. The wariness that hit her gaze. Like he was a bad guy and was out to hurt everyone who stepped into his path. Like he shouldn't even be here and around such good, law-abiding people.

Whatever. Each and every one of them could go screw themselves. His sister was so lucky he loved her because otherwise, he would've left the minute he finished putting the water in the cooler. Hell, he would've left that water to sit in the heat, that's how much he wanted to leave right away.

"What's up?" Ethan prodded.

Dare wasn't in the mood. Not today. Or any other day.

He took a long pull of his beer instead of answering.

"Go ahead. Ignore me all you want. I won't quit."

Dare chuckled, despite not meaning to. "This I know." He took another large gulp before saying, "I don't want to talk about it."

Ethan nodded his head as if knowing no matter how much he poked and prodded, Dare wouldn't give in until he was ready. It didn't mean Ethan would forget; he'd just let it go for the time being.

"So Penelope and I finally decided on a wedding date. In April."

Almost a whole year from now. He was surprised they hadn't gotten hitched already. They lived together and had since close to the time they reconnected back in October. They'd talked about getting married often, yet could never decide on a date. He was happy for Ethan.

Maybe he'd even come back for it.

No. He'd have to come back for it. Ethan was a good friend. Better than he'd ever had in his life. Even before he went to prison. He'd had friends, but not good ones. Not that he was blaming any of his old friends, but hanging with them and doing what they had done had led him to the path he was currently on.

"Congrats, man."

Ethan fiddled with his bottle. "I love my brothers. They mean the world to me."

Dare twisted his head toward him, nodding. "They're good dudes. You're lucky."

What an odd thing to say. He knew Ethan and his brothers were close. At times, Dare was jealous of them and how close they were. Sure, he loved his sister, but he didn't like getting too close to her. Not like they used to be before he went to prison. Because all he'd end up doing was hurting her once again.

"I want you to be my best man."

Dare flinched. "What?"

"I could never pick between Emmett and Gabe. I'd hate for one of them to get hurt by it or something. When I thought about who else would be perfect, you're the first person that popped in my head. So what do you say?"

Be his best man? Shit. Didn't that role come with responsibility and shit? Like planning a bachelor party and whatnot? How could he do all of that when he didn't plan to stick around town?

"And you're not saying anything?"

"Your brothers might be hurt you aren't picking one of them."

When Emmett got married to his sister, Austin and Sophie also got married. It had been a double wedding. They had decided not to have any attendants in the wedding. The four of them stood at the altar, and it had been a beautiful affair. Ethan never had to worry about who Emmett might've picked as his best man. Dare figured if Emmett had picked Gabe, Ethan would've been hurt, though he might've never voiced it. Ethan was right to be leery about choosing between his brothers, but it didn't mean picking him was a good choice.

"They won't be. This is what I want."

"They're your brothers."

"And so are you," Ethan all but snapped.

Dare tilted his head, shock reverberating around him. Did Ethan honestly see him like that? In a way, they were brothers by marriage. That's what he had to have meant.

"I tell you things that I don't even tell my brothers sometimes. You're an important part of my life—even if you haven't been in it long—and I want you standing up next to me when I get married."

Dare looked away. Ashamed. Disgusted with himself.

"I don't deserve that honor. I'm leaving."

He heard Ethan inhale a sharp breath. Then a hand hit his shoulder softly.

"What are you talking about?"

"This town. I'm leaving. Soon."

"Why?"

Dare didn't want to answer the harsh question that snapped out of Ethan's mouth with such venom. Not because he was afraid to tell Ethan, but because he had no idea why. He still couldn't explain to himself why he felt the need to flee.

The hand on his shoulder turned from soft to fierce. Ethan shoved him hard enough so he was looking straight at him and almost fell off the bench.

"You're off parole and suddenly you want to leave. What the hell?"

"I don't fit in here." Dare look down because he couldn't stand the hurt in Ethan's eyes. "I don't fit in anywhere."

"Knock it off. Stop this self-pity shit right now."

Dare snapped his gaze up. "That's not what I'm doing."

Ethan rolled his eyes. "Okay, you keep telling yourself that. Did you tell Deja yet?"

"No. You're the first person."

"Good, don't say a word to her because you're not leaving. Because it'll crush her, and then you'll be answering to Emmett."

Dare snorted. "I'm not afraid of Emmett."

"I know, but you should be very afraid of me. Because I'll step in to stop Emmett and really show you the pain."

It was hard to imagine Ethan getting so pissed. Yet, he remembered when Ethan shoved Gabe against the wall a few months back after finding out he married a random woman and that he might leave town with that same random woman. The rage. The fear. Dare had felt it clear across the room. He'd finally stepped in and grabbed Ethan off Gabe and had to use all his strength to hold him back. He knew how strong Ethan was. It didn't matter. If he wanted to leave, he'd leave, even if he had to get into a fight about it. He'd take the beating, but it wouldn't stop him.

Yeah, if they ever got into a brawl, it'd be a helluva fight. Neither would give in, doling out a world of pain.

"You'll be my best man. You'll stay in town. You won't break your sister's heart."

"Is that right?"

Nobody told him what to do. Not even a good friend— damn near close to being a brother.

"Yes, that's right."

They stared at each other, both breathing heavily, as if waiting for the other to throw a punch. Start the fight right now and get it over with.

"Is it okay if I sit here?"

They both jerked their attention to the other side of the picnic table where Julie—the one who thought him a loser

—stood looking apprehensive. No doubt she felt the tension swirling around the table. Why was she even over here? There were plenty of tables scattered around the yard to pick and she had to pick this one. What was her endgame?

"Yep. Please have a seat," Ethan said with a charming smile, switching his expression like a damn light switch. Dare wanted to punch him for that annoying trait.

She sat down, barely making eye contact with him. Shit. First arguing with Ethan, and now he had to endure sitting with a woman who judged him without even knowing him. Same old shit, new person. He could only assume Ava told all her friends about his past. They knew he was a felon and made assumptions about him—like everyone did.

That was why he wanted to leave.

Make a fresh start. Meet new people who had no clue about his past. Not unless he chose to tell them about it. What right did Ava have to share things about him with people he didn't even know? Damn nosy busybody. Always getting into people's shit like she had a right to.

Ethan turned toward the red barn where Penelope stood, waving at him. "I'll be right back."

"Whatever." He didn't care that made him sound like a petulant child.

"I'll take that as the conversation is over."

He snorted again, giving Ethan the middle finger. "That's what I think about what you had to say. Nobody tells me what to do, Ethan. Not even you."

"Watch me." Then he threw a charming smile at Julie. "Ignore his sour attitude. The heat always makes him cranky."

Dare rolled his eyes at that but didn't look at Julie to see what she thought of Ethan's words. He didn't care what this woman thought of him. Or what anyone thought of him.

They'd think what they'd like about him, regardless of anything else. So why should he care what they thought? Nothing he did ever changed their mind anyway.

"I'm sorry."

At that, his gaze drew to hers. Her golden-hazel eyes were filled with regret. Why? What the hell was she apologizing for?

"Mom? Dad?"

The ringing in his ears drowned out any other sounds besides the pounding of the rain on the roof of the car. He tried blinking, but his eyes felt glued shut.

No.

Covered with something.

Dare's arm ached as he reached up, wiping at his eyes. He blinked a few more times, finally able to see.

An icky crimson stared back at him as his hand wobbled in the air. Blood. The world went black again as more trailed down his head over his eyes.

"Shit..." He reached up, swiping his sleeve against his forehead, crying out in pain.

Now he knew why his head radiated with pain. He had a huge gash, which was gushing blood down his face.

A groan next to him startled him.

"Dad?"

Preparing for the pain, he reached up and smoothed his sleeve across the wound and his eyes once again. His dad was hunched over, his seatbelt holding him in place.

"Dad?" Dare shook his dad's shoulder, eliciting another groan but nothing else. "Shit."

Rain continued to pour from the sky, beating on the hood. He flinched when he realized it was also hitting him. Turning toward where the windshield should've been, he blinked rapidly and leaned forward, jerking when the seatbelt stopped his momentum.

"Mom!"

His vision blurred again, but this time not only from the blood still pouring down his face—from the image before him.

His windshield was busted, the rain saying hello with a vengeance because it could. It had a large opening to do whatever the hell it wanted.

On the ground, several feet from the car, lay his mother. Her right arm was bent in an unnatural position, as was her left leg. Her eyes stared straight ahead, right at him. Yet, he knew she wasn't seeing him. She wasn't seeing anything. Her neck was also bent in an unnatural position.

His mother was dead.

Because of him.

His arm lifted, feeling like lead, as he swiped across his wound, excruciating pain vibrating across his entire body as he did so. Yet, he didn't cry out. He didn't bellow in pain. He took it, every moment of it, because he deserved it.

"Dad?"

Dare tried shoving his shoulder again, garnering another moan.

"Dad, wake up!"

His dad lifted his head, groaning. "Donna, baby?"

It didn't matter Dare had told her to put her seatbelt on. It didn't matter his dad had agreed with him and told her as well. She didn't listen. That didn't even matter.

The only thing that mattered was he crashed and he caused this.

His dad would never forgive him.

"I'm sorry."

His whispered words were drowned out by the torrential

downpour. Even that didn't matter. Because his dad made a face after looking out the window, his body seizing up and slumping once again against his seatbelt.

THE LOOK of disgust on his face in the house earlier should've warned her to keep her distance. The look of pure hatred right now said she should get up and walk away before something terrible happened.

But she couldn't. A part of her refused to listen to the sensible side.

The party had been going on for a few hours, and this was the first time she had a chance to get closer to him. She felt terrible about how she must've reacted when Ava introduced them. Julie told herself to stay away from him, but as she saw him sitting by himself for a while, she knew she couldn't. She had to apologize for her reaction. It was rude and uncalled for.

Ethan joining him had put a damper in her plans. When it looked like they were arguing, she thought it was a good time to join them. The last thing she wanted was something ruining Ava's party. Or her vacation. She was here to enjoy herself, not witness a fight—because she had felt the war brewing even from across the yard.

Of course, it didn't seem like the tension had wavered, even though Ethan walked away. If anything, it had increased.

His piercing blue-eyed stare unnerved her. She couldn't say why. Not much scared her. She'd come face-to-face with her share of bad people in her line of work. She even had to pull her gun once—thankfully didn't have to shoot it. But the way he glared at her unnerved her down to her very soul. As if he could carve her to pieces with his penetrating gaze.

His jaw was clenched hard, the muscles contracting in his cheek. Although his deep, hard gaze frightened her, the man himself didn't scare her. She felt secure in his presence that he might lash out at her with words, but not with his hands.

She cleared her throat when he didn't say anything.

"I'm sorry for our introduction earlier. Ava's told us about everyone in her family, and I let my mind wander to..." *Your past* sounded so wrong and disrespectful, but it was the truth. "I'm sorry if I looked shocked. She shared your wonderful news that you're off parole. Congratulations. Not that it's any of my business. And I'm muddling this up. I just...you looked angry at me when you walked out. You don't look very happy with me right now, and I want you to know I'm sorry. That's all."

She added a smile at the end as if that would help any of the word vomit that spewed out of her mouth sound better.

He continued to stare at her for the longest time. For the life of her, she couldn't look away. She didn't touch the sandwich on her plate or the chips piled high next to it. She didn't wipe the strand of hair that blew into her face and then back out as the wind lightly whipped around them. She held his strong gaze, refusing to look away.

"Okay."

Okay? That's all he was going to say? What did it mean?

She twitched, forcing her smile to remain. "Okay."

If he could use the simple word, well, so could she.

A hint of a grin emerged on his handsome, scruffy face. So subtle, if she hadn't been maintaining eye contact with him, she would've missed it.

"Care to share what you two were arguing about?"

"Nosy much? I see why you're such good friends with Ava."

She chuckled, despite knowing he hadn't said that as a compliment. It was true. She was being nosy. Maybe it was her line of work, always looking for the truth, looking for clues and evidence to bring the perps to justice. She had a hard time keeping her nose out of things she should. With him almost displaying a smile—sort of a peace offering— she figured why not jump right in. She was never one to mince words—with anyone.

"Well, you did have words in front of me at the end. It's not as if I eavesdropped in the beginning."

"It's none of your business what we were talking about."

"Okay."

He took a sip of his beer, another grin hiding behind the bottle. She would swear on it.

"Okay."

She couldn't hold back a smile at his response.

Silence grew between them. She picked up her sandwich and took a bite, chewing before deciding she should say something. She came over here to apologize, which she did. She could now make small talk and act like there wasn't a weird, icky tension still swirling around them.

"So what do you do, Dare?"

He snorted. "You know what I do."

Well, okay, she did. Ava had mentioned he worked for Emmett mowing lawns and such. Of course, he knew Ava had shared that, just like she shared about his prior history with the law. She was only trying to be nice and pretend she hadn't known. So they could have a pleasant conversation.

It wasn't going to work. Not if they weren't on the same page to wipe away the history.

"Let's pretend I don't know."

"Why the hell would I do that?"

Could he make this any more difficult for her? Did he enjoy torturing her?

"I'm trying to be nice and have a conversation."

"Why? You don't have to pretend to like me. My feelings ain't hurt."

Somehow she doubted that. He hid it well, though. Behind his tough exterior and bad attitude. Pretending like nothing hurt him.

She blew out a breath, a low chuckle releasing. "Let's start over. Please. I'm not pretending to like you. I don't even know you. So that's why I'm trying to have a conversation to get to know you, so I can decide whether I want to like you or not. You're making it very difficult."

The irritating man simply stared at her with a sly grin on his face. As if he was thoroughly enjoying making every moment of this painful.

She held her hand out across the table. "Hi. I'm Julie Russo. I'm Ava's friend from New York. We've known each other since we were eleven. Nice to meet you."

He continued to stare at her.

Wow.

He was going to be a jerk and not meet her halfway. She was trying here. To make up for her rudeness in the house.

Well, she didn't get to where she was in life by giving up.

She kept her hand in the air, waiting for him to make the next move.

THIS CHICK WAS WEIRD. Why did she care so much about talking with him? She apologized. He accepted it. End of story. Now he wanted her to go away and leave him alone.

No matter how much she wanted to act like his past didn't matter, it did. It always did.

But she clearly wasn't going to get up and walk away. Her hand still hung in the air, and the longer she held it out, the more he looked like a jackass.

Fine. He'd play her dumb game.

The moment his hand curled around her delicate fingers, the air around them electrified with energy. He swore he even felt a jolt run through his arm and down his body to his very toes. The way she subtly jerked, she had felt it, too.

He had a strange urge to rub his thumb against her hand. Feel the softness of her skin. Maybe even pull it closer so he could—

"This is where you introduce yourself."

Her voice startled him. Enough to realize he'd been holding her hand and saying nothing.

But this was dumb, and he felt stupid introducing himself like she had.

Of course, her grip was strong, despite how tiny her fingers felt in his large palm. She wasn't about to let him get out of this.

Say something, idiot.

Because the longer they held hands like this, the more likely someone would see them and come over asking what the hell they were doing.

"I'm Dare."

He tried to extract his hand, but she wouldn't let him go.

"This is not how introductions go. You're supposed to let go of my hand when I want it back," he said with gritted teeth as if holding her hand were bothering him.

And damn it, it was, but not the way she thought. His body was starting to react in a way that hadn't happened in a very long time. His senses were charged and ready to go. He wanted to stand up, pull her closer, and kiss her.

Which would be the worst kind of move in history. He didn't even like her. She judged him without even knowing him. It didn't matter how much he thought she was one of the most gorgeous women he had ever met. Her long brown hair. Her hazel eyes. Sweet, kissable lips that enticed him to move closer every second that passed.

"You didn't fully introduce yourself."

"You're being ridiculous. Let go before someone sees."

She leaned forward and smiled—a wicked, delicious smile that had him wanting to inch closer himself. Snatch a kiss like he had a right to. "Are you embarrassed if someone sees us? We're shaking hands."

"There is no shaking going on."

Like the annoying ant she was being, she started to move their hands as if shaking in greeting. "Hi. I'm Julie—"

"Stop. Fine." He groaned and rolled his eyes. "Hi. I'm Darrian Wilson. People call me Dare, though. My sister is married to the idiot Emmett, who's cousins with your friend's husband. I spent ten years in prison for killing my parents. Nice to meet you, too."

Her eyes rounded and she trembled, finally letting go of his hand.

"That was not the sort of introduction I expected."

He shrugged. "That's the sort of introduction I give."

"Seriously?"

"Yep."

She cocked a brow, making her look even more attractive for some odd reason. Damn it. He didn't want to think anything about her was attractive in any way. What he wanted was for her to go away.

"You're telling me you tell people you were in prison. Just like you did. That you killed your parents."

"Well, I did."

"Ava said—"

"Ava needs to keep her damn mouth shut. It wasn't her business to tell any of her friends about me." His jaw was tight, his teeth grinding against each other. It hurt, but he deserved the pain. "I've been on a few dates since I've been released. I've found it's easier to tell the truth upfront. This way I'm not wasting my time. They don't stick around after hearing about my past. So yeah, that's how I introduce myself."

Her mouth opened wide. "Yeah, idiot, because you say it so brutally."

Now she thought he was an idiot. At least she wasn't afraid of him.

He frowned. "How should I say it? What's a good way to say I killed my parents? Tell me. So I know for next time."

She sat back, slouching some, her lips pressed together instead of wide open with shock. "I don't know. But there has to be a better way."

"Because once people know they'll accept me and like me anyway? Like you did. I didn't even tell you myself, and you proved it doesn't matter how I say it—or if *I* even say it."

She cast her eyes down to her plate before meeting his gaze once again. "You're right. And I said I'm sorry."

He wanted to mutter 'okay' like he had the last time, but he couldn't get the simple word out. Because was it okay? Was it okay to keep being treated like an outcast? Like he was a villain who could never be turned into the hero?

Villains were never heroes. No matter how hard they tried.

He wasn't sure how to respond, and clearly, she was baffled herself because they simply stared at each other.

Then a slow smile built on her lips.

Laughter bubbled up his throat and escaped. "Please tell me you're not about to say let's try this damn introduction again. For the third time."

"Why do you ask?" Her laughter sounded sweet and melodic and he wanted to hear it again, despite reminding himself he didn't like her and her judgmental ways.

"Because you started to smile and it had a craftiness hiding behind it. I'm not doing that shit again."

"Well, I wasn't going to say that. Although I wouldn't be opposed to it."

He rolled his eyes. "What were you going to say?"

She shrugged. "Nothing. I was smiling, and you jumped down my throat about it."

He wasn't sure if he believed her or not. But he wasn't opposed to her smiles. How could he extract another one out of her?

Wait, what? Did he want to keep talking to her? Maybe a small part of him did. This was the most interesting conversation he'd had in a long time. Kept him on his toes.

"So what do you do?" he asked, taking a drink of his beer.

Bingo!

A beautiful, brilliant smile lit up her face. Because despite not starting the dumb introductions over, he was attempting the conversation she so wanted. It was worth asking the question to see her red, succulent lips curl upward.

"I work for the FBI."

He nearly spewed his beer everywhere but managed to keep it in, which made the liquid go down the wrong tube.

He started coughing and didn't manage to clear his throat for a good minute. The entire time, she sat there eating and chewing her sandwich like he wasn't having a mini choking attack.

"Should've known. You've been interrogating me this entire time."

Her brow rose in that adorable, sexy way only she could do. "I've been trying to engage you in conversation, not interrogate you."

"Could've fooled me."

"You are the most exasperating man I have ever met."

That deserved a grin because, oddly enough, he was proud of that fact. He imagined it took a lot to ruffle her feathers. Especially being an FBI agent. She needed to be levelheaded and cool, be in charge and not afraid.

"I'll take that as a compliment."

That delectable brow, still arched, told him it hadn't been one.

3

"**E**ww. I have so much new respect for you."

Ava laughed as she poured the chicken feed into the troughs. "Don't you get up at like six every morning to run?"

Julie pulled her hair back into a ponytail and tied it together. "Yeah, but we're up at five and it stinks in here."

They'd been taking turns helping in the mornings to see the inter-workings of the farm. Today—on day four of their vacation—was her turn. She helped Ava feed the chickens, goats, and then watched her say good morning to all the pigs. Julie didn't know why Ava tortured herself so, naming and talking to the pigs like they were pets. They were all going to get butchered at some point because that's how they made the bulk of their money on the farm. But she didn't say anything. Just followed Ava, silently laughing— and crying—inside. It was pitiful and sad in a way.

They had three more days before they left for home, and Julie was more miserable thinking about it than she anticipated she'd be. Yes, she missed Ava living in the same city, but she'd had a few years to get over it. While this was the first time everyone had visited Ava on her turf, Ava came to visit New York every few months to see her dad. Julie saw her plenty enough that it was okay one of her best friends lived so far away. She still had Ashley close by. Plus, she worked so much these days, she rarely saw Ashley, who lived in the same city.

The misery that had been gradually building and burning a hole in her gut got larger and larger as the end loomed closer. She couldn't say why. So she ignored it because there wasn't anything she could do about it. Once their time was up, she'd leave. She had to.

The party had been wonderful. Julie enjoyed getting to know the McCords and some of Ava's friends she worked with. Of course, her highlight of the day had been chatting with Dare. They'd sat at the picnic table for over an hour talking about...too much it was hard to navigate through it all. She couldn't remember a time she'd enjoyed herself so much *and* was aggravated beyond belief. Dare knew how to push her buttons without even trying. It had been a challenge, and heaven help her, she had a hard time resisting a challenge.

That was the last time she'd seen him. He left the party without saying good-bye, and she hated to admit how much it hurt. She thought they'd connected—in a weird, odd way. Not that he had to say good-bye or owed her anything, but it would've been nice.

"I have to go into work today for a few hours. I hope that's okay."

Like she'd tell Ava it wasn't. She'd already replied to a few emails and chatted with her partner, Tom, several times since she arrived. Work was work, and it was hard to ignore it, even while on vacation.

"Totally fine. Need help?"

Ava froze, her brows arching high as a silly smile emerged. A mixture of dismay and humor. "You're on vacation. You're not coming in to help me. I don't even want to go in, but one of the officers asked me to look at something, and I couldn't resist saying no."

Julie wanted to argue but decided against it. Ava was like her in a lot of respects—probably why they were such good friends. Once they had their mind set on something, it was hard to budge.

But she didn't want to go fishing, which was what was on the agenda today. Austin and Zane were planning on taking them out on the boat to catch some fish and enjoy the sun. It already felt like it was going to be a brutally hot day again. They had gone fishing yesterday. On the dock at a nearby lake. Today they wanted to go on a boat. Julie had never been fond of boats. The rocking motion always made her sick to her stomach.

"You don't have to go fishing today if you don't want."

Ava had finally figured out why she asked to join her at work. Julie appreciated she saw behind the mask, but she also didn't want to be the lone person sitting back. She might need to take some medication before they left on the water, but she could keep everything in—hopefully. How embarrassing to puke in front of her friends and Ava's family.

"In fact, why don't you come into town with me today?"

Ava headed for the exit so she didn't see Julie roll her eyes. "Now you're saying that so I don't make a complete fool of myself."

The humid air hit her face as Ava opened the door and stopped. "Nobody would laugh at you. Ashley knows you get sea sickness, too. I'll be honest, I completely forgot about it when we talked about going fishing on the water. I'm sorry."

"It's okay, don't worry about me."

"No, you're coming to work with me."

Julie laughed as she followed Ava toward the house. "No, I'm not. You already said no, and you can't change your mind."

Ava scoffed. "Watch me."

For the life of her, she couldn't figure out why she insisted on arguing with Ava when she didn't want to fish.

"I'm not going with you."

"Stop being stubborn."

"You're the one being stubborn."

"You've been semi-moody these past few days. Vacation time is supposed to relax you, not make you tense." Ava shoved open the back door, stepping into the cool kitchen.

Julie rolled her eyes again, not even caring that Ashley and Markus had seen the gesture where they stood around the island. Mahone and his girlfriend didn't seem to be in attendance yet. She wasn't going to ask why Ashley and Markus were already up. They were early risers anyway, so it wasn't surprising to see them in the kitchen.

"I'm not moody. I've been enjoying myself."

And she had.

They had relaxed around the house, enjoying each other's company. They had the party, of course. One night they had a bonfire and enjoyed s'mores and beers with the mosquitos being such a nuisance. They had gone fishing and even went on a hike at a nearby trail. All in all, there wasn't anything to complain about or to be moody about. It had been nothing but relaxation since she arrived.

Maybe too much? She was used to being on the go every

single day of every single minute from the moment she woke up. Relaxing was a hard business for her.

But she would not say she had been moody whatsoever.

"What are you two arguing about?" Ashley asked with a gentle smile hiding behind her coffee mug as if that would lessen the tension in the room.

"I told Julie she could come into work with me today because you're all going fishing...on a boat."

Ashley's eyes lit up with recognition. "It completely spaced my mind. You don't have to come with, Julie."

"Ava fails to mention she first told me no I couldn't go to work with her when I first asked. Now she's doing it out of pity."

Ava's mouth dropped open. "Am not."

"Are to."

"Nope."

"Yeah."

"Definitely not."

"You so—"

Markus cleared his throat, stopping the argument. "Why don't you go into town with Ava and do some shopping? You mentioned on the plane getting some trinkets for your nieces and nephews, and we haven't had a chance to shop yet."

It was just like Markus to be the peacekeeper. This wasn't the first time she and Ava—or even her and Ashley— had gotten into a tiff about something so ridiculous. Not that it ever affected their friendship. They argued, they discussed, they spat back and forth, and then they moved on like it never happened.

"I think I will. I'm not in the mood to work anyway."

"Ha!"

Julie smirked at Ava's lame response, knowing quite well

she would've enjoyed helping Ava with whatever she was working on.

"So glad we settled that," Markus said with a devilish smile. Ashley jabbed him playfully in the ribs not to gloat too much.

"What are Eleanor's plans with the kids today?" Ashley asked. "She mentioned the playground."

"Oh, she has a whole list of fun things for them. She is soaking this up. She adores Jimmy and having a little girl to spoil." Ava shook her head. "She's been hinting Zane and I need to try for another one. She wants a little girl."

Eleanor, besides being their longtime housekeeper, was also part of the family. A grandmother of sorts. Since Ava's mom had passed away when she was younger, Julie imagined Ava loved the doting Eleanor displayed. Julie knew she'd hate it if her mother constantly badgered her about kids. Julie already got the badgering about when she was going to get married—of course, so the kids part could come.

She'd get married when the time was right. And when she actually found a man worth marrying. For the kids part, she wasn't sure she wanted any. Work consumed too much of her time—time she didn't mind being consumed—and kids would disrupt that. She wasn't sure she wanted it disrupted. It wouldn't be fair to her kids to work too much either.

"Well, maybe I'll spoil them, too," Julie piped in. That was the perk of being an honorary aunt.

The conversation moved on to the plans for the evening. Another cookout with fish this time instead of hamburgers. They had a nice fire pit set up in the backyard. Julie was curious to find out how fish tasted cooked over a fire. Of course, if they caught enough for them to even have a fish fry.

Before long, Markus, Ashley, and the rest of the gang were on the way to the lake, and she and Ava were headed into town.

"Drop me off at the coffee shop. I could use another cup. Call me when you're done."

Ava found a parking spot not far from the shop. "This town doesn't have a ton of stores to browse. Call me when you get done."

Instead of jumping on a new argument, Julie smiled and hopped out. She waved good-bye, with Ava shaking her head and laughing.

The line wasn't long, and she had her mocha latte in hand and found a table in the corner near the window.

She flinched when a shadow passed over, not expecting anyone to step into her area. Then held in a gasp when she saw who stood in front of her.

Dare.

Her heart pitter-pattered for the first time in regards to a man. She was always cool, calm, and collected. It took a lot for a man to make her unsettled. But one glimpse, one tiny look from this sexy man before her, and she could feel her palms start to sweat and her nerves playing havoc on her senses.

"Hi."

His hello was tentative as if he wasn't even sure he should've come over to speak to her. She understood the hesitation because she could feel it filling her up, but she wouldn't let that stop her from enjoying his company. She'd missed him more than she realized. No way would she admit that's why she'd been slightly moody the past few days.

She nodded, waving a hand at an empty chair. "Join me."

She could still see the hesitation written in his eyes, in the way his body was half-turned toward the door as if ready to flee. But he chose to take a seat. He had a large cup in his hand when he sat down. He lifted it, blowing on the small hole in the lid, and then took a sip. She couldn't look away. Her eyes followed his movement, his lips as they formed a circle to blow and then pressed them to drink.

Oh, dear. She was making a complete fool of herself. Staring like a psychopath ready to make a move.

She looked away, staring at her cup. Fishing was suddenly sounding like the better option. Even with the threat of puking her guts out. She would even take her mother badgering her about settling down over this embarrassment.

"Oh, you know who I saw the other day. David. You remember David from the high school football team?"

Julie barely resisted rolling her eyes. Yes, she remembered David. He was a stuck-up jock who had thought his shit didn't stink back then. She didn't imagine his attitude had changed any. He didn't seem like the type.

"Yep, I do."

"He's a doctor now."

So impressive. Of course, if her mother heard her sarcastic thoughts, she'd never hear the end of it.

"That's nice."

"He's single, too."

Now that was going too far.

"Why does that concern me?"

"I mentioned you, and his eyes seemed to light up."

This time she didn't try to hold back the roll of her eyes. "Mom, I don't need your help finding a guy."

"Well, at this rate, I'll be six feet under for fifty years before you settle down."

"Oh, geez, dramatic much." Julie picked up her glass of water and silently prayed the waiter would come back for their order soon so she could order a glass of wine. If her mom was going to stick on the dating kick the entire lunch, she needed fuel for it.

"Your brother has been married three blissful years and given me two beautiful grandkids. Your sister has been married ten happy years and given me three wonderful grandkids. It's time you joined them."

Her mother was always blunt. No doubt where she got the trait. Julie would agree her brother, Julian, was blissfully married. It was still early in the marriage. His wife, Becky, was an angel. He'd do anything for his wife and kids.

Her sister, Juniper, on the other hand, she wouldn't say she had a happy marriage or wonderful kids. Her kids were the most rambunctious bunch of children she had ever met and they loved to back talk. Her husband, Philip, didn't seem to care about any of them. He was one of the most self-absorbed men she had ever met. Although, Julie doubted Juniper complained to her mother about any of it. She rarely said anything to Julie. But she saw. She always saw everything.

"I'm not ready to join them, Mom. When it's time, it's time. I'll know."

"You won't. You ignore what's in front of you half the time. I got David's number for you. Call him."

"I'm not calling him."

Her mother fiddled with her phone, and a few seconds later, Julie's phone pinged with a text message.

"Call him."

Julie didn't look at her phone or acknowledge her mother again. It was pointless to argue with her. She'd never stop.

"I've always wanted ten grandchildren. It's a nice number. So you better get to it."

Julie laughed. "I'm not having five kids."

"I never said you had to have five, but I don't foresee Juniper having any more. She's getting up there in age. Julian might have one or two more, so that leaves you having at least three. You're not getting any younger either, dear."

Just what every woman wanted to hear. How old they were getting. Three kids! Ha! Julie wasn't even sure she wanted one. Work was her life, and she had no ambition at the moment to have a child. Having a man would be nice—sex was always good to have—but it didn't mean kids would be in her future, even if she found a man she wanted to marry.

"Please, Mom, tell me what you think. I hate reading between the lines."

Her mom waved her hand in the air, shaking her head in disapproval. "Don't get that tone with me. You know I'm only looking out for you."

This she knew. Although her mother could be harsh and downright cruel sometimes with her words, Julie knew she only wanted what she thought was best for her. Her mom loved her. That was never the problem. It was keeping her nose out of her business that she struggled with.

"Call him."

Julie smiled, but not at her mom. The waiter had arrived.

"I'll take a glass of Chardonnay. Largest one you have."

DARE ALMOST DIDN'T STOP and say hi when he saw Julie sitting by herself. But then his nightly dreams—very erotic and oh so naughty dreams—swam through his mind, and he knew he couldn't walk away without saying something to her.

She'd been on his mind since the moment he left the party how many days ago. It aggravated him beyond belief. He didn't like things consuming his energy, especially not a woman who got on his nerves more than anything.

He could feel the awkwardness between them. Sort of how it felt when she first sat down at the picnic table. The longer they had chatted, the more it had dissipated. It was as if they were starting all over again.

"You're by yourself."

Well, duh. Any idiot could see that. Why did that have to be the first thing out of his mouth?

She smiled, finally lifting her gaze back to his. For a moment there, it was as if she had fled the table, lost in her thoughts.

He inhaled deeply, trying to keep his emotions in check. Her smile, with her brilliant hazel eyes, hit him square in the gut. Damn, but he wanted this woman with every breath in his body. Foolish of him. Because it would never happen. She'd never be with a loser like him. He didn't blame her one bit.

"Everyone went fishing today. Again." She chuckled as if he knew the hidden joke.

He forced a grin, although he didn't know why it was funny.

"You don't like fishing?" He could take it or leave it. The McCords loved to fish, so he'd been forced to go more than he liked to.

A shiver touched her body, and he ached to reach out and comfort her somehow. Stop the tremble. Or make her tremble in a completely different way.

Idiot! He had to stop those ridiculous thoughts. It'd bring him nothing but pain.

"I don't like boats. Fishing is okay."

Why didn't she like boats? It took him longer than he cared to admit for it to click. She got seasick. By the slight tint of red on her cheeks, it embarrassed her. It was the first time he'd ever seen such vulnerability from her.

So he decided not to continue with that line of conversation.

"Coffee's good here."

Another gorgeous smile lit up her face and he couldn't help the giddiness that spread through his system. He put that smile on her face. He made her happy with—a pretty lame comment.

"It is. You come here often?"

Idle chit-chat. How odd for them. But refreshing compared to their last interaction.

"Every so often. When I need the extra kick to the system."

Interpreted as he hadn't gotten much sleep the past few nights because his mind had been wide awake thinking about her.

She picked up her phone sitting on the table and glanced at it. "It's only about ten o'clock. You don't have any jobs today?"

Beginning of summer? Hell, no. He always had jobs. Too much sometimes, but he never complained to Emmett. He was grateful for the job. He wouldn't have been hired anywhere else. Not with his record.

"I do. Except the house I normally go to today around this time canceled their contract. My buddy and I decided to swing by for some pick-me-ups."

Dare didn't ask why they canceled their contract either

when Deja called him with the news. He said 'okay' because it wasn't his business why someone wanted to stop the service.

Unless it had something to do with him.

He never thought of that.

He couldn't imagine why it would be because of him. He did his work without bothering anyone, and he did a damn good job of it, too. His mowing was excellent. His trimming precise. Never left a blade of grass behind, blowing that shit smoothly out of the street and off the sidewalk. He did an impeccable job, not caring how much he tooted his own horn.

"Lucky me."

On the contrary. Lucky him. But her words filled him up with even more desire. She hadn't said it with revulsion or sarcasm. It had sounded like she meant it.

"I should go."

The words slipped out of his mouth before he could take them back. The way her eyes filled with hurt, he wanted to kick his own ass for saying it so abruptly. He did have to get going to his next job. But the way she said 'lucky me' hit him so strongly, if he stayed in her presence any longer he'd end up making a fool of himself.

"My buddy is waiting in the truck for me." Not that Tyrone would mind if he stayed a few extra minutes. Even he had commented about how beautiful Julie was when Dare mentioned saying hi to her.

"Of course. Nice to see you again."

He stood up.

"Yeah, you, too. Enjoy your day."

She smiled, but it was half-hearted compared to the others she had bestowed upon him.

"Do you wanna catch a beer later or something?"

Catch a beer? What the hell did that even mean? It was like he'd never been in front of a beautiful woman before and asked her out. Well, to be fair, he hadn't. The few dates he had been on since being released were all set up through Ethan or Deja. He had never asked a woman on his own. Before prison, he didn't date. He'd had sex with two girls that he didn't even remember their names now. Young and dumb. Trying to fit in with his friends. Now that shit didn't even matter.

And why was he even asking her out? It's not like he had a chance in hell with her. For one, she didn't live in Minnesota. It would never work out. For two, she was an FBI agent. The law didn't date felons.

"We're having a fish fry tonight. You can come."

With the McCords? Without Deja or Emmett there? Unless they were invited, too. Which he didn't think so because then Deja would've forced him to come with as well. She liked him to be a part of everything when it came to family events. Like he was a part of their family as well. He wasn't.

She must've seen his wince at the prospect because her weak smile morphed into a real one along with an adorable giggle escaping.

"Looks like that is a torturous prospect."

"The McCords aren't that bad. I don't hang with them often, though." *If I can help it.*

"I'd like a beer later. I can meet you somewhere."

But what would she tell everyone?

Hell, he didn't even care if she made up some excuse and didn't tell them the truth. His need to see her, to be with her, was too strong to worry about how she might approach it. He was shocked as hell she even agreed to meet him for a beer.

"Haverty's Bar. About nine." That would give her time to enjoy the fish fry and then have a beer or two with him.

Maybe more. If he was truly lucky.

He might not be able to date her, but there was nothing wrong with having a bit of fun. Didn't women like bad boys? He could be the baddest boy there was if she wanted.

"Sounds good. I'll see you then."

He nodded and walked out of the coffee shop filled with anticipation...and dread.

It'd been over ten years since he'd been with a woman. He didn't want to screw a moment of this up.

Knowing him—the colossal screw-up he was—he would. Epically.

4

"You look nice. All dolled up...even wearing lipstick," Ava noted as Julie finished the last curl in her hair with the curling iron.

"She never wears lipstick unless it's a date," Ashley added, her head peeking out from behind Ava in the doorway of the bathroom.

"Which is odd because she didn't say it was a date."

"No, she said she was going out for a beer. With a friend."

"And she wasn't even alone that long this morning in town. It was only a few hours in the office before I called her for her to make a friend."

"A friend she hasn't told us about either."

"Odd."

"So very odd."

She sighed dramatically at her friends' irritating conversation meant to get on her nerves and unplugged the hot device.

Twisting their way, she pinned a smile on her face like

she wasn't bothered by their nosiness. "You said you didn't mind if I borrowed your car."

"And I don't," Ava confirmed. "We're curious who you're meeting and why it's a secret."

Julie wouldn't say it was a secret, per se. She just wasn't sure how Ava—she didn't care what Ashley thought—would react.

"You met a hot guy in town and there is nothing wrong with that." Ashley wiggled her eyebrows playfully. "You're a grown woman who can do whatever the hell she wants. We, as your friends, want the juicy details."

Ava laughed and pointed at Ashley. "What she said."

"I'm going for a beer, not sex."

Maybe.

Who knew what the night entailed. She wouldn't say no if Dare made the suggestion. Would he? Julie had to admit she couldn't read him as well as she could other guys. He was an enigma. A mystery. He held himself in check so rigidly and so well it was hard to decipher what he was thinking.

He was a challenge in so many ways, and it was difficult to resist that. She loved a challenge. She wasn't assuming sex was on the table tonight, but she definitely wouldn't say no if the need arose.

"When's the last time you had sex?" Ava asked, as if asking whether it was going to rain later. It wasn't. She knew because she looked at the weather app earlier. Because after making a billion excuses about why she was looking at her phone, waiting and searching for a text from Dare, she realized she'd never get one. They never exchanged numbers. She'd have to rectify that mistake.

"Why?"

"It's been quite a few months," Ashley answered for her.

Her mouth popped open. "As if you would know."

"Uh, you tell me everything. Your last date with snort-man didn't end in a round between the sheets. So it puts it a few months before that when you went out with jockey-man. You said he had a small penis and it wasn't even good."

"I never heard about snorter," Ava said, appalled, changing Ashley's ridiculous nickname for her past dates. Julie did like snorter better than snort-man, but that's what Ashley did. She gave every one of her past dates a dumb name and added *man* behind it.

"Because he was so insignificant it wasn't even worth mentioning." He snorted every time he made a comment. She almost walked out on him before their meal had been served.

"Is jockey-man the one who also had smelly feet?" Ava asked Ashley instead of her. As if Ashley knew more about the men she had dated than herself.

"Yeah. I think if he hadn't had that problem, she would've dated him longer."

Julie crossed her arms and rolled her eyes. "Or the sex was appalling and I didn't want to waste my time anymore. I could've handled the stinky feet."

"No one should have to *handle* stinky feet," Ava said, disgusted, then shivered as if smelling something rotting that very second.

"You two are ridiculous." Yet, Julie loved them so much. She didn't know what she'd do without her friends.

"And you're not leaving until you give us something." Ashley mimicked her stance, crossing her arms and spreading her feet a bit as if preparing for Julie to run head-first into her like a linebacker.

Should she? Dare didn't say not to tell anyone. It wasn't a

big deal. It was a beer...or two...or sex if the night went extremely well.

"It's Dare."

There. She said it. Because she didn't keep secrets from her friends and she wasn't going to start now.

"What's a dare?" Ashley asked, confusion settling on her determined face.

Ava, however, met her stare head-on, the knowledge twinkling in her eyes. She had heard her correctly.

"I didn't know you two hit it off so well."

There wasn't any accusation in Ava's tone, but Julie heard the hesitation. As if she had weighed her words carefully before speaking.

"We didn't, actually. It was a very tense conversation when I sat down at the picnic table. I saw him in the coffee shop today. He asked if I wanted to get a beer, and I didn't want to be rude."

Because I really wanted to join him. I like his company.

Ava continued to stare at her—hard. "You like him."

"He's not a bad guy."

"I never said he was."

Julie tensed, tilting her head slightly. "It's the way you said it."

"You said you didn't get along with him at first."

"Yes, but I didn't say he was a bad guy."

Ava huffed. "I didn't either."

Ashley swiveled her head back and forth between them.

"You put lipstick on," Ashley finally said when neither she nor Ava continued in the argument.

"So?" What did that have to do with anything?

"So you consider it a date." Ashley said it so matter-of-factly.

"He's—" Ava stopped.

Julie frowned. "He's what?"

He was a lot of things that she couldn't begin to describe —none of them bad—but she wasn't going to stand around and let anyone put him down. He didn't deserve that. They might've had a few tense conversations, but he had never been rude to her. He'd only stood up for himself when she'd been the rude one initially judging him.

Ava sighed, her body relaxing from the tense stance she had. "I don't want to see you get hurt."

"What about him? Aren't you concerned about him? He's family, after all."

"Very extended family, if that. You're my friend, and I'm going to worry about you more."

"Would you be having a problem with this if he didn't have a record?"

There. Julie finally put the real issue out in the open. Because, while she tried to tell herself it didn't bother her either, it kind of did. She took pride in her work, in following the law. She'd never even considered trying an illegal substance in her life. She wasn't about to judge him— any more than she already had—but she couldn't comprehend what would possess him to do drugs at such a young age. And she couldn't begin to understand because she hadn't asked him yet. Maybe she would tonight, and maybe she wouldn't. She'd play it by ear.

"I don't know." Ava shrugged. "I'm also thinking of Deja. She's very protective of her brother."

Ouch.

"Meaning she doesn't like me? Wouldn't approve of me?"

Ava threw her hands up in the air, nearly hitting Ashley in the face. "You're making this more than it should be."

"You're making this more than it should be," Julie accused, pointing in her direction.

"You look beautiful, and we expect all the details when you get home," Ashley cut in, defusing some of the tension. Yet creating a new bout of it with her words.

"I do not want to hear if she had sex with him," Ava said, shaking her head as if wiping out mental images that had appeared.

"Well, I do." Ashley smiled at Julie, bobbing her brows up and down with a smirk.

Julie couldn't help it. She laughed. "I'm going for a beer. That's it."

"But you're wearing lipstick and the shortest dress you brought with you. You say 'just a beer.' I hear 'do me, baby.'"

At that, Ava snorted.

Then all three of them busted out laughing. Tension erased.

Until Ava spoke again.

"Be careful."

———

DARE WAS SO glad he was sitting down when Julie walked into the bar. Holy. Hell. The woman was drop-dead gorgeous.

She wore a soft-purple sundress that cut low on her thighs. Thin straps on top and the front scooped low, show-casing her breasts that he ached to touch with every fiber of his being. Her hair was in curls that laid prettily on her shoulders. Her lips were painted bright red, and she had a light shading of eye shadow he noticed as soon as she reached the table. He couldn't recall her wearing that much makeup at the party. Did she doll herself up for him? His heart thumped wildly at the thought.

He stood up, yet didn't move from sight of the table. She

would've seen how hard as a rock he'd gotten at one look of her.

"Hi."

She smiled, making his cock twitch even harder. "Hi."

He took a seat when she did. "I didn't know what you liked, so I didn't order anything yet."

The waitress appeared, giving him a short reprieve. To get his breath back, his wits about him. She was dressed like a queen, and he felt ridiculous compared to her. He had thrown on a pair of jeans—one of his nicest pairs—and the only buttoned shirt he owned. He almost put on a T-shirt but thought better of it. Now he was glad he did, although he still felt underdressed compared to her. Her beauty took his breath away. This was never going to work. He was way out of her league.

It wasn't uncomfortable in the bar, but he had rolled up his sleeves halfway, baring his forearms. He'd left the top button undone and the shirt itself untucked. Now he wished he would've tucked it in and kept the sleeves rolled down.

They both ordered a beer and oddly enough stayed silent until the waitress returned less than two minutes later with their drinks.

"So how was your day?" she asked before taking a sip of the cold beer.

He watched her lips touch the bottle and his mind veered to territories he should avoid. But damn it was hard to erase as he imagined her lips curling around his cock instead. Maybe that was bringing naughty too much to the forefront of his mind.

He cleared his throat, realizing she had asked him a question. Right. How did his day go?

"Fine."

She frowned, yet he saw the laughter in her eyes. So,

okay, he could try harder to make polite conversation. He was the one who asked her out. Idle chit-chat was not something he was good at. Chatting in general wasn't his forte. He liked to keep to himself. Less talk meant fewer ways for him to screw up.

"It was hot. One of the yards I had to take care of was a bitch today. Very hilly. It's always a pain in my ass. And yours?"

"Good."

This time he gave her a look. A mixture of mock irritation and delight.

"I bought a few trinkets for my nieces and nephews. Learned how to milk a goat from Ava while everyone else went fishing."

From there, they went into an easy chatter, as if this were a real first date getting to know each other. She told him she had an older brother who had two kids—one daughter, one son. An older sister who had three kids—two daughters, one son. Her time at college and a few crazy stories as an FBI agent. Maybe she sensed his edginess at that part because she kept it short, moving on to New York and how he should visit it at some point.

He'd never been anywhere but Minnesota. He'd never had a chance to travel. His parents didn't give a damn about taking family vacations, and then, of course, ten years of his life was ripped away by one tragic mistake.

She instinctively knew to move on from that as well and asked if he enjoyed baseball when his eyes glided to the TV hanging behind the bar.

"I do. Sorry, I was just checking the score."

Minnesota was up two runs against Detroit. That's all he needed to know.

"Oh, I'm a diehard fan myself. New York, of course."

He rolled his eyes in jest. Her beautiful laughter filled up the space, making his heart skip a beat and his cock twitch in delight. He could listen to her laugh all day long and never tire of it.

"Holy shit. Are my eyes deceiving me? Is that you, Dare?"

Dare looked to the right of Julie at the sound of the voice. Holy shit was a good description. His old buddy Rick was walking up to their table. He stood up, and they grabbed each other's hands, pulling in for a one-armed hug, clapping each other on the back.

"Damn good to see you. When'd you get out?" Rick asked him.

"Over a year ago."

Dare didn't miss the flash of hurt in Rick's eyes, but he ignored it. Rick never once came to his trial. Never once visited him in prison. Never once showed his support the moment he got locked up. Considering Rick had been one of his closest friends back then, it hurt. So he could deal with the pain if he didn't like the fact Dare hadn't reached out when he was released. Not to mention, Rick was a part of his old life and he was trying to forget all about that. Move on and build a new life.

"Well, it's good to see you."

Dare nodded. "Same to you."

Honestly, Dare would've never lost sleep over not seeing Rick again.

Rick turned his attention to Julie. "And who is this angel? Hello, love, I'm Rick."

He held out his hand, a slight predatory look in his eyes. Dare didn't like it or the way he addressed Julie. Love? Who in the hell did Rick think he was? She was with *him*. Sitting at a table with *him*. For all Rick knew, she was his girlfriend, so he should be watching what he was saying.

Julie smiled, and it grated on Dare's nerves she bestowed one of her beautiful smiles at an old friend who didn't deserve it. She shook hands with him and managed to extract her hand with ease. Though, Dare swore Rick had tried to hold onto her longer.

"I didn't get your name, love."

Dare cleared his throat, though it came out sounding more like an annoyed grunt. "Stop calling her love."

Rick tore his gaze off Julie, who had looked shocked that Dare had said something. Did she think he'd stand by while someone spoke to her that way? Rick laughed. "I didn't mean nothing by it."

"Don't matter. I don't like it."

Did he have a right to say something? Hell, he didn't care if he did or not. She might not be his—as much as he ached for that to be different—but he wouldn't abide by someone, especially someone like Rick, talking to her that way. Rick didn't know her. He had no respect calling her such an endearment when they'd just met.

Another smooth laugh left Rick's mouth. "You were never one to shy away from anything. Nice to see you haven't changed. I wasn't trying to step on your toes with your woman. We cool?"

Dare stared at him for a few beats longer than was necessary, but he needed to get his point across with Rick that he wasn't playing. He'd knock him on his ass if he called her something other than Julie again. Not that he intended to tell Rick her name. He didn't want to hear her name on his lips either. Maybe he should punch him on the principle of the matter.

Or not.

He'd rather not see the inside of a jail cell ever again.

"We're cool."

Rick nodded and clapped him on the back. "Let's get together soon. Catch up and shit."

"Yeah, sure."

That wasn't going to happen, despite what he said. Rick was his supplier back in the day, getting him all the drugs he needed. Dare could only assume Rick hadn't changed his ways. He had the look about him that said he'd gotten far worse. He was dressed nice, maybe a little too nice. Slick-backed hair, smooth, greasy smile. Dare didn't trust him one bit.

"It was a pleasure," Rick said with a sly smile at Julie, then smirked at Dare before venturing away toward a table in the back where he took a seat next to some other guys that looked like they were up to no good.

Dare reclaimed his seat, avoiding Julie's gaze, embarrassed beyond belief. This was why he needed to leave town where nobody knew him. Shit like that could continue to happen. He was surprised to see Rick in St. Joe. His normal stomping ground was St. Cloud. What was he doing in this small town?

"You okay?"

He looked up, surprised to hear the concern in her voice.

"I'm fine. Sorry about that. I knew him way back when. He was a jerk to women then, too."

The sweet, slow smile that punctured her lips made his gut clench with anticipation. Which was dumb. She'd never do anything with him but have a beer. No kissing. No touching. No sex.

"I thought you were going to hit him. You looked very upset."

"I thought about it." The smile remained on her face, making him think she wouldn't have minded.

She twisted her empty bottle but didn't say anything

else. His beer was gone, too. They could order another one. Without glancing toward Rick, Dare knew he didn't want to be in the same place as him. He might change his mind and show Rick some pain.

"Do you want to leave?"

Her eyes held his. "Together, or separately?"

Wow. She still wanted to be in his presence after that fiasco. He figured she'd want to get as far away from him as possible. His past didn't paint a pretty picture of him. One reason he was glad she talked more tonight about herself than he did.

"We could watch the game at my place."

She stood up, snatching her purse from the table. "I'd like that."

Well, shit, she kept surprising him. He wasn't going to ignore the luck landing in his lap.

He couldn't help it. His gaze swiveled toward Rick, who happened to be looking his way. Rick nodded as if saying good-bye, and Dare gave a slight tilt to his head as well. For some reason he couldn't explain, he grabbed Julie's hand as they walked outside. She didn't try to remove it.

She stopped at Ava's car she'd borrowed tonight and turned toward him. His hand still held hers. They stood close together, barely a breath away, but not quite fully touching body to body.

"I don't live far. I walked here."

Her head bobbed up and down.

His eyes glided to her mouth, then up to her golden depths that told him she was feeling the desire brewing between them as much as him.

He lifted his hand and brushed her cheek. "I really want to kiss you. I know I shouldn't."

"Why's that?" she asked breathlessly, her eyes glancing at his mouth, begging for his lips to touch hers.

She knew why but needed him to say it out loud for both of them to hear. For both of them to be reminded.

"Because I'm no good. You're all that's good in this world, and I'm nothing but bad news. I have a feeling one kiss won't be enough."

"Oh, I know one kiss won't be enough."

His cock jumped at her honesty. She continued to shock him again and again, and it shouldn't. She'd been nothing but forthright with him since they met. He liked her honesty. It was so damn refreshing and he'd always know where he stood with her.

"You should go home. I'm sorry I ruined the night."

She grabbed the front of his shirt and squeezed, pulling him closer so their bodies were finally touching.

"You didn't ruin the night. Your friend didn't help it, but you didn't do anything wrong."

He wanted to believe her. For a millisecond he did, until his past slammed into him, reminding him of all the bad choices he'd made and why those choices would always haunt him.

"You should still go home."

Her grip tightened. "You said we'd watch the game. I was looking forward to it."

His nostrils flared and his eyes narrowed, and he damn near licked his lips thinking of the things he wanted to do to her. None of it had to do with watching baseball. "You know we wouldn't actually watch the game. I don't know what's happening here, but we can both be honest with each other that something is. Before we do something we'll regret, we should stop it. Go home, Julie."

"If you'd let go of my hand you're holding and got free of my grip,"—she shook her hand that held his shirt—"I might believe you want me to go home. But you don't, and you haven't tried yet. I know exactly what I'm doing, with no regrets."

"I'm a felon."

"You're a man who made some terrible mistakes. You say people don't give you a chance, judging you as soon as they know your history. Here I am giving you a chance, and you're not giving yourself one. Stop pushing me away."

He stepped closer, pushing her up against the car. Her sharp inhale told him she felt how hard he was. How much he wanted to touch her in ways he hadn't touched a woman in far too long.

"You leave in a few days. It'd just be sex."

She flinched, blinking a few times. "I can do just sex. Can you?"

He wasn't sure. If he was being fully honest with himself, he was afraid once with her would never be enough. He wasn't only talking about a kiss. She'd been on his mind since the moment he left the party last weekend. Igniting his senses, overtaking his thoughts, making him go crazy missing her when he barely even knew her. One day and he was a goner. One time between the sheets and he feared he'd never recover. Never look at another woman again.

"I can."

Not that he'd ever tell her any of that. She wanted sex, he'd give her what she wanted. He'd always give her anything she wanted. He knew deep in his heart he'd never be able to say no to her. That was a first for him, well, besides his sister who he'd do about anything for as well.

She pulled him until her lips met his, setting his body ablaze. Then she let go with a wily smirk and pushed against his chest, making him release her hand.

"I'll drive you home. I don't want to miss a moment of the game."

Neither did he.

But he knew in the end, he'd lose this game, and he never wanted to win more than he did now.

5

A light breath released before she opened her car door and smiled at Dare, who looked at her from across the hood.

"Nice house," she remarked, following him to the front door.

He shrugged. "It's Ethan's. He offered me a room when I got out, and when he moved in with Penelope, he said I could stay."

"You don't live as close to the bar as I thought you did. That had to be at least two miles or so."

His shoulders lifted in a careless gesture again, but he didn't look at her as he did so. "I like the fresh air. It's good exercise, too."

Julie wouldn't deny he had a wonderful physique. She could tell he worked out. Lean and toned. She supposed if he walked a lot that would account for such a toned body.

"Have you driven since..."

Dare twisted his head, staring at her with sorrowful eyes.

Way to bring down the mood. That was a terrible question to ask. She could see the answer in his eyes.

"No."

Then he turned back toward the door and shoved the key into the hole.

The lock didn't click when he turned the key, and he swung the door open when he realized he hadn't locked it. Light illuminated the foyer as she shut the door. She noted the alarm panel close to it, yet it hadn't been set.

And he forgot to lock the door. She locked it because it was a habit.

"You didn't lock your door. Or set the alarm."

"Forgot, I guess." His entire body looked tense, his eyes darting to the knob as if he wanted to unlock it. She did that. Asking questions and making statements that weren't helping the atmosphere between them.

Now she had to change the mood. To something much better and much lighter.

"Which house are they keeping? Ethan and Penelope. They've been engaged a long time. I'm surprised they still have both houses."

Maybe Dare would buy this house from Ethan. It was in a nice neighborhood. Small and quaint and perfect for a bachelor. She assumed a two-bedroom house, since Ethan had offered him a room. Based on the tiny foyer with the living room to the left and a short hallway leading toward bedrooms, she didn't think it was larger than two bedrooms. Of course, she could be wrong.

Dare shrugged again. "No clue. Ethan hasn't said."

Still not a good mood changer. She sensed it was a touchy subject, so she didn't pry. She'd had that feeling a lot tonight with him, interpreting his moods when the conversation shifted. His jaw would lock, his eyes shimmering with pain. She didn't want to bring the mood down or force him to talk about things he wasn't comfortable with, so she usually switched gears to remove those emotions. He didn't smile enough. She relished in trying to get those smiles to appear. She was failing miserably at finding a good topic to chat about. Everything seemed to bother him.

Oh for two so far.

"Do you want a beer?"

"I want you to show me your house."

His eyes flashed with a moment of hurt as if stating it was his house was too much for him to handle.

"The bedroom, to be specific." Her lips curled up into a saucy smile. The sorrow filling his eyes disappeared and desire took its place. That's it. That's what she wanted to see from him.

"You're not shy. With anything. Are you?" Though he asked it seriously, one of his rare brilliant smiles lit up his face.

"I have my moments." Right now wasn't one of them.

"You still have a chance to leave, Julie."

"Do you want me to leave?"

His jaw clenched hard before she swore he murmured "I'm going to hell for this" and then surprised her by swinging her up into his arms.

"You had your chance. You're mine now."

Her heart skipped a beat. She knew he meant for the moment. For the night. But that hidden romantic side of her wanted it to mean more. That was an absurd thought. They lived worlds apart—not just a few states between them either.

He walked with steady footsteps to his room, the first door on the left. The first door on his right had been another bedroom—Ethan's room, most likely. She had spied another door on the left as well and assumed the bathroom. Another doorway in the living room indicated the kitchen lie that way. So like she had surmised, a two-bedroom house. She loved being right.

She didn't want to let go when he set her on the bed. It was silly, but she didn't want to miss a moment of his touch. It had been hot and electrifying. She wanted to imprint it everywhere, so later she could take it out of her memories and relive each moment.

He turned on the bedside lamp and immediately started to unbutton his shirt, which was one part sad and one part exhilarating. Sad, because there was something about a man with his sleeves rolled up. It wasn't difficult to see he worked hard every day exerting his strong muscles. Well-toned forearms that had her drooling at the sight. And definitely exhilarating because she was ready for everything between them.

She slipped her sandals off, each one hitting the floor with a soft thud. His gaze followed her movements as she lifted her dress and threw it to the floor. His eyes dilated with pleasure, his fingers stalling on the button of his jeans when he saw she wasn't wearing a bra. She wasn't well-endowed, which proved to be handy when wearing certain clothes. Dresses with thin straps for one. Didn't take much to hold her babies up. He said she wasn't shy, but when it came to her breasts, she wanted to curl up and cover herself. Not all men liked tiny-breasted women. At least, dickwad-man—aptly named by Ashley—had made her self-conscious about it when he said he didn't like flat-chested women.

His pants disappeared quickly along with his boxers, and then he was joining her on the bed, smoothing his body across hers.

"You're blushing," he whispered, feathering light kisses across her cheek and down her neck.

"It's the way you looked at me."

He lifted his head. "I want to devour you from head to toe. I've looked at you like that on several occasions since I've met you. You've never blushed."

He had an intensity about him. She knew this was inevitable because he was right. He *had* looked at her like he wanted to eat her up, and she had ignored it, knowing it shouldn't happen. Yet, when he looked at her naked breasts, her mind veered to other men and the way they looked at her. With disinterest. Like she wasn't good enough.

"My boobs are small, okay."

His eyes glided to her chest, and she wanted to slap her hands over them, yet he was in the way, and she could tell by the way he tensed, he wouldn't allow her to anyway.

"They're perfect."

Before she could protest, his mouth claimed a nipple, sucking hard at first, then turning soft, his tongue swirling, his teeth nipping. Her body arched off the bed, her nerves dancing with bliss she knew was on the horizon. Holy hell, he had only kissed her nipple. She couldn't imagine how much more electrifying his touch would be anywhere else.

One of his hands reached up and ensnared her hair, gripping lightly but with possession, while his other hand made a trail down, snagging her panties. She lifted her butt to help him remove them, and then nothing but cool air and his hot body touched her. She continued to move with his ministrations, aching—no, needing more.

Except she couldn't find her voice. She was so focused on his touch. The way he gripped her hair, the way his lips devoured her breasts, taking turns on each one as if to make it fair. The way his fingers found her core and turned up the desire in her. The only thing she found herself capable of was moaning and whispering his name in a plea, letting him know in the only way she could she had to have more. All of him. Now.

"God, you're perfect in every way." His low masculine voice filled her soul with beauty. She knew she wasn't ugly. Finding a date was never a struggle. It didn't mean she didn't have body issues now and again.

The magic his fingers were creating with the tender kisses on her breasts was enough to hit her peak, especially when his teeth dragged across her nipple before his tongue soothed it. She cried out in pleasure, squeezing his biceps, her nails digging in.

"I need to hear that again," he rasped out as he reached over to his nightstand, then swore under his breath. "I'll be right back."

He slid off her and rushed out of the room. She had closed her eyes to let the bliss wash over her, but opened them when she heard the crinkling of the condom package. He ran to the bathroom fast to grab a condom. She loved that he was as excited as she was for this to happen.

He covered himself, then held himself still, his brows pleated, his jaw hard. He looked like he was in pain, which filled her with pain. Had she done something wrong?

"What's the matter?" She smoothed out his brow, then brushed her hand down his cheek.

Dare swallowed hard. One hand still held his cock while the other was buried deep in her hair again. While he'd had a firm grip on her hair from the beginning, it never hurt. He never pulled or yanked on it. It's as if he needed to claim a part of her, keep a hold of her in some way, to prove he had her, to possess her.

"Dare?" This time she brought both hands up and brushed them across his head, loving the soft, fuzzy feeling of his hair.

"It's..." He swallowed again. "It's been a very long time for me. I'm afraid I won't last long."

Ah. He was admitting he hadn't had sex since being released. She couldn't help the happiness that filled her up that he had picked her to share this moment with. He could've slept with anyone to get it out of his system, but he didn't.

Yet...

He said this was just sex. If that were the case, wouldn't he have released his pent-up tension a lot sooner? Like right after he was released from prison.

"It's a good thing the night's still young. You do have more than one condom, don't you?"

A slow grin grew on his nervous face. "A whole box."

"Then I don't see the problem."

At that, he positioned himself and slid inside, groaning deep. She grabbed his ass, pulling him closer.

"Careful," he hissed with a strained breath.

"No, I want to see you lose control. You're always so controlled and mannered in everything you do. Let go."

Then she lifted up, relishing in the low growl he emitted and the way he closed his eyes in pleasure. Her hands tightened on his ass, her nails digging in. He took the cue and started pumping hard, in and out. As he predicted, it didn't last long. He tensed, groaning, dipping his head into her shoulder when it hit him.

His hot breath hit her neck, soothing in a way, yet rousing her senses, tempting her. She wanted more. That barely scratched the surface.

"That wasn't even close to losing control."

He lifted his head, swiping a kiss before grinning wildly. "Challenge accepted. Watch me lose it with you."

Exactly what she wanted.

They were more alike than he realized. They both couldn't resist a challenge.

This night was only beginning.

DARE CRACKED HIS EYES OPEN, unable to hold back a grin when he saw the beauty lying next to him. His hand was pressed against her stomach, and he wanted to scoot closer and pull her all the way into his arms. But the light filtering through the window said the morning had sprung and he more than likely needed to get his ass into gear so he wasn't late for work.

If he did what his body ached to do, he'd be late. Not that it bothered him to be late for that reason, but he'd rather not hear his sister harping in his ear for it and asking why he was late. That's if Tyrone tattled on him about it.

Julie had spent the night. It stood to reason everyone would find out where she had been all night long. Unless Ava and her friends didn't spread it around the family. He didn't think Zane would say anything, but Ava had a way about not keeping shit to herself.

Whatever happened, he wasn't going to regret last night. It had been one of the best nights of his life. They'd used quite a few condoms from the box he had purchased a while back thinking he might have sex with a few of his dates at some point. Now he was glad he had saved them for Julie. It wouldn't have been the same with any other woman.

His fingers started to brush her stomach with soft strokes when he heard a door slam.

Shit.

Ethan was here.

He had remembered it was garbage day today and rolled

out the garbage can late last night before they finally decided to call it a night. He forgot to lock the door...and set the alarm last night. Not that he felt unsafe, but Ethan paid for the alarm system, and he felt like he had to use it because of that. Something he failed at. Not something he wanted to admit to Ethan.

Extracting himself from the bed as quietly as he could, he sighed that their time was up. He wasn't foolish enough to think he'd ever have her in his arms again. The bedroom door closed with a soft click, and his feet barely made a sound as he padded toward the kitchen where he heard Ethan making a racket.

He obviously walked a little too quietly because when Ethan turned around from the pantry, he jumped, putting a hand to his chest.

"Shit, dude, you scared me. I thought you'd be at work by now."

A glance at the microwave clock said he'd be getting an earful from Deja later—if Tyrone told her. He was definitely going to be late. It was 8:07. Did Tyrone knock on the front door and he didn't hear it? Did he even call him? Dare would have to check his phone to see if he missed his call. His phone was still in his pant pocket lying in a messy puddle on his bedroom floor. Something else he rarely did. Leave his clothes lying around. He was lucky he remembered to bring the garbage can out to the end of the driveway. Everything else left his mind last night but Julie.

"I overslept. What's up?"

Ethan popped in from time to time. Although he lived full-time with Penelope, he hadn't officially moved all of his stuff out yet. Plus, he came over on occasion to hang out, watch baseball, have a few beers. He never knocked, and it had never bothered Dare—until today.

The guilty look on Ethan's face said whatever he stopped by for Dare wouldn't like.

"Dropping off a few things."

Ethan was standing by the pantry.

"Like what?"

"Just things."

He clenched his jaw before taking a deep breath. Dare knew Ethan meant well, but it didn't mean he appreciated half the shit he did sometimes. He didn't want handouts like he was hurting for shit. He wasn't a charity case or someone who needed looking after.

"I hope you didn't drop off food like I'm some poor joker."

Ethan huffed. "Penelope went overboard when she went shopping. I thought I'd share with you."

And he was supposed to believe it was by accident. Whatever. They all thought he was a fool. He might not make a lot of money working for Emmett, but he got by. He paid Ethan rent—a lot cheaper than he deserved—he paid for his phone bill and cable, and besides that, he didn't have much to worry about. He could afford groceries.

He turned around toward the coffee pot and started preparing it.

"Don't be pissed. It's like two boxes of cereal, some crackers, and a box of noodles. It's not that much."

"I don't need handouts."

"It's my house. I was dropping it off for myself. Okay."

Dare whipped around. "You haven't slept in your *own house*," he said, emphasizing how ridiculous Ethan sounded trying to make his dumb point, "since the moment you got back together with Penelope. Don't give me that shit. First, it's for me, and now it's for yourself."

"It's not a handout."

"You came when you knew I wouldn't be home. Like I wouldn't notice extra shit in my cupboards."

"They are pretty bare."

A hollow laugh filtered out. "Because I haven't been to the store yet this week, asshole."

He turned back toward the coffee pot, scooping grounds into the device, not even caring he wasn't being gentle about it. Grounds fell and scattered around the counter.

"When do you plan to go?"

He half twisted, glowering menacingly at Ethan. "Why do you care when I get my damn groceries?"

This time, Ethan clenched his jaw, breathing deeply before responding. "If you're not restocking, then it means you don't plan to. Which means you still think you're leaving town." Ethan took a step around the island separating them. "And you're not."

More empty laughter fell out. "You don't tell me what to do. Nobody does."

"You will devastate Deja if you leave. Do you understand that? Do you even care?"

"*WILL THE DEFENDANT PLEASE RISE?*"

Despite the tremors filling his entire body, Dare stood up with steady legs. Or maybe he was visibly shaking, embarrassing himself. It didn't matter. None of it mattered.

Judgment time was about to begin.

Although it sounded like the judge asked him to stand, like he had a choice, he ordered him to stand to his feet. Face his consequences like a man.

He was far from a man. He was a complete and utter failure.

"*Darrien Wilson, you have been found guilty of criminal*

vehicular homicide, driving under the influence of a controlled substance, possession of a controlled substance in the fifth degree, and reckless driving."

Yeah, he knew all of that. He listened to the jury tell him how guilty he was when they listed the same guilty verdicts. No one cared it had been raining that night. No one cared he had to drive because his dad was having a heart attack. They had no phone to call an ambulance. He had no choice but to drive his dad to the hospital. His mom hadn't been in her right mind to handle the task.

No one believed him that a dog had run into his path and he was forced to swerve. The rain, with the jerk of the car, sent him straight into a tree. Killing his mom on impact, and his dad's heart attack completing its job before help arrived.

No one cared.

Except his sister.

And he didn't have the courage to turn around once while the court proceedings went on to look at her. To see the disappointment on her face. To see the hatred. To see the rage he had ruined not just his life, but hers as well.

"In consideration of no prior record, I'm sentencing you to eleven years in prison instead of the maximum penalties."

He flinched when the judge slammed his gavel down hard. Not from the amount of time he was losing from his life, but simply from the loud noise. It had startled him. Came out of nowhere.

Eleven years didn't seem like enough for his actions. Not that he was about to disagree with the judge. With all the charges combined, he could've been looking at twenty years or more. The criminal vehicular homicide charge itself was a maximum of fifteen years. All in all, he was damn lucky with the overall outcome.

He felt numb as his public defender—he couldn't afford his

own lawyer—mumbled nonsense in his ear. Not even the rest of the judge's words filtered into his brain. The only thing he could hear were the quiet sobs coming from behind him.

His sister was truly alone now. He had always promised to protect her and keep her safe, and he'd broken that promise without effort.

The bailiff motioned for him to follow him.

"Dare! I love you."

He moved around the table without looking at Deja. He didn't deserve her love—or her forgiveness. Something she had said several times to him when she visited him.

She was better off without him. Forgetting he ever existed.

DARE RETURNED his attention to the coffee pot, pouring water in. What right did Ethan have to ask such a question? Of course, he cared about his sister. Did he always do what was right by her? Hell, no. He screwed up all the time with her. That's why it was better he left. If he wasn't around her, he couldn't mess up. He couldn't hurt her. Like he hurt her so many years ago, deserting her, getting sent to prison.

"I'm sorry. I shouldn't have said that. I know you love your sister. You won't just be hurting her if you leave. You'll hurt me, too. I'll miss you. I don't understand why you have to leave. Why you think you have to."

Neither did he sometimes, so how could he begin to explain it to Ethan? Although last night proved a good reason why he should. Running into his old life was not something he wanted to continuously happen.

"Why is Ava's car in the driveway?"

Well, he didn't want to answer *that* question. Why the shift in the conversation? Probably because Ethan knew he wouldn't win against him. If his mind was made up about leaving, he'd damn well leave. Why hadn't Ethan asked that question from the moment he found him in the kitchen?

"Maybe she's letting me use it."

"You're going to drive? Did you go for your license and not tell me?"

Yeah, that did sound unbelievable. He wasn't ready to drive, and if he did, he'd have to find a car somewhere, not borrow other people's. He couldn't afford to buy one right now. Well, if he bought a very used, very cheap car, he might be able to afford one. What was unbelievable about the questions was him actually driving a car. He'd yet to get behind the wheel of a vehicle since being released. He wouldn't say it was because he was afraid to...or maybe he didn't want to admit to himself he was afraid of what might happen if he did.

He got by without a vehicle. It didn't make him nervous to be a passenger, but every time he thought about driving, his hands started to sweat, and his mind veered to things best left in the past. It was enough to keep him in check and away from the wheel.

"Why'd you stop by when you knew I wouldn't be home? Putting food in my cupboards isn't going to make me stay."

"If you're so hell-bent on leaving, then why haven't you yet?"

Because he didn't know how to tell Deja. Because he didn't know where he wanted to go.

Because it scared the shit out of him.

"How about you mind your own damn business."

"You are my business. You're one of my best friends. You're my best man for my wedding."

Dare put the pot back on the burner and looked at Ethan. "I never agreed to that."

"I won't accept no for an answer."

He hissed in a sharp breath, trying not to let out a mangled laugh, or worse, a scream. "That's not going to make me stick around either, Ethan. I don't need you pitying me."

"Oh, for fuc—" Ethan drew in a rough breath then let it out slowly. "I'm going to pretend you didn't say that to me. I would never ask you to stand up with me if I didn't mean it."

Dare didn't doubt that. He should've never said it, but it slipped out. Because he was done with this conversation and he'd do—or say—anything to get it to stop. Pissing off Ethan, which was rather hard to do, would work.

"You never answered my question. Why do you have Ava's car?"

He had no intention of answering that either.

Ethan could badger him all he wanted, but he wasn't about to admit he made love to the most amazing woman on the planet all night long. That was his secret he'd keep to himself. Unless it came out amongst the family. Still didn't mean he had to share how it made him feel. Like he could be the good guy for the right woman.

"I'm using it. Good morning, Ethan."

Dare swiveled his direction to Julie, who looked beautiful and sexy with her rumpled hair and the happiness in her eyes. She looked like she'd been thoroughly loved—which she had been—and like she wanted more before she left if the twinkle in her eyes were true. She walked up to him, kissed him on the cheek, and pulled a mug from the cupboard.

"I hope this works its magic fast. I need my coffee in the mornings." Then she hit the on button to the pot since it was something he had failed to do.

Standing in front of the coffee pot like an imbecile.

"Good morning, Julie."

Dare turned around, wanting to laugh at the shocked expression on Ethan's face, even though his greeting had been as if everything were normal.

Why was he shocked? Because he managed to snag a gorgeous woman like her, or shocked because that gorgeous woman happened to also be friends with Ava—and an FBI agent.

"What time do you have to get to work?" Julie asked him, ignoring the awkward tension in the kitchen.

"About ten minutes ago."

She frowned. "I'm so sorry."

"It's not your fault. I should've set my alarm."

"Well, I can get out of your hair. This way you're not even more late on my account."

That was the last thing Dare wanted. He'd never called out before. Luckily, he'd never been sick, and it never occurred to him to take a day off and play hooky. Until today. Would she stay if he asked her to?

"Don't rush. I know the boss pretty well." Dare smiled, though he knew she saw how fake it was. He could feel it. The force it took to move his lips upward took more energy than he cared to admit.

As much as he wanted to spend the day with her, he knew he couldn't. Not because he shouldn't call out of work, but because it would never last between them. He had one night with her, and he'd have to live off that, even as it pained him.

A throat cleared, prompting both of them to turn toward Ethan.

"I'll just leave then. Have a wonderful day. I'll call you later, Dare."

He glared at Ethan. "Don't bother."

If Ethan thought he'd forgive and forget what happened this morning, he had no intention of doing so.

"You're so prickly in the morning. Drink your coffee." Ethan pointed a finger at him, smiling like there wasn't still tension floating between them.

"Stop telling me..." his words trailed off because Ethan had walked out of the kitchen and he would've never heard the rest anyway.

Silence filled the room. Although Ethan had left, an awkward vibe still lingered in the kitchen. He couldn't look at Julie. She had to have heard them arguing. He grabbed a mug from the cupboard and nearly dropped it when she touched his shoulder. Her touch always sent the desire straight to his cock. But this touch was more than that. More comfort rather than desire. He wasn't sure he could handle something like that from her.

"Do you want to talk about it?"

Hell, no. Talk about his shitty past and how much it was affecting his future. How much of a loser he was. How his past would never let him go. Why he'd never get someone as good and pure as her—for the long term. He was good for a quick lay, but nothing else.

Talking was the last thing he wanted to do.

6

J ulie shut the front door and didn't suppress an eye roll when Ashley and Ava strolled into the living room. She was smiling as she did it, so she knew they understood she was jesting, but part of her was annoyed. She didn't want to share the wonderful night she had with Dare. It had been one of the most wonderful nights she'd ever had, and it pained her she couldn't have another with him.

One night was truly not enough.

"You spent the night." Ashley's entire face lit up with happiness. "I honestly didn't expect that."

"Me neither." Ava wore a smile, but not as bright as Ashley's.

Figured. Ava might not have come right out and said it, but she had an issue with her hooking up with Dare. She pretended like she approved of him, but she didn't.

"I fell asleep. I should've called."

But not once had it crossed her mind to let her friends know she wouldn't be coming home. Everything but Dare had fled her mind.

"Well?" Ashley asked.

Julie dropped her purse to the couch and couldn't keep the wacky smile off her face. "He's amazing."

That was all she was going to say. Normally, she didn't mind giving them a complete rundown of the night, but with Dare it felt...wrong. Especially with Ava.

"That's it? I need more details," Ashley pouted.

"Amazing is a pretty strong adjective. It says a lot." Ava's smile disappeared. "You like him more than I realized."

Her own smile drifted away. "Unfortunately, I do. And we live far apart, so I know it'll never work."

Not to mention the whole felon thing. She wasn't sure her place of employment would be happy to hear she was dating someone with a record. Good thing she didn't have to worry about it.

She was going home in a few days, and she'd never see him again. Unless she visited Ava and happened to give him a call. She did manage to get his number before leaving, even though she knew it would only set her up for heartbreak. Chatting now and again would not ease the pain settling in her chest. It would only make it worse.

Even if they could figure out a way to make things work between them, she wasn't sure she wanted to start a relationship with someone who couldn't talk to her. Share their feelings. Because when she asked Dare if he wanted to talk to her about what happened between him and Ethan, he ignored her. Said 'It's all good. Nothing to talk about.' As if she hadn't heard them shouting and arguing with each other. He wanted to leave town, and Ethan wanted to do every little thing—even ridiculous things—to change his mind.

That wasn't all good. That was far from good.

And the sappy, sorry part of her heart thought if he had

told her about it, she could've suggested New York as a place to move.

So it was a good thing he chose not to talk to her about it. Because nothing could happen between them.

"Do you want to talk about it?"

Julie let out a boisterous laugh, covering her mouth in shock when she realized that was a terrible reaction to such an innocent question. Ava's brows rose, and Ashly squinted as if trying to decipher the specific laugh.

"Well, that deserves an explanation," Ava said more lightheartedly than most of her previous comments.

She didn't want to betray Dare. Not that he had asked her to keep anything to herself.

"As long as you promise to keep it to yourself."

Ava cocked a brow but nodded. Ashley agreed as well.

"Ethan dropped by this morning. He and Dare were arguing. I asked Dare the same question."

"And did he talk about what they were arguing about?" Ava asked.

"No, he said everything was good. I don't know why I laughed." Julie shook her head as if that would release all the turbulent thoughts floating around. "It's not that funny. I didn't believe him when he said it was all good."

"Please tell me you're going to tell us what they were arguing about." Ashley gave Ava a stern glare, telling her she had to keep her mouth shut and not share the details.

Julie had to agree. It was Ava she was worried about spreading the gossip, not Ashley.

"It's not my story to tell. I didn't hear all of it."

Ava crossed her arms. "You're also one of the best FBI agents there is, so I know you figured out, for the most part, what it was about."

This was very true. She was proud of her skillset within

the FBI. She didn't have a hundred percent closed case rate —nobody did—but she had a high number of cases she closed compared to not.

"Dare wants to leave town. Start fresh somewhere else. Ethan doesn't want him to go."

Ava's arms fell to her sides. "Does Deja know?"

Julie shrugged. "I'm going to guess no." She twisted her lips before smoothing them out with her tongue. "We had a small run-in with an old buddy of his. Before prison. I can sort of see why he'd want to start over somewhere else. That can't be easy running into his old life all the time."

"Was it bad?" Ava inquired, concern written all over her face.

Ava might not always appear like she approved of Dare, but when it came down to it, she'd defend and protect him. Julie knew it by that simple question.

"Not terrible, but not pretty." A wistful smile touched her lips. "The asshole called me love two times. Grated on my damn nerves. Dare told him to knock it off. I swore he wanted to punch the guy, but he held back. There was tension there because of that, but otherwise, I think Rick was happy to see Dare. Not so much the other way around."

"Rick?" Ava's expression perked up. "Rick Toro?"

"I have no idea. He didn't offer his last name and Dare didn't say. Why?"

"The drugs in this area has had a slight uptick in the last few weeks. Remember when I went into the office yesterday to check out a new case? It was an overdose. Though the officer that responded wasn't convinced it was a simple overdose. He suspects murder."

This perked Julie up. "Was it?"

"I couldn't tell by the little I was given. We have to wait on the tox report. The victim had multiple signs of previous drug use. There was a needle on the scene, and all points lead to overdose. I told Officer Marcos I'd look further into it."

"Why does he think it's murder?"

"Gut feeling." Ava shifted on her feet, crossing her arms. "Which I would never ignore. He also said he knew the victim. Tamera something. I can't remember her last name. He's arrested her a few times on drug possession. Last time was five months ago. She has a five-year-old little girl. The threat of losing her opened her eyes finally. She went into a drug program and had been clean since the last arrest. Or so he thought. That's his main reason for not believing it's an overdose."

"And Rick Toro? What does he have to do with anything?"

"He's the bigwig in St. Cloud tossing drugs around. If it's seeping into our town, he's behind it. Did he say anything specific to Dare?"

"Just that they should catch up soon." Julie's eyes narrowed. "I don't like how you're looking right now."

Ava winced and popped a shoulder up carelessly. "I got a dead woman and an increase of drugs in my town. If Dare can help me, I can't pass it up. Can I?"

Damn it. No, she couldn't. Julie would do the same thing for a case if she had the opportunity.

"Well, if you're going to talk to him about it, I want to come with."

Ava stared at her for a long time before nodding. "Fine."

"Good."

Of course, there was nothing good about how this conversation veered into such dangerous territory.

EMMETT HAD four crews working at any given time. Each crew had a trailer filled with every piece of equipment a person needed to make someone's yard look brand new. Mowers, trimmers, leaf blowers. Dare usually worked with Tyrone, who kept one of the trailers with him. Tyrone usually swung by his house and picked him up. After Julie left, he grabbed his phone, which he had put on silent the night before, and saw several missed texts and one phone call from Tyrone. He'd stopped by, and when Dare never answered his phone, he left.

Of course, being late today, he had to meet Tyrone at the job site. He'd had to call a cab, because after ignoring all of Tyrone's texts, Dare didn't think Tyrone would pick him up again. He wasn't going to whine about it. It was nice of Tyrone to pick him up anyway.

Dare wasn't late, ever, so he was surprised by the cold-shoulder by Tyrone when he finally showed up, but whatever. He didn't let it bother him while they worked. Not even an apology had helped. When lunchtime rolled around, he offered to buy Tyrone's meal. That finally sparked some forgiveness. When Tyrone asked why he ignored him, Dare didn't go into detail about Julie but mentioned a woman had held him up. The same woman he said hi to in the coffee shop. That got a sly smirk out of Tyrone and the rest of the forgiveness he wanted.

He hadn't needed it, but it helped to have a smooth working relationship with his partner. When Deja asked him to come to the office after work, he didn't hesitate to ask Tyrone to drop him off there. They both knew why she wanted to see him. Tyrone had, unfortunately, told her he didn't answer, and Deja would ream him out for being late. Just because he was her brother didn't make him exempt from her wrath when it came to the business. She ran a tight ship and expected everyone to follow orders without question. He wasn't pissed at Tyrone for ratting him out either. He needed to do his fair share like everyone else.

The door shut with a loud bang and he lifted a hand in thanks before Tyrone pulled away and out of the parking lot. A rush of cold air greeted him when he opened the door, and Deja's cool stare helped to chill him out the rest of the way. She had a way of looking at a person and decimating them with ease.

"Care to explain yourself? Tyrone was pissed this morning."

Dare took a seat in front of her desk and slouched into a comfy position as if he didn't have a care in the world.

"Don't know why. I've never been late before when he picks me up."

"You weren't answering your phone. You didn't answer when I called either."

Yeah, he had seen she called him twice this morning but knew returning her phone call wouldn't help him any. How did he explain he slept with Ava's friend? Ha! He'd never explain something like that to his sister.

Deja gulped in a large breath as if preparing herself for a huge blow she was about to deliver. Dare felt his entire body tense.

"Tyrone mentioned this morning that he's not always happy being your chauffeur all the time."

Dare rolled his eyes. "He picks me up and drops me off. I wouldn't call that a damn chauffeur service."

Maybe Dare had misread him this afternoon. Tyrone hadn't forgiven him at all. The asshole knew his sister was going to have this talk with him.

"Have you thought about taking the driver's test and getting your license back?"

He gritted his teeth together, crossing his arms. "So did he say he doesn't want to work with me anymore? Is that what you're getting at?"

"Don't ignore my question."

He abruptly stood up, making the chair skid back a few paces. His sister jumped in her chair.

"He either said he doesn't want to work with me anymore or he didn't."

Deja stood up. "Answer my question."

"Fine. I won't work with him anymore if he doesn't want to work with me. "

"Why do you do this? Why do you ignore me when I bring up driving again? If you're not comfortable—"

"Don't." His jaw tightened.

Deja's expression softened, and Dare hated the pity he saw in her eyes.

"Why didn't you answer my call this morning? Is there something I need to know?"

"Like what?"

Deja flinched at his sharp tone, and he immediately regretted it.

"Emmett heard Ethan talking to Penelope about asking you to be his best man and how you declined because you aren't planning to stick around town. He almost didn't tell me, but I made him tell me what was bugging him. I've been waiting for you to tell me and you haven't. Is this you finally telling me? By ignoring me? By being late for work? Are you going to run off and not even say good-bye?!"

Rage filled him. As much as he wanted it to be directed at Emmett, he couldn't blame him. Everything happening was all his fault. He was pissed at himself. Every harsh, broken word Deja threw at him, he deserved. But it didn't mean he wanted to talk to her about him skipping town. He wasn't ready to have that talk. To see the disappointment in her eyes, the despair. The hurt.

Of course, he was already seeing it.

"I'm late once, and that asshole has to blow it out of proportion. You want me to quit, fine. I quit."

Deja slammed her hand down on the desk hard. "Stop it! That isn't what I said. Tell me the truth for once."

Dare stepped forward, the anger fueling him. He was beyond controlling his emotions, and when it came to his sister, he tried so hard to keep them reeled in.

"I can't stand this town. I can't stand the constant reminder that I messed up your life. That I hurt you. I can't go anywhere without my past shoving a fist in my face. I'm a charity case to the McCords, and I'll never be able to do anything that makes what I did to you better. I'm scared shitless to get behind a wheel again, and I don't know how to fix that. And as for being late, I slept with Ava's best friend, Julie, and had one of the best nights of my life. She slept with a loser, and I wish I could regret it but I don't." He let out a pained breath. "I tried for you. I tried so hard to be the brother you want me to be, and I can't do it anymore. I've never been that guy. I never will be."

He turned around and didn't stop, even when he heard his sister shouting after him. His house—no, Ethan's house —was a good ten miles from this location. It would take him a long time to get home, but the walk would do him good. Maybe it'd help to erase the heartache he had put on his sister's face.

It took almost three hours to make it home. The whole time his phone rang. First Deja, then Emmett. Then Deja again, and one call from Ethan. He ignored them all. Nothing they said would change anything. He'd still be that guy. The felon. The loser. The screw-up. The boy who killed his parents with his reckless behavior.

When he turned the corner to his block, a smile grazed his lips—home finally—before disappearing into a scowl. Ava's car sat in his driveway. She was the last person he expected to come console him or whatever she was here to do after walking out on Deja. Unless it was Julie.

As soon as he got closer, the door to each side of the car opened. Ava stepped out of the driver's side, and Julie stepped out of the passenger side.

This was even more surprising than thinking it was Ava to hound him about the argument with his sister.

He found himself stopping in his tracks before he could pass Julie. All he wanted to do was get to his front door and slam it shut, locking them both out. But his feet were frozen and his eyes zoomed in on hers.

Julie frowned and took any sort of option out of his hands when she approached him, standing in his path.

"You're sweating." Her hand brushed his forehead. "How far did you walk? Where were you?"

Ava didn't come as close as Julie, but she didn't hesitate to speak. "Deja said you left the office over three hours ago. You didn't walk from there, did you?"

A tired, disgusted laugh escaped. "Now my sister tells you everything like it's your damn business."

He couldn't look at Julie and see the disappointment in her expression. He stepped around her and shook his head.

"Well, it's not your damn business, Ava. I don't have anything to say to you."

"She was worried about you. We all were."

Were? So they didn't care anymore? There was nothing to be worried about anymore? Well, good riddance to all of them. He continued to shake his head and headed for the front door. Whatever. He wasn't going to try and interpret her words and the meaning behind them.

Could he get inside without them trying to follow him? Highly doubtful. When Ava got a bug up her ass, it was hard to stop her. And Julie, well, he wasn't sure about her in any aspect other than she had been blunt thus far. She'd no doubt be a force to be reckoned with like Ava. He wasn't even sure why she was here with Ava. They slept together. It had just been sex.

He shoved the key in the lock and realized he didn't lock the dumb door again. Why did he even bother carrying the key with him? Locking the door wasn't a habit he was good at doing anyway. Before he could open it, a hand touched his arm, curling around his bicep. His eyes closed as her soft, yet strong grip washed over his senses. One touch and he wanted to drop to his knees and give Julie anything she asked of him.

"Let us in."

Such good intuition she had, knowing he was about to shut the door on them. Although she didn't say as if asking, it also didn't sound like a demand. She was leaving it up to him whether he'd allow them inside.

He twisted, jerking at the concern in her eyes. Why was she worried about him? What the hell did his sister say to them? He left—sure, angry. But...this was all very confusing.

"You shouldn't be here," he whispered, for some reason not wanting Ava to hear.

"I can't seem to stay away."

He opened the door and stalked inside. Though he wanted to shout vile things at Ava to get out of his house, he allowed them to enter. If he was going to listen to Ava bitch at him for hurting his sister's feelings then he'd do it while chugging a beer—or two. He didn't wait for either of them.

Beelining it for the kitchen, he groaned when he heard them follow.

He grabbed a beer, not bothering to offer them one, knowing he was acting like an asshole, but unable to stop it. Even with Julie. And he knew he shouldn't treat her with disrespect. She hadn't done anything wrong to him.

He crossed his arms after taking a long pull of the beer and waited for the beratement to begin.

7

Dare was definitely giving off 'don't touch me' vibes along with the 'don't talk to me' vibes. She'd gotten past the front door, and she'd get through this other bullshit he was trying to portray.

He was hurting. That was obvious. From the fight with his sister, no doubt. Based on the conversation Ava had with Deja, she finally knew her brother wanted to leave. The talk obviously didn't go well. Julie still couldn't believe he walked as far as he did. But it made sense, she figured. He didn't drive. He hadn't since being released from prison. Of course the big dummy could've called a cab or something.

Damn it. Dare would not like knowing everything Ava kept telling her. She wasn't going to stop Ava from giving her the information because she wanted to know every little thing there was about him. He wasn't likely to give anything up. But she also wanted to respect him and have him tell her everything. How he was feeling. What happened with his sister. The things in his past. When he might feel comfortable enough to get behind the wheel again.

But would he ever provide any part of his feelings

without prying it from his mouth like a crowbar trying to open a locked treasure chest?

Julie ached to move closer to Dare. Take his hand and offer support to what Ava was about to spring on him. Feel his roughened touch because she missed it. It hadn't even been a full twenty-four hours since he last touched her, and she missed it like she missed her favorite java joint on the corner from her office. Such magnificent coffee.

Except she stayed on the far side of the kitchen, Ava near her, to give him the space he clearly wanted.

"Get it over with and then get out of my house."

She flinched at his harsh tone, hating herself for the reaction. He had looked at Ava as he said it, but she knew she had been included in that. She had arrived with Ava, after all.

Since he walked away from the front door, he hadn't looked at her once.

"Are you okay?" Ava asked tentatively, as if she knew as Julie did that he was barely hanging on to his control.

He smirked. "I'm fine. Good talk. Bye."

"Well, that's good to hear." Ava beamed a bright smile as if she believed his bullshit. "I'm not here specifically about what happened with Deja, though."

Dare blew out a strong breath, like a bull gearing up to attack. Then his sharp gaze finally hit her. She flinched at the hatred she saw in his steely blue eyes. Why was he looking at her like that?

"Well, gee, Ava. Sorry for sleeping with your friend. Especially with a loser like me. Won't happen again. Now get the hell out of my house."

Enough was enough. Julie could only stand to take so much. She was more than happy to give him space when it came to his feelings about his sister, but not when it came to her. She refused to let him demean what they shared last night. It had been more than sex, even if neither of them wanted to voice it.

She stormed his way, shoving him hard in the chest. He had nowhere to go, so his back hit the counter.

"Say that again. Tell me what you really think about me. To put yourself down like that says more about what you think about me than anything." She spoke low, each word tinged with venom. He wanted a fight, she'd give him one.

Dare's hands were down by his sides. She could feel the beer bottle resting against her thigh. His blues eyes bore into her, his hot, sultry breath teasing and tempting her to lean closer. Yet she didn't move a muscle. Her right hand held his chest, the pressure hard, yet not hurtful.

"It's easy to say something clear across the room, but you got nothing to say this close to my face? Huh? Tell me!"

Her hand rose up and down as rough, harsh breaths left his mouth, yet he didn't say a word.

"Go on. Tell me what you think. What last night meant to you. Was it good enough for your first time after so long? Or maybe I—"

His lips slammed down hard on hers as his one arm snaked around her back, pulling her closer. Her hand curled into his shirt as she opened her mouth, letting him devour her unlike anything he did last night. Every hurt, every ache he endured today poured out into the kiss. He didn't have to tell her with any words what last night meant to him. She felt it in the brutal kiss.

Last night had been everything. It had been too short and not enough.

He broke the kiss first, leaning his forehead against hers. His heavy breaths made her ache inside. She could feel his pain bleeding through every tiny movement in his body.

"Why are you here?"

She wanted to shield him from what Ava wanted but knew she couldn't. If he was as good of a man as she believed he was, then he'd see—though she predicted he'd resist at first—what they wanted to do was for the greater good.

"Well, I'm not here because my friend's not happy I slept with you, so don't go saying shit like that again. Or calling yourself a loser. I won't stand for it."

His hand on her back tightened, yet he didn't move away from her, his forehead still against hers.

"So she isn't happy?"

"That's what you focus on?"

He leaned back, his intense blue gaze searing into her like a hot poker. "I know I'm not good enough for you, but I don't need that shit thrown in my face."

"No one's throwing anything in your face, and you are good enough for me. Stop putting yourself down."

"So you'd date a felon?"

Oh, he had her there. She wasn't sure how to answer that loaded question.

"That's what I thought."

She hesitated too long, not sure how she could word what she felt correctly, but what he believed was far from the truth. She would date him...if she could.

"Listen to what she has to say and think about it. Okay?"

His eyes narrowed as if trying to decipher what Ava wanted to speak to him about.

"Please."

He shook his head, and she wanted to pound her fists into his chest to make him see reason. For him to listen instead of jumping to the defense all the time. He wasn't a bad guy, despite thinking he was.

"I hate that I can't say no to you. I hate what you make me feel."

As long as he didn't hate her.

Now she wanted to know what he felt. What did that mean? They only spent one night together. His feelings couldn't be that strong.

But he felt something.

Like she did.

While she wanted to lie to herself and say she only felt extreme lust—she wasn't opposed to telling Ava to leave her here when she was done and have her naughty way with him again. But she couldn't say it was just lust. It was...an intense emotion that she couldn't find the right word for yet. It was something she hadn't ever felt. He made her feel things that were new and exhilarating and terrifying.

Maybe that's how he felt, too.

"Well, just don't say you hate me."

Before he could respond—she didn't want to know what he had to say to that—she yanked the beer out of his hand and took a long swallow, turning toward Ava as she did.

"Can't promise he won't bark at you, but he's willing to listen."

DARE SNORTED at what Julie said to Ava. Not that it wasn't true. He'd listen to whatever the hell it was Ava wanted because Julie asked him to. And he didn't know how to tell her no. He should've never admitted that. They barely knew each other for him to feel so strongly about her. Would she use it against him? Would she test him to the limit?

He hoped he never had to find out.

Ava stepped closer to them. Her steps were tentative,

which looked so odd on her. He'd never seen her be anything but strong and confident. It wasn't as if he'd physically strike out at her. He might holler and posture and put up a tantrum worthy of an Oscar, but he'd never lay hands on a woman.

"For the record, I deduced on my own Julie slept with you because she didn't come home last night. Not because she told me anything. Whatever happened between you two is between you two."

Dare nodded. Fair enough. He knew they couldn't keep it a secret, but it wasn't anyone's business but their own. He was grateful to know that Ava respected that.

"She did mention you had a run-in with an old buddy, though."

He glanced at Julie, who blushed with embarrassment.

"I told her how nice it was that you stood up for me when he kept calling me love. It grated on my nerves."

Rick was lucky Dare didn't beat him to a pulp for calling her that endearment he had no right to do.

"What about him?"

"I'll cut to the chase, okay?" Ava asked, nodding as if he were agreeing.

And shit, he did agree. He wanted this conversation over with and them out of his house.

Maybe not Julie, but he didn't have high hopes she'd stay. They had one magical night and he'd have to live off that for the rest of his life. He didn't think he'd ever meet someone as special as Julie again. Someone who would overlook his record. She might've judged him in the beginning, but she apologized and that was that. He believed she was sincere.

"I think he's running drugs in this town. There was an overdose yesterday, and we have reason to believe it could've been murder. That Rick had something to do with it. I need to arrest him. I need to get him off the streets."

But she needed him to help with that.

Rick might've touched a nerve. He might've wanted to beat up his old friend. But he wanted nothing to do with that old life.

He didn't want to ruin his friend's life either. It wasn't his business.

"I don't think that's cutting to the chase."

He needed Ava to spell it out completely for him before he told her where to go. Preferably out the front door never to come back.

Better yet, he'd leave and disappear. No one could bother him then. No one could make him feel like he was pathetic and unworthy. No one could remind him daily of his failures. No one could pretend he was better than anything but the loser he was.

"I want you to go undercover as an informant. Find out anything you can about his business and report back to me and the chief of police. I already ran it by him, and he's all for it. Right now, that woman's death is being labeled as an overdose, but if one of my officers thinks it's murder, I need to trust his instincts and look harder into it."

My officers? Ava thought she ruled everything, everywhere she went. That trait had always bothered Dare. Not that he ever voiced it to anyone, even his sister.

"No."

He wasn't getting involved. He didn't think he had it in him anyway. He'd been clean for the past ten years, and being surrounded by drugs...well, that could end his sobriety. Urges didn't hit him often. Not as often as he assumed it would hit once he was released. He hadn't been using drugs that long when he was younger before he got locked up. Sure, it was easy to get contraband into prison if you knew the right people. He had. But he didn't touch anything in prison. He wanted to forget that life and move on. Why test himself? Being around Rick, he'd expect Dare to do whatever the hell he did, which meant getting high, and once he started, he didn't know if he'd be able to stop again. Not that he ever did heavy shit back then, but who knew what Rick was into these days. He'd been dressed sharp like he was bringing in some good dough. Dare could only imagine what kind of dugs Rick was supplying.

"Dare, please, think about—"

"I don't need to think about shit, Ava. I'm not someone you can push around. I said no."

A warm hand touched his shoulder. *Don't do this, Julie. Don't say a word.* He tensed, waiting for her to land the blow.

He had no idea why she had such a powerful control over him. Why he knew deep in the pit of his stomach, if she asked the same question Ava had, he'd reverse his answer.

"I'll do it with you."

Ava gasped as he whipped his direction to Julie.

"Excuse me?"

Her touch was light on his shoulder, but he could see the emotions she was holding back. So many swirling in her velvety hazel eyes.

"I'll do it with you. We'd be a team. You wouldn't be alone."

But he was always alone, even when surrounded by people. Why did he sense her words held more meaning than just the assignment Ava asked of him? As if she knew how he felt. That he didn't believe he belonged anywhere.

"You can't do that, Julie," Ava butted in.

Dare crossed his arms. Julie let her hand fall as he

moved. He didn't say anything as he waited for Ava to say more, which she did when Julie scoffed.

"You work for the FBI. He'll know something is up if you go with Dare."

Julie's stance went rigid as she stood taller. "You work for the police. His sister married into your family. Like Rick isn't going to find that suspicious."

"That can't be helped. Plus, it doesn't mean Dare shares the same views as us. He can convince Rick he's..." Ava's voice trailed off as she realized what she was saying.

Dare wasn't one of them. One of the good ones.

He was the bad guy. The felon. The one who didn't belong in the family. Something he knew all along. Ava was finally admitting she knew it, too.

He was a murderer.

"No, you are not!" Julie snapped, slapping him in the chest.

He shook his head, it dawning on him that he said that last bit aloud. He hadn't meant for it to slip, but whatever. It was true.

"Ava seems to think I'll fit right in with Rick and have no problem getting in. Because I'm just like him. I fit in that world more than I fit in this dumb one I keep pretending I might fit in one day. It's the truth, even if you want to ignore it."

"You are more than what you think you are. You made a mistake—"

"I killed my parents, Julie. That's beyond more than a mistake."

She let out a slow breath as she smoothed her fists out. A sly smirk emerged on his face as he realized she wanted to hit him again. Knock some sense into him. But he didn't need that. He knew who he was. Nobody needed to convince him otherwise. He wasn't the one having a problem hearing it. She needed to accept the truth. He was a killer, plain and simple.

Was he tempting the beast inside her? Maybe. But she had wanted him to lose control last night and he had. He did her bidding. Now he wanted to see her lose control. He wasn't the only one always keeping his emotions in check.

"You didn't do it on purpose. There were a lot of factors involved, and it was a terrible tragedy. I don't want to hear you call yourself a murderer again. Do you hear me?"

"I heard you."

He'd acknowledge it, especially since she was breathing heavy and her fists were clenched again, but it didn't mean he wouldn't say it again. He just wouldn't say it in front of her.

Julie looked at Ava. "Rick has already seen me with Dare. At a bar. We left together. We can set this up where Dare doesn't reach out to Rick, but Rick does to him. Nothing suspicious with that."

"How do you propose we do that?"

Ava sounded like she was being convinced. What. The. Hell. He never agreed to it. In fact, he had said a big fat no. He didn't want Julie anywhere near Rick. Who knew how dangerous he had gotten. He'd been a low-time drug dealer ten years ago. Dare didn't know how far he'd climbed that ladder. The higher he climbed, the more dangerous he'd be.

"We'll figure out where to find him and be there at the same time. A coincidence. A place that Dare has frequented before so it's not too much of a coincidence. It's a small town, so it shouldn't be too hard."

"And your work?" Ava asked, looking more and more convinced.

"I'll take care of it."

The hell she would.

"I said no." He shook his head and backed up a step, away from the counter and away from Julie. "I said no."

She didn't make a move to come closer, but she didn't need to with her next words.

"Aren't you tired of running away from yourself? You can tell yourself you want to get away from this town because your past keeps haunting you everywhere you go. But it's still going to haunt you, even if you move halfway across the world. You want to run, but not from this town. You're trying to run from yourself. It's impossible."

She didn't know what she was talking about. And he didn't have to listen to it.

He couldn't walk around her because he knew she'd stop him, so he turned the other direction and pulled open the door to the backyard, slamming the sliding door shut.

Chased out of his own house.

Because he couldn't say no to her again, and she knew it.

8

J ulie bit her bottom lip, staring at Dare as he stalked out of the house. She moved to follow him, but Ava's voice stopped her.

"I've never seen anyone but Deja get in his face like that, and he allows it."

Emotions were high. She'd been so tense, more wired than she'd been in a long time. Her job put her in some very sticky situations at times. Nothing compared to this moment.

But she could make this right with him. She could...

"Maybe this isn't the right avenue to take."

Ava sighed. "You might be right. I won't force him to do it. Deja will have my head when she hears about this. I can't ask you to stay..."

Julie swiveled her head toward Ava, knowing she had more to say. It was the way she paused as if waiting for her to look.

"But you're looking for an excuse to stay, aren't you?"

She shrugged. "That man aggravates and frustrates me

more often than not. I don't know what it is about him that makes me—"

Ava was her best friend. She should be able to be honest with her. But Ava was also the most judgmental, opinionated one out of the three of them. Not to mention, she was related to Dare in a roundabout way and it made everything a bit more tricky.

"What?"

"Makes me wish for..." *What you have.* "More than what I have now."

She wasn't ready to be completely honest with her best friend. Maybe not even with herself.

"I should go talk to him."

Ava nodded. "I can't ask you to stay."

"You're not. I'm volunteering. Let me talk to him, and we'll go from there. You should..."

"Leave." Ava giggled.

Julie hadn't meant for that last part to come out. She was in town to visit her friend, not continuously hook up with a guy.

It was what she wanted—ached for, though.

A slow grin emerged. "I don't know what I'm doing. This is silly."

Ava walked toward her and pulled her in for a hug. "No, this is you finally doing something for yourself. I thought work could—should—always be my sole focus. I was wrong. It shouldn't be for you either." Ava took a step back. "I'll be honest, I never pictured a guy like Dare being the one to make you stop and think."

"Because of his record?" Ava gave a tight nod. "Yeah, that has me hesitating, but only because of my job. I'm not holding it against him. I wish he'd open up more, though. I meant what I said to him. He can't keep running away."

"Well, if anyone can get him to stop running, it's you. You love a challenge."

This time she joined in with the giggles. Ava knew her so well.

The kitchen fell silent. She frowned as it all whirled around her mind.

"I'm afraid this one I might fail. He's so..." Not the kind of challenge she'd ever been up against.

Part of her wanted to wrap him up in a big bear hug and let him have his way, hide from himself and the world. The other part wanted to beat all kinds of sense into him.

"Look, I can see you have feelings for him. I'm not against that. He's a good guy...when he's not being a crank pot." Ava's brows rose as if waiting for Julie to argue that point. No way was she going to. "But bottom line, he lives here and you don't. And if the solution is him moving to New York, would that be because he wants to be with you or because he's running? You'll always wonder. Not to mention, that would be moving super fast, and I've never even seen you move in with a guy, let alone let one follow you home."

All good points. Ones she'd give serious thought to. Not right now, though.

"One thing at a time. Let's not get ahead of ourselves. He hates me right now."

Ava rolled her eyes. "Uh ah, and I hate New York."

Yeah, okay, Ava's sarcasm wasn't necessary. Dare didn't hate her, but he wasn't happy with her. They both knew if she kept pressing about the drug thing, he'd cave. He already admitted he couldn't say no to her. Should she use that to her advantage? Was it worth it?

"Call me when you need a ride home." Ava looked out the window. Dare wasn't in sight. "Good luck."

Julie wasn't sure if Ava meant that for convincing him to

bring a bad guy to justice or in general—the relationship developing between them.

Ava left, and Julie didn't know where to go. Sure, outside to find Dare. But more so, about the drug issue. Did she continue to keep convincing him it was the right thing to do? Or let it go?

In the end, she was terrible when it came to relationships with guys. Because she never put forth the effort.

It was time to put some effort into it.

THE SCREAMING GRATED *on her nerves, but she ignored it like her sister was doing. Because if her big sister could ignore the chaos surrounding them, so could she.*

"Kim, Karter, and Kortney, if you don't stop making a ruckus, you're gonna see my wrath!" Juniper finally hollered from the kitchen to the living room where the kids were arguing over a video game.

At ten, twelve, and fifteen, one would think kids would stop screaming like they were a toddler when it came to games, but not her sister's kids. They didn't like something, they blew the roof off to let you know.

Of course, they knew once their mother used a certain tone, if they didn't calm down, they would see the wrath and that was never pretty. Even Julie hated when Juniper yelled, and being the younger annoying sister, it had been known to happen growing up.

"So, back to what we were talking about," Juniper said, picking up her glass of wine and taking a sip.

Julie would rather listen to the screaming than continue their conversation.

"Don't give me that look." Juniper's brow rose. "You know how much Mom worries about you."

"I don't need a man to make my life fulfilled." Or kids, but Julie would keep that to herself.

She loved her nieces and nephews, but they could be a little too much for her at times. She loved that she could spend time with them, but when she had enough, she could go home and leave them where they belonged—with her sister. If she had her own kids, she wouldn't be able to do that.

When Juniper didn't say anything, she continued. "And Mom worries more about when she's getting her total of ten grandkids than being worried about me."

"Well, she isn't getting any more from me." Juniper shivered as if the thought of even having sex disgusted her.

"Things still weird with Philip?"

While their mom liked to think Juniper had a wonderful, happy marriage with her husband, Julie knew better. They argued more often than not. The last time she stopped by to visit Juniper—over two months ago—she confessed they hadn't had sex in three months. Julie wondered if that was still the case.

"He works a lot. I don't see him much."

"Are you going to be okay, Juney?"

Her sister swiped at her eye, sniffing once. She'd never break down and cry, not with the kids home, but sometimes it was hard to hold it in.

"How did we switch this conversation from you to me? Let's go back to you."

As much as she hated to do that, she would if it made her sister feel better. But it wouldn't make her feel better; it would only help her avoid the situation she was in. Sometimes, the best thing to do was confront the problem head-on.

"I know I'm not the best to give relationship advice."

"You're totally not." Juniper laughed, and she couldn't help but join her.

"But I'm going to."

Juniper rolled her eyes but didn't protest. Because she needed this, even though she didn't want it.

"If you're not happy, leave him."

"It's not that simple, Jules. We have kids. We have a mortgage that I would never be able to handle on my own. Mom loves him."

"Who cares what Mom loves or doesn't!" Julie wanted to slam her hand on the counter. It was better than throwing her wine glass with rage that their mom had such influence over the decisions they made. "She's not the one living with him. She's not the one dealing with the hurt. Do you love him still?"

Juniper was silent for a moment, tracing the rim of her wine glass. "I love parts of him. I hate the other parts. It's those parts I love that make it hard to quit. I want to make it work, but he makes it so difficult."

"Well, the Juney I know wouldn't let him keep getting away with his behavior. One holler and those kids quieted."

"Some things are hard to fight."

Julie knew she didn't know the whole story of the problems in Juniper's marriage, but she sensed it had to do with infidelity. While she hated to think her sister would be the one to cheat—blaming it solely on Philip—she wasn't positive who might've been the culprit. She was too scared to confront her sister about it. Sometimes knowing the truth was worse than being in the dark.

"Then my advice is to do what is best for you. Not the kids. Not Mom. Not Philip. But you. You're never looking out for yourself. Being unhappy isn't going to make anything better. Whatever decision you make, you know I'll always be by your side."

Julie reached out her hand across the table. Juniper took it and squeezed.

"I know, Jules." Juniper squeezed her hand again. "Same goes for you. If you're happy single, then that's okay."

Well, Julie wouldn't say she was completely happy single, but for the time being, she was content. She hadn't found that person worth fighting for yet. Not like Juniper had.

DARE DIDN'T TURN his gaze toward Julie as she took a seat next to him on the ground. He'd had nowhere to go, so he'd plopped down on the side of the house—where they couldn't see him—and leaned against it. Walking was the last thing he wanted to do, so he figured he'd wait them out. They'd eventually leave. Ava knew when he'd had enough and she wasn't going to win.

Julie obviously didn't know him.

His knees were raised, his arms outstretched with his forearms resting on his knees. He jerked, yet said nothing when Julie took one of his hands and interlocked her fingers with his, laying their joined hands between them on the ground.

An array of orange, red, and yellows permeated the sky as the sun made its descent for the night. Soon, they'd be plunged into darkness. Dare didn't care. He didn't have the energy for much. He definitely didn't have any energy for more arguing.

They sat there in silence, watching as the sun disappeared and the moon made its entrance.

"Are you hungry?"

He wasn't sure how long they'd been sitting outside— at least thirty minutes—but he finally turned to look at her.

"I guess."

A corner of her lip tilted upward. "You're such a conversationalist."

He produced a grin as well. "You didn't ask an open-ended question."

"Feed me."

"You're so demanding."

Julie leaned closer, brushing a light kiss to his lips. "You're frustrating as hell."

Somehow, they fit perfectly together. It didn't take much for him to realize she was the one, and it hurt deep inside that he'd never be able to keep her. That they'd never be together forever. Not like his sister had with Emmett. Or Ava had with Zane. And everyone else in the McCord family that was happily in love.

"I got noodles and crackers in the cupboard. That's about it."

Sweet, melodic laughter filled the night air. "You should go grocery shopping."

"So I've been told."

She started to stand, not letting go of his hand, which forced him to stand as well. "Are you going to let me spend the night again?"

Of course he would. Like he'd waste another chance to spend time with her. Each moment was precious, and he'd cherish every second he had with her.

Did that mean she was done arguing about his friend Rick and what Ava wanted him to do? He doubted that, but he wasn't going to bring it up.

He wrapped his free arm around her waist and pulled her closer. "You're always welcome to spend the night."

His lips descended, and she immediately opened up, kissing him with the passion that always exploded between them. Despite having a fence around the yard and no one likely to see them, he didn't want to go much further than kissing her. Though his body ached to do so much more. Plunge deep inside her and show her how much he cared about her. Release all the emotions he was barely holding onto inside.

The kiss slowed, but their bodies stayed molded together.

"I'm sorry, Dare," she whispered against his lips.

What was she sorry for? A lot had happened in the house. Too much was said. He didn't have the power to take it on right now.

He stepped away, pulling her back toward the door. "Let's feed you."

Cool air hit his face when he opened the door and stepped inside. He let her hand go, and she closed the door. More cool air hit him when he grabbed two beers from the fridge. One slid across the island when he pushed it toward her. She stopped it before it hit the edge just as he knew she would.

"Are we going to ignore it all night?"

He twisted open the beer, took a large swallow, and went to the pantry, opening it up. "What do you want with noodles? I think I have butter. No sauce or anything. Are buttered noodles fine?"

His entire body tensed when she wrapped her arms around him, resting her head on his back. "Don't ignore me, please. I tried to apologize. You didn't say anything."

"I forgive you."

Even though he wasn't sure what the hell she was apologizing for. There was a lot she had done to piss him off, but he'd forgive her for it all—if they could move on and never talk about it again.

"You're just saying that. I can tell."

"Are you looking to keep on fighting? Because I think you can figure it out I don't want to talk about any of that shit anymore."

Her arms tightened around him. Her grip was strong but not painful, yet he still wanted to pull away from her. He could if he tried, but he didn't want to accidentally hurt her in the process. They were standing between the pantry and the island. Someone was bound to get hurt if he tried to shove her off. Because that's what he did. He hurt people even when he wasn't intentionally trying to.

"I'm not going to let you keep running away from everything."

"Julie...don't." He gritted his teeth, forcing himself to not say anything else.

"I'm staying for a while in town. You said I'm always welcome to spend the night, so that's where I'm spending my nights."

Was he going to regret saying that? He had a feeling he might.

He inhaled a large breath, letting it out with slow precision. "How long are you staying?"

"As long as it takes."

What the hell did that mean?

He was afraid to find out, so he didn't ask. He simply turned around in her arms, leaning past her to set his beer down. Then he surprised her by picking her up, making her wrap her legs around his waist.

"I'm done talking. And so are you."

Before she could protest, his lips covered hers, muffling whatever she was going to say. He started walking, bumping into a few things as he made his way to the bathroom. When he set her down in front of the shower, she cocked a brow.

"I thought we were eating."

"First, I need a shower." His eyes grazed up and down her body, loving every delicious curve he saw. "And so do you."

"Now who's the demanding one? Whatever you say. We can argue later about everything else." She grinned wickedly, then whipped off her dress.

Nothing else mattered when such perfection stood before him. He got naked just as quickly as her, and soon hot water was raining down over them as he loved her thoroughly in the shower.

9

He whipped his jacket off, throwing it, not even caring where it landed. Why should he? It's not like his mother would care. She hadn't bothered to clean the house in over three weeks, and the dishes, if he—or Deja—didn't do them they'd would pile up until they were forced to clean them or eat off dirty dishes.

Deja sat at the kitchen table, her head buried in her math book. She looked up when he stormed by.

His hand tightened on the fridge handle as he inhaled a deep breath and let it out gradually. He knew without turning around that his sister had followed him into the kitchen.

"Why aren't you at work? You always work Thursdays."

The icy cold water slid down his throat, soothing the ache that had attacked him biking home. It did nothing to calm the rage simmering on the edge.

"Not anymore."

There was silence for a beat.

"What happened?"

Damn it. He didn't want to talk about it. He didn't want Deja to know what a failure he was. How big of a loser her big brother could be. They needed that money. Not only to keep them surviving—because his parents scarcely helped—but so as soon as Deja graduated high school, he'd have enough money saved up for them to hightail it out of this crappy town.

"Dare?"

The fridge door closed harder than he intended, so he took a few more calming breaths before turning toward Deja.

"Boss thought I was stealing money from the register. Let me go."

The instant fury on Deja's face made the rage filling him up simmer down some. He could always count on his sister to have his back.

"How dare they accuse you of something like that!"

They were a team. Always had each other's back. Dare might not have a lot in life, but he'd always have his sister and her full support and love. In the end, that's all he needed.

"Whatever. I'll find a new job."

Where, he wasn't sure. Another garage again, working on cars, even though he didn't have a real passion for it. He was good with machines, knowing the mechanics of how everything worked. It seemed like the best option for an eighteen-year-old who had no ambition to go to college. He couldn't leave Deja alone with his parents anyway. She'd never survive on her own with them. They barely survived together.

"They can't do that to you. Why would they even accuse you of something like that?"

Probably had something to do with the fact the boss's daughter hit on him last week and he turned her down flat. She was twenty-one, loved to cause trouble where she went, and he hadn't wanted to risk his job sleeping with the boss's daughter. Guess it didn't matter he took the high road. She set him up to take the fall for something he didn't even do. He knew without a *doubt she took the money herself. Spent it on booze and drugs because that was all the ambition she had in life.*

"I didn't like it there that much anyway. It's not a big deal."

They both knew it was, but Deja was smart enough to know when to back off. Nothing she said would change the outcome, so why argue about it?

"What's for dinner, D? Your turn to cook tonight."

They swapped every other night cooking dinner. On the nights he worked, she always made sure to make enough leftovers for him so he had something to scarf down when he got off. His parents sometimes joined them, but most often than not, they did their own thing, expecting their kids to fend for themselves. They'd been doing it so long, it was odd when their parents joined them for a meal.

"I was thinking spaghetti, but I hadn't made up my mind."

"Sounds good to me. We'll cook it together tonight."

Because they were a team.

Always.

A WARM HAND landed on his stomach, smoothing up and down his chest before landing on his cheek. Then soft lips hit his own.

"Morning."

He returned Julie's greeting with another kiss. "Morning."

"What time do you have to be at work today? I can cook breakfast while you grab a shower."

His entire body tensed, and her hand took another path caressing up and down his body, knowing she had upset him. They'd just woken up and already the tension returned. He hated how he could react to the littlest thing. A simple question shouldn't affect him so much.

After showering last night and eating a quick bite, they relaxed in front of the TV watching a movie. Nothing more was said about Rick and what Ava wanted him to do. But it simmered and swirled around the air like smoke filling a burning room.

But did it matter the strain between them had returned? No. Because it would've anyway at some point. Julie was here for a reason—well, maybe two—and she wouldn't leave without saying her piece about the real reason she was here.

"I don't shower before work because I get dirty during the day." He moved her hand away from his chest and sat up, scooting to the edge of the bed. "Not going in today either."

Because he had quit. Sure, he had said it in the heat of the moment, but if he was going to make good on his word that he was leaving town, he had to quit. It's not like he could keep working with Tyrone when he didn't like chauffeuring him around. He wasn't about to start problems at the job. Better to cut ties and make his sister's life easier.

He grabbed a shirt from the closet and flung it on. Julie sat up, brushing her hair behind her ear.

"Why not?"

"I quit last night."

She frowned. "Why?"

"Because."

Then he walked out of the room knowing he was acting like a petulant child. But he didn't want to talk about it.

Julie found him making a pot of coffee. When he looked at her, he had a hard time keeping his feet grounded and not moving her way to wrap her up in his arms. She wore one of his shirts, her thighs just peeking through, showing off way too much creamy skin. He'd loved her several times last night, and he wanted to do it all over again. Soak up as much as he could with her because soon it would all end.

"You need to stop walking away from me. I don't like it."

He crossed his arms and leaned against the counter. "Stop questioning me about shit like you have a right to."

"Act like a grown man and maybe I will."

A fake laugh escaped. "You just love starting fights."

"You make it so easy."

Then she mimicked him by crossing her arms and leaning against the counter on the other side of the kitchen.

"You look good in my shirt."

Her eyes flashed with heat, yet he could still see the fight lingering in her depths. She wasn't ready to concede.

"It's soft. I'm keeping it."

His lips widened, liking the thought of her in his clothes. All the time. "You didn't even ask."

She shrugged with a devilish smile planted on her lips. "You told me to stop asking questions."

This time real laughter came out. "You are the most difficult woman I have ever met."

"Well, someone has to keep you on your toes, otherwise you'll just think you can keep getting away with shit. You can't."

"I've never gotten away with anything in my life. I always take the fall, always get screwed, always pay the price, even when it's not my fault."

He tensed, then swiveled around before he could see her reaction to the confession he hadn't meant to slip. The words flew from his mouth before he could stop himself. His hand stalled on the mug he was reaching for when Julie's arms slid around his waist.

"I pictured this morning going so differently. Can we start over? Good morning, Dare."

Several breaths released before he felt his body relax and the tension dissipate. Not completely, but enough for him to turn around and look at her.

If she could pretend everything was okay, then so could he. For now.

"Good morning, Julie. Would you like a cup of coffee?"

"Yes, please. I like creamer. Do you have any?"

His lips pulled up into a grin. "That would be a no."

She kissed him, then patted his chest and walked to the fridge, pulling it open. "Well, you have some milk left. As long as you have sugar, I can work with that. First thing on the agenda is the grocery store."

He inhaled a large breath, anticipating another mini fight to ensue.

"The store is about a mile from here. I usually walk."

She set the milk on the counter. "You must not buy a lot of groceries at one time, then."

"About two bags worth. I only have to worry about myself. I don't need much."

Julie started searching through other cupboards, presumably to find the sugar. He found it adorable the way she scrunched up her nose while looking around each cupboard, so said nothing about where she could find the sugar. Plus, the ball was in her court now. He wasn't going to start this fight. Because he didn't want to argue about the fact he didn't feel comfortable driving yet. He might never drive again.

"I could use the exercise. I like to run most mornings. I haven't done that on this trip. My body is feeling neglected. Want to run there and walk the way back?"

Uh. She wasn't going to question him why he walked

everywhere. That he didn't even want to think about driving again. Well good. He didn't want to have to explain himself.

But running?

"I'm not much of a runner."

She cocked a brow. "You walk everywhere. You're in shape. You can handle it. We can compromise and jog."

Jogging still sounded terrible. That was running in his eyes, but he told himself he wouldn't start a fight.

"I can do that."

The beautiful, bright smile that lit up her face was worth the horrible thought of jogging.

He set two mugs on the counter and was about to pull her in for another kiss as they waited for the coffee to finish brewing when the doorbell went off.

"I'll be right back."

That was code for 'stay here' but he had doubts Julie would listen. He disarmed the alarm, setting it for once thanks to Julie for reminding him. As soon as he opened the door, he wanted to slam it shut when he saw Emmett and Deja on the porch.

"Emmett's here to pick you up for work. I'm here with him so you don't argue about it." Then Deja stepped inside, brushing past him. For a moment, he thought she was going to circle him and push him outside so he had no choice but to leave with Emmett.

He moved away from the door, giving leeway for Emmett to enter. Emmett shut the door with a quiet click, yet didn't say anything yet. Deja stood by the couch with her arms crossed.

"I quit last night."

"You were an idiot last night, and we both said things we didn't mean."

More like he said things he shouldn't have said.

Oh, he meant them, but he should've kept them to himself. All Deja did was pluck a nerve by repeatedly asking whether he'd drive again. She didn't do anything, but like usual, she let him get away with his behavior. Let him hurt her over and over like her feelings didn't matter.

"I quit."

Despite knowing he was hurting his sister, he couldn't stop himself. He couldn't work there anymore. He couldn't stay in this town any longer, seeing his failures over and over.

"You do not quit."

"I won't be a burden to anyone, and clearly I am. Tyrone doesn't want to lug me around. I'm sure in the hell not going to make Emmett do it. And I'm—"

The tears coating Deja's eyes made him pause.

"You're not leaving. I won't allow it," she spat. Emmett walked closer to her, but she waved him off. "Say it right now. Say you're not leaving. Where would you go anyway? Where would you work?"

Because no one's likely to hire a felon like Emmett did were the unspoken words he heard. It wasn't untrue. He knew he'd have a difficult time finding a job. Not many people were good-hearted like Emmett. And shit, Emmett said he didn't do it because of Deja, but more than likely, he had only hired Dare because of his sister.

"Look, Dare..." Emmett's voice trailed away when Julie walked into the room.

She took a spot next to him, curled her hand into his, and smiled at Emmett and Deja, but didn't say anything.

He didn't want to have this conversation in front of Julie. Hell, he didn't want to have it in general. Why couldn't she have stayed in the kitchen and let him pretend she wasn't hearing any of this?

"You can't quit." Emmett held up his hand to stop him. "Not because I'm telling you you can't, but because I don't want you to. You're good at what you do. But if you don't want to work for my company anymore, I respect that."

Deja opened her mouth to dispute that, but Emmett grabbed her hand and squeezed, stopping her, then continued. "Nobody in this family wants you to leave. Not just Deja. And we sure in the hell don't think you're a charity case either."

Dare flashed his eyes to the ground, embarrassed. Emmett had been at the office last night and heard everything. Of course, Dare hadn't seen him. He'd been too hyper-focused on Deja to notice anything else. He had probably been hiding in his office where he couldn't see him.

"Dare?"

The plea in his sister's voice gutted him. He wanted to turn away and pretend this conversation wasn't happening. He knew if he walked out of the room, not only would Deja give him an earful for that, so would Julie. Tell him again he's always running away from his problems. He wouldn't dispute it. It was easier to run away. Safer.

"I don't know what the hell I want. I don't know where to go. I know I don't feel like I fit in here. In the town, in the family. In everything."

"Fine, okay. I'll help you find another job. One in walking distance."

Dare wanted to laugh at Deja glossing over one big glaring fact he stated. He wanted to leave. Yet, he'd give her credit for letting the driving argument go. She respected his fear of getting behind the wheel again.

"D, there's not much—"

"There's an auto shop less than a mile from here. You liked working on cars."

He shook his head. "I was good at working on cars. I never liked it."

"What are you going to do, Dare? Move to New York?" Deja threw a hand in Julie's direction.

The sudden outburst and switch of the conversation had Julie flinching. Yet, she still didn't say anything or drop his hand and move away from him. What was there to say? Even if he did do something crazy, like move to New York City, it would never work between them. She'd never date a felon in her line of work. She pretty much confirmed that last night when she couldn't even answer his question about it.

When he didn't say anything either, Deja swallowed and shook her head. "I apologize. I shouldn't have said that."

"It's all good, sis. It's just sex anyway."

Julie flinched again. He regretted the words even before he said them. But it was true. They said that's all it was going to be. Why hope they could have more?

"I'm going to pretend you didn't say that," Julie said with a sharp tone, her lips in a thin line. She still held his hand, her grip tightening as if warning him to tread lightly and not say any other dumb shit.

He looked at her. "But—"

She put a finger to his lips. "I said I didn't want to fight anymore, so don't say anything else that will start it back up. Please."

He backed away, letting her hand fall away.

"Dare…"

This time Julie's low plea gutted him. He wasn't sure which one was worse. Hearing his sister beg him or Julie?

"Let's just get it all out of the way." He looked at Emmett. "You know me and you wouldn't even like each other if it weren't for my sister. We hated each other in the beginning."

"I never hated you. I didn't care for the way you treated Deja, though."

"You pity me, Emmett."

"You pity your damn self, Dare! Stop blaming others for how you're feeling," Emmett threw back.

Dare ignored him and turned his attention to Deja. "I don't do anything but mess up your life. You know it's true. I've been doing it since forever. It's better when I'm not around. Let me go, D."

Before Deja could respond, he met Julie's irate expression. "There's nothing to argue about with me saying it's just sex, because that's what we said it would be. Why get pissed? Why are you staying here? Extending your stay? For more sex, or to convince me to help Ava? Either way, you're getting something out of it, and I'm the one left dealing with the aftermath of it all. You'll go back to your pretty little life, and I'll still be stuck in my shitty one."

Her anger had morphed into hurt as his spiel went on. He didn't need to stick around to see tears hit her face. He had nobody to blame but himself for hurting her.

Hurting her with the truth. Because the truth could be brutal as hell.

"You all know where the door is."

Then he walked out of the room. Silence followed him.

JULIE WAS SHAKING LIKE A LEAF. A mixture of rage and agony. How dare he reduce what happened between them to sex only. Sure, they might've said that in the beginning, but every time they came together it was beyond the simple act. It was more. It was everything. He was simply too scared to admit it. Like he was scared about so much more.

She had to clench and unclench her fists a few times to stop herself from following him and beating some sense into him. And to stop the wall of tears she felt pounding on her eyelids.

"My brother can be—"

"Please don't, Deja," Julie interrupted. "Don't make excuses for him. I might not have known him long, but I know him." She wouldn't pretend to know everything, but she knew enough to know everything he said was a defense mechanism. He was afraid of his feelings and lashing out. To everyone.

Deja nodded, conceding. "What did he mean by helping Ava?"

Well, this was awkward. She might believe she knew Dare well, but she didn't know his sister at all. Ava had made the comment Deja wouldn't be happy to hear about it. Julie didn't want to be the bearer of bad news.

"On a case."

Of course, she also didn't want to lie to Deja either. Julie always thought honesty was the best policy, even when it could be difficult. Being a liar didn't get a person anywhere in life.

"Please elaborate. I don't know what that means."

The steely gaze Deja threw her way made Julie hesitate.

"She wants him to reacquaint himself with an old friend. Possibly get some dirt on him relating to a recent drug overdose. An officer suspects murder."

Deja took a step toward her. "You're telling me that Ava wants my brother to get involved in his old life when he's trying to get on a new path."

Julie gave a tight nod.

"And what's your involvement? My brother was correct in his assessment. You're either staying for more sex or to help Ava. She is your best friend. So I'm thinking it's more like you're here to help Ava. Not going to happen. I think it's best you leave."

Not how Julie wanted this to go, getting on Dare's sister's wrong foot, but nobody talked to her that way. She might have let Dare speak his mind, but nobody else had the right.

"My feelings for your brother are none of your business. The only person I'll share them with is him. You can keep your opinions to yourself."

"Nobody messes with my brother." Deja took another step closer. "I don't care who you are. Nobody hurts my brother."

"Okay, before my wife gets her trusty tire iron out and uses it for the first time, how about we take a breather?" Emmett stepped in between them, looking more at Deja than at her. "You want to take your anger out on someone, you can with Ava. I'll go with you."

Deja snorted. "To stop me?"

"To help you." Emmett glanced at Julie over his shoulder. "I don't know what you think about it, but I think it's a terrible idea. He's worked hard to move on, even if he's not showing it right now. Asking him to do something like that is asking for trouble."

"A woman lost her life. If it's murder, someone should pay for that."

Although, Emmett's words held a ring of truth—and doubt. Was Ava doing the right thing asking for Dare's help? Was she doing the wrong thing trying to convince him it was right?

"I agree, just not at Dare's expense." Emmett's gaze was stern, but not as hateful as Deja's. "Come on, let's go."

Before Deja could argue, he grabbed her hand and

pulled her toward the door. They left without another word. Which was for the best, Julie thought.

Now time to face Dare. Make him stop running from her.

She searched everywhere in the house.

Gone. No sign of him.

Still running. Would he ever stop?

10

J ulie was right. He ran when things got tough. It didn't mean knowing and admitting that made it easier to stay. The minute he left the room, he escaped the house. He was smart enough to grab a pair of shoes and his wallet and phone, but otherwise, he hightailed it out of there before anyone could stop him.

No one did.

No one followed him.

They were finally sick of his shit. Well, good. It would make leaving town easier, saying good-bye to his sister easier. Never see Julie again easier.

Yeah, right.

None of that would be easy, but it was nice to pretend otherwise.

He kept his head down and his eyes on the sidewalk instead of everything going on around him. Cars coming and going. One person getting their mail. Another walking their dog. People going on with their lives as if they didn't have any problems. Not like him.

"Dare? You need a ride somewhere?"

He froze, hating getting caught. But there was nothing but sincerity in Emmett's brother, Gabe's, voice. Dare didn't think Emmett called Gabe either. He'd happened to be driving by and saw Dare, stopping to see if he needed help because he was a nice guy.

"You okay?"

Gabe no doubt asked that because he still hadn't lifted his head or turned in his direction. Was he okay? Shit, he had no idea how he was. So many erratic emotions were swimming through his veins. He was afraid he was going to say or do something to hurt Gabe, the nicest, quietest guy in the McCord family.

Instead of answering, he pulled open the passenger door and slid inside. Then sighed, releasing a small bout of tension, but not enough to even feel close to being better. He screwed up and there was no coming back from it. Like always.

"I could use a drink. You want one?"

His head swiveled so fast at Gabe, he was surprised he didn't get whiplash. For the first time, Dare heard a hint of anxiety from him. Gabe was usually the calm one in the family. The one who didn't make waves or cause problems. Who went with the flow. He didn't get into trouble, and he certainly didn't drink at eight in the morning.

"Yeah, sure. Olivia at work?"

Because the only thing Dare could think was going on with Gabe was problems with his wife. They had an interesting relationship. Getting married in Vegas completely drunk and forgetting it ever happened. Reuniting nine months later and deciding to stay married because they fell in love in a few short days. Olivia, who had been born and raised in Vegas, now lived here and worked as an arson investigator in St. Cloud. Gabe was a lawyer. They had a new house, a new life, and living the honeymoon stage of their marriage. What could have happened?

"She has the day off. I was on my way to work, but I'm thinking about playing hooky. You wanna do the same?"

No doubt, Gabe heard about his tantrum last night with Deja. Not much stayed a secret in the McCord family. Gabe was also the kind of guy who didn't pry. He'd want to know what was going on, but wouldn't ask. Dare would have to provide it if he got the nerve to talk about it.

"Well, I quit, so no need for me to play hooky."

Gabe nodded and pulled away from the curb. Twenty minutes later, Dare found himself at a bar he hadn't visited before in a smaller town near St. Joe. It was a rinky-dink place, a little sketchy looking from the outside. But Gabe didn't hesitate to get out and head for the door like he felt secure they were safe here. Dare followed without arguing.

The inside looked much better than the outside. Nice hardwood floors, old-looking but shined with cleanliness. High-top tables were scattered around the perimeter, and a large dance floor sat empty in the middle. There was one other guy who sat at the bar; otherwise, the place was empty.

"Hey, Frank, how's it going?" Gabe said to the older gentleman behind the bar who was drying glasses with a white rag.

Gabe took a seat, and Dare followed suit.

Frank smiled and pulled two shot glasses out, setting them in front of them. "I'm good. And you, Gabe? Haven't seen you in forever."

"It's been a busy time. Got married and bought a new house."

Dare sat without making a peep, while Gabe and Frank chatted for a few minutes, catching up on each other's lives.

Gabe informed Frank why he had to buy a new house. Getting targeted by an arsonist a few months ago and it burning to the ground. Gabe also introduced Dare, though Dare didn't offer his life pleasantries, even though he could see it in Frank's eyes he wanted to know his story.

After their chatting died down, Frank grabbed his best whiskey and topped off the two shot glasses.

"First one's on me."

Then he walked toward the other end of the bar to chat with the other lone customer.

Dare picked up his shot glass first and downed it in one swallow. It burned the entire way down. It felt good, yet painful. Because he wanted another one...and another...and another, until the ache deep inside him disappeared. Even then it wouldn't go away. It never did.

Gabe joined him. They sat in silence for a while.

"Emmett says you want to leave. But I already knew that. You know I'll help in whatever decision you make."

Dare nodded, appreciating his support. He never once doubted he'd get Gabe's support. Back when he first found Olivia, Gabe talked about moving to Vegas. Only to Dare, that he knew of. Dare told him to do it. Do what was right for him. Nobody else would've said it to Gabe. Dare knew Gabe respected the honesty he got from him. At the same time, Dare had mentioned his need to leave. All those months ago, he had wanted to leave even then. Hell, as soon as he got released from prison, he wanted to hightail it out of town.

He couldn't.

One, because of parole.

Two, because of his sister.

"I don't know what the hell I want, Gabe. Everything is so damn confusing." He turned his head toward Gabe and tilted his lips up by one corner. "Thanks, though. It means a lot."

"That's what family is for."

Dare nearly snorted at that. He wasn't so sure the McCords would've been that willing if Gabe had wanted to move halfway across the country. Hell, he knew Ethan would've hated the idea.

"You want to talk about it?" Gabe whispered. Not because he didn't want Frank and the other guy in the bar to hear, but because he wasn't sure he should've asked.

Dare shrugged. "I have no idea where to start. I feel like I can't live up to my sister's expectations of me. Not that she'd ever say she has any, but she should. She should hold me accountable for my actions and the shit I say more than she does. Ava wants me to visit my old life, and I'm scared of what that'll do to me. I can't drive because the thought of getting behind a wheel scares the shit out of me. Might end up killing someone else. And I'm pretty sure I fell in love with the one woman who I can never have a life with. So to sum it up, my life sucks and leaving would solve it all."

Gabe nodded as if processing it all, his eyebrows low, thinking and contemplating with so much concentration.

"Well, Deja loves you, and sometimes we're blind when it comes to our siblings. We let them get away with more than we should. She probably worries if she fights back, she'll lose you. That's the last thing she wants. Don't be surprised when she finally puts up a fight. A person can only take so much."

Honestly, Dare would welcome it. Not that he wanted his sister to get so upset she said or did something to hurt him, but he deserved it. He deserved her wrath, her anger for everything he had ever done to her. Abandoning her when she needed him the most.

"I have no idea what you're talking about with Ava, but if you don't want to do something, don't. She can be pushy, but no one has the last say but you." Gabe shrugged. "I don't know what to say about the driving. I can't imagine how that must feel. So no help there."

Dare was enjoying Gabe's advice. Of course, it was things he had already told himself several times, but hearing it from someone else always helped. Curiosity got the best of him when Gabe didn't continue on the last point he had made.

"And my love life?"

Laughter fell out of Gabe's mouth. "I don't even have a handle on my own."

"What does that mean?"

Gabe rubbed a finger over the top of the shot glass, avoiding eye contact. "I think Olivia is pregnant."

"Why do you think that?"

Not that Dare knew everything that went on in each relationship in the McCord family, but he figured Olivia and Gabe had a solid relationship. They had to if they stayed married not even knowing each other that well. Why else stayed married to a stranger?

"I saw the pregnancy test in the trash can. Hidden under some tissues."

"Did you ask her about it?"

Gabe shook his head before Dare even got the last word out.

Dare chuckled, slapping a hand on his back. "Are you stressing because Olivia hasn't told you or because you're about to be a dad?"

A slow grin emerged on Gabe's face. "A bit of both. We're usually good about communicating, but she has me all worried why she didn't tell me yet. Like, how long has it been in the trash? I have no idea how to be a father. We haven't even talked about having kids yet. I mean, we've grazed the surface, but nothing like we said let's do it now."

"Gabe, you are going to be the best father. That is, without a doubt, a no-brainer." When Gabe's smile inched up a notch, Dare continued. "And maybe she hasn't said anything yet because she's freaking out herself."

"I'm losing it for no reason is what you're saying?"

"No, you're worrying tells me how much you're going to be a great father."

Way better than mine ever was.

"Thanks, Dare. I needed someone to talk to about it. I didn't know how to bring it up to her. It seems so silly now when I think about it."

"Anytime."

He meant that. Even if he wouldn't always be around, he needed Gabe to know he'd be there for him no matter what. No matter where he was.

"So who's this woman you love?"

Dare snorted. "What, it hasn't made the rounds in the family yet that I slept with Ava's friend Julie?"

Gabe's eyes rounded. "Not to me."

"You look surprised. Is it because she's so beautiful or the fact she's an FBI agent?"

"More like that you love her so soon. But I get that feeling. I got it with Olivia. I didn't know her very long, but I just knew. It felt like she was the one. That I wouldn't be able to live without her."

Well, Dare would have to learn how to live without her. Even if they could overcome the obstacle that was her job—and his record—she'd never forgive him after the things he said this morning. He intentionally lashed out at her to push her away. No doubt it worked.

"What do you plan to do?"

"Nothing. Even if I could do anything, I ruined it this morning."

Gabe held up two fingers to Frank, who nodded. "Nothing's ever officially ruined. You might need to do some serious making up, but it's not hopeless."

Dare sighed. "How does someone with a record make it work with someone who works with the law? Tell me. How do I say sorry for the cruel things I said?"

"You know what I noticed there. You didn't mention the whole living states apart problem, which means you have it half figured out. You're willing to be with her no matter what. Flowers are usually good to say sorry. Chocolate. Or whatever her favorite thing is. Groveling like you never groveled."

They both laughed, though it wasn't that funny, then Gabe continued.

"For the first part, no clue. It's only an issue if you both make it an issue. So you have a record. That doesn't define who you are."

"It sure feels like it, Gabe. Everywhere I go, it defines me."

"It's a part of you, it doesn't mean it is *you*. You're more than just something on a piece of paper. You're a person that made mistakes, paid for them, and now you want to live life like the rest of us. We all make mistakes, Dare. Some are more egregious than others. It doesn't mean that mistake has to live with you forever. You learn and you move on."

"You make it sound easier than what it really is."

Frank re-filled their shot glasses.

Gabe picked his up, nodding. "Yeah, I know. But if I'm going to make it through fatherhood, I have to be confident about it. Like you have to be about your life. Your life is only shitty if you keep thinking it is."

Gabe held his shot glass in the air.

Dare weighed his words. They tumbled around his mind like an out-of-control twister hell-bent on destruction. He'd lost his confidence a long time ago. The bravado he put on most of the time was an act. Fake, pure and simple.

Because in the end, he ran. Ran from everything.

He picked up his glass and clinked with Gabe's.

"Here's to liquid courage for what I have to do." Dare downed his.

"It's gonna take more than two for me." Gabe did the same.

Julie sat by Ashley and Markus in the comfy lawn chairs as Deja and Emmett went toe-to-toe with Ava. They'd been at it on and off all day long about Dare helping Ava with the drug problem. Considering Deja and Emmett had come to Dare's house earlier this morning, she figured those two would've headed to work after reaming Ava out. Except they didn't. Now it was nearing lunchtime, and Zane and Austin were firing up the grill to cook for everyone. Mahone and his girlfriend had borrowed a car and went sightseeing on their own. Julie figured it was more to get away from the tension than actually wanting to see the town more than they already had.

"How long do you think they're going to argue about this?" Ashley didn't quite say it in a whisper, but she said it low enough so none of them turned their attention toward them.

Julie had tried one time to say something about the

matter, and the look of disgust thrown her way by Deja had her shutting her mouth real quick. She liked Dare. She had no idea if anything would develop between them further—because, despite the way he hurt her this morning, she wanted more. What that more was, she wasn't exactly sure. And if she wanted more, she wanted his sister to like her. She wouldn't if she continued to argue for the wrong side.

Honestly, Julie saw both sides of it. She saw the law side where they could put away a bad guy for murdering a single mom looking to better her life. Of course, if it turned out her death was a simple overdose and not murder, then they were getting another drug dealer off the street. She also saw the other side. The side where this could ruin Dare's life and send him in the opposite direction. That, she didn't want.

"I imagine it won't be solved until Dare gives his final say."

Because in the end, that's what mattered—what he had to say about it—and so far, he wasn't a fan of the idea. Ava would lose this battle, and Julie was okay with that. She might've been more on Ava's side in the beginning, but it wasn't difficult to convert to Dare's side, especially seeing the way it was affecting him, and he hadn't even said yes.

"Anyone know where he disappeared to?" Markus asked. Not as quietly as Ashley had. Though no one turned in their direction like Julie feared. They were too engrossed in arguing to pay attention to much else.

"No. He's not answering his phone."

She knew he had it with him. The house had been empty of that and his wallet when she did another cursory search for him. She'd left a voicemail along with a few texts, as had Ava, Deja, and Emmett. Even Ethan tried calling, despite being at work today. The only people not in atten-dance were Sophie and Penelope—who were shopping together in the Cities at a craft fair—and Gabe and Olivia. Julie assumed both of them were working.

Dare didn't respond to anyone.

"So, you still staying tomorrow, or flying home with us?"

Julie didn't know how to answer Ashley's question. She hadn't had time to change her flight yet, so she could fly home with them tomorrow. Even if Dare didn't go through with Ava's plans, a part of her wanted to stay.

Which was silly. They hardly knew each other, and as he put it, it was just sex between them. Nothing more.

Before the tears could gather at that cruel thought, a car pulled into the driveway. She'd never seen it before, and she had a habit of taking note of everything, even the cars people drove.

She hid her surprise well—as least, she thought so— when Olivia climbed out of the driver's side and Gabe and Dare tumbled out of the back seat. She almost questioned why they both sat in the back. Then they stumbled around the car, laughing and throwing a haphazard arm around each other. She deduced the answer without thought.

They were drunk as a skunk.

Everyone—even Ava, Deja, and Emmett—grew quiet as the three drew closer.

"I'm gonna be a dad. Holy shit." Gabe's eyes rounded, then he and Dare busted out laughing as if everyone else couldn't be privy to the joke.

Julie, Ashley, and even Markus stood up and walked closer to the group.

"What's going on with them?" Ava asked, pointing her question to Olivia. "Was he being serious?"

"Gabe called me for a ride home. As you can see he needed one." Her brows drew high. "He found my pregnancy test this morning, and instead of asking me about it, he got drunk with Dare. It was the first thing that popped out of his mouth when I picked him up. Not exactly how I imagined telling him, but it's okay. Yes, we're having a baby."

The way Olivia glanced at Deja, then a glance at her, she had a feeling Dare had blurted out a few things in the car as Gabe had.

"Congrats, bro!" Emmett threw his arms around Gabe and squeezed him hard. "So happy for you." He looked over his shoulder at Olivia. "And you, of course."

"It's so exciting. And nerve-racking." Gabe laughed, then froze. "I think I'm going to puke."

"Dude, not in the yard," Zane said, tossing an arm around his waist as Emmett took hold of his other side and they half-carried him to the side of the red barn.

"How much did you two drink?" Deja asked Dare. Her arms were folded, her stance was rigid, and she wasn't smiling. Not even at the good news. Besides Emmett congratulating them, no one else had said anything. They should.

Dare shrugged. "Lost count after shot number five. What's it to you, sis?"

Deja's nostrils flared, and Julie didn't blame her for the sudden rage. He might be drunk, but he didn't have to be a jerk.

"Dare, why don't we go get some water?" Austin suggested, walking toward him as if he'd need help getting inside the house.

It wasn't a ridiculous thought. He appeared to be wobbly on his feet. Swaying so much she was surprised he hadn't fallen on his ass yet.

"Don't want any. Don't want shit from you. From any of yous." He snapped his fingers. "Nope," he continued popping the 'p'. "Not what I meant ta say. I had a whole speech." He drew his arms wide. "Big one."

"How about another time?" Austin said, though more tentatively and didn't make a move closer to him either.

Dare ignored Austin and pinned his gaze to her. "You hate me?"

She shook her head. "I think water would be good, though."

He sighed, his eyes glossy and heavy-lidded, his lips in a grim line. "Fine. Water me. I can't say no to you. I hate that. Just like you hate me."

Giggles escaped before she could stop herself. Drunk Dare was interesting. He wanted to start a fight, even half out of his mind, she'd give him one.

"Whas soooo funny?"

"I know you're piss-ass drunk right now, but I'm tempted to water you like you asked."

Dare frowned.

"In fact, I think I will. You deserve it. You hurt my feelings today. I don't hate you, but you hurt me."

Dare didn't respond, though he kept squinting his eyes as if having a hard time keeping them open, and he still wasn't steady on his feet. He didn't attempt to stop her as she went toward the side of the house. Not that she thought he'd be able to stop her in his state.

"What are you doing, Julie? Should I be worried?" Austin's tone of voice already depicted he was worried.

"About yourself? No, but I'd move out of the way. Should Dare be? Oh, yeah."

Then she grabbed the hose and turned on the faucet and sprayed it directly at Dare, right in his face.

11

He shifted in the chair but made no sound. There was no way in hell he'd let anyone know how uncomfortable he was at the moment. His clothes were still damp, although a few hours had passed since Julie had doused him with the hose. As much as it hurt his pride, he could admit—to himself only—that he deserved it. His face still stung from the direct hit, too. He'd take the pain—any pain—as long as it meant Julie didn't hate him for the way he treated her this morning.

The effects of the alcohol were still running rampant through his system. His mind was hazy, and he could feel a headache coming on, subtle, sitting on the edge of a ledge waiting to blast him with the weight of it. That's what too many shots did to a person. The bottles of water he had pounded along with the hamburger he had eaten didn't even help the feeling of heaviness weighing him down.

Maybe that wasn't solely from the alcohol.

Dare sat in his own little corner of the yard away from everyone else. On purpose. Since the dowsing incident, besides Austin bringing him food and bottle after bottle of water, everyone left him alone. His sister. Ava.

Julie.

He wasn't so far gone anymore that he couldn't have a conversation with any of them. But it was for the best they all stayed away. He couldn't guarantee nothing crazy wouldn't come out of his mouth.

Olivia had taken Gabe home about an hour ago. Gabe was definitely in a rougher state than he was. He'd puked his guts then promptly passed out. Olivia let him sleep it off for a bit before rousing him and having Emmett help him to the car. Dare stayed in his corner the entire time. He didn't even have the nerve to congratulate Olivia as everyone else had. He figured he had in his drunken state in the car anyway.

It was his fault Gabe couldn't even string a complete sentence together without throwing up or saying something idiotic. The man didn't drink to excess like Dare could. Not that he'd ever gotten this drunk since being released. He'd overindulged before, sure. But not to this extreme.

Not to the point he felt sick to his stomach. Not the puking kind of sickness either.

Disgust with his behavior. For ruining Gabe and Olivia's moment.

Dare finished off the bottle of water and nodded at Austin, who approached with another full bottle.

"Thanks."

Austin took a seat in the empty lawn chair next to him. There were quite a few scattered around him, yet no one else wanted to risk coming closer.

"How are you feeling?"

"Like a house fell on me."

He could use some aspirin, but he wasn't about to ask for

any. Not when he had told Austin he didn't want shit from him. From any of them. Here Austin was still being a nice guy and helping him out.

"Need anything else?"

He shook his head once, hoping that would persuade Austin to leave it be. To leave him be. He wasn't ready to apologize, even though he needed to.

"I can grill another hamburger or something for you."

Dare stared off into the cornfield behind the house. Last year they had planted alfalfa, but he couldn't remember the reason why they had decided to switch it up this time. Zane had droned on about it, but it wasn't something he particularly cared about, so his mind had wandered.

"You don't have to pretend to be nice to me."

"Well, that's where you're wrong, Dare. I'm not pretending. I care about you, and I'm worried. So get your head out of your ass and stop whatever the hell this is."

That was just like Austin—like all the damn McCords—to let the behavior slide. To be firm, yet endearing in the same sentence.

"I know Ava can be a little too much sometimes. She can't help herself, even when she knows she should back off. You don't have to do anything you don't want to do. Emmett and Deja have been arguing with her all morning about it. That she's wrong. I agree with them."

How laughable. Because Dare had come up with a decision while drinking his problems away with Gabe.

"I'm going to do it."

Then he did start laughing. Low chuckles until a full-on burst of laughter came out.

"You're all worried about me for no reason. That's the guy I am. The druggie. The loser. It should be a breeze getting back into the swing of things with my buddy Rick."

"Do you really believe that?"

Dare looked Austin straight in the eye. "How do you *not* believe that?"

"Pretty simple. I see the kind of guy you are. Caring. Kind. Thoughtful. Hard-working. Dependable."

How could Austin believe those things about him? He wasn't anywhere close to any of those descriptions.

Austin could see the disbelief in his eyes because he continued. "You're very intuitive when it comes to Sophie. She's had a rough life and you treat her with...not kid gloves, but with a level that most don't. You're great with little Jimmy. You think Ava and Zane would've ever let you babysit if they didn't think you were trustworthy." Austin sighed and looked up at the sky. "You might've been released from prison, but you're still living in your own kind of prison. You won't let yourself out. Until you do, you're going to be stuck in this limbo you've found yourself in. Is helping Ava going to help you? Or are you doing it because that's all you see yourself as? A druggie, a loser?"

Definitely the latter question, but he wasn't about to say it out loud. Austin knew the answer. It had to have been a rhetorical question.

Maybe there was another part of him that had to do it for a completely insane reason as well.

For Julie.

To keep her here in his domain.

To find a way to keep her forever, even though he knew it would never work out in the long run.

"I'm sorry for what I said earlier. Thanks for the water."

Austin grinned. "How hard was it for you to say that?"

Dare matched his grin. "Don't expect me to say it again."

"As much as you want to think you're not a part of this family, you are. Once you're in, you're in. You're stuck with us, Dare. Get used to it. We fight. We argue. We make up. That's how it goes."

His eyes trailed to the field once again. "It's going to be hard for me to accept that."

"Yeah, well, we won't ever let you forget it, so take your time. We're not going anywhere." Austin paused. "Even if you do. We're still your family, even thousands of miles away."

It was nice to know he had their support to leave. He knew Deja would hate the decision, but she'd eventually back him up. Here he was getting approval and support from one of the McCords. Which meant he had it from all of them.

He didn't deserve this family.

But deep down inside, he wanted to feel like he did.

THE SUITCASE STARED at her as if it were as confused as her.

I thought we were staying?

She thought so, too.

But how could she stay and continue to mess up Dare's life? According to Ava and his sister, he'd never done what he had today. Drink to excess. And with Gabe of all people. Look what she was doing to him.

Perhaps in the beginning she thought she knew what the right thing to do was. To help out a poor single mom who lost her life too soon. Find justice for her. In any way.

Now she realized it couldn't happen at the expense of Dare's life. One simple question to help out and he was spiraling out of control. Quitting his job. Getting drunk. It was better if she left.

It wasn't like they had a future anyway.

She jumped when a knock sounded on the door. Thankfully, whoever was behind the door didn't see her moment of weakness. The door swung open before she could tell whoever it was to enter—or go away. They didn't give her enough time to decide which option she preferred.

Ashley's concerned face met hers.

"How long are you going to hide away in here?"

Julie rolled her eyes for added effect as if that would hide her true feelings. They were best friends for as long as she could remember. It was impossible to hide anything from her.

"I'm packing."

Ashley cocked a brow and glanced at her empty suitcase sitting wide open on the bed. "Yeah, you've gotten super far. Good job."

Julie sighed. "I can't go out there right now. Dare is super pissed at me."

Ashley sat on the edge of the bed. "He's still sulking like a baby in the chair."

"Sulking?"

Ashley didn't know him well enough to know what he was thinking or doing in his little corner. Hell, neither did she, but she doubted he was sulking. More like brewing on the edge of madness.

"That's what Deja said." Ashley looked at the suitcase. "Are you going to leave without saying anything to him?"

Wasn't dowsing him with water saying enough? Did she need to add more?

She wasn't even sure where that came from. One second she was feeling sorry for him in the drunken state, the next she felt a surge of rage and irritation bubble up inside her. It felt cathartic as the water poured out and hit him in the face. The way he jerked and sputtered. He didn't even fight her off, and that didn't stop her. It was when he fell on his ass and didn't try to move out of the way that had her stopping. It was as if all the fight in him had died.

And it felt like all her fault.

He even admitted it. He couldn't say no to her. So if she asked again if he'd help, he'd do it because he wouldn't be able to deny her. That wasn't right. It wasn't okay to ruin his life for the sake of another's.

A pair of socks hit her face, jarring her out of the trance she had fallen into.

"What are you thinking?" Ashley asked with a whisper of a smile on her face as if she were contemplating throwing something else at her.

"That it's better I leave without saying anything to him. I haven't said anything good lately."

"So you both said shit you shouldn't have. I don't recall you being a chicken shit, though. Walking away when things get rough."

"I mean, what is going on here?" She was so confused.

Ashley stood up. "Well, if *you* don't know, then how can I know?"

"We came here for a vacation. That's it. And now it's time to go back home."

"Yeah, sure, that's what it started as. A vacation. And then it morphed into something else. Something you jumped in with both feet, without even blinking. You can't just jump back out now."

"Why not?"

Julie knew she sounded way whinier than she should've.

"Because it's not how you deal with things. So get your ass outside and go talk to him. If the conversation leads you back into this room to this suitcase, then fine. It does. If it leads you somewhere else, that's okay, too."

"Okay, fine." She turned around and walked out of the room before she could change her mind again. "I need a vacation from this vacation."

"I heard that," Ashley shouted from behind her.

Well, whatever. It wasn't as if she whispered it. It wasn't a secret. It was just the truth.

Something she had to do with Dare. Tell the truth.

Hot air blasted her face when she stepped outside. It felt refreshing for a brief moment, and then she wished she could march right back inside the house for cool air—and a good escape route.

But she was no coward, and this had to be done sooner rather than later. He'd had time to settle down, to let the alcohol run through his system. He wasn't so drunk that he wouldn't be able to have the conversation.

She bypassed Ava and everyone else sitting around the bonfire they made a little bit ago, right before she decided to go inside and pack.

Then she plopped down into a chair right beside Dare, who looked at her but didn't say anything.

Neither did she.

They stared at each other.

The wind blew through her hair, whispering words of encouragement. The birds chirped in the distance, chanting she could do it. The sun beat down, making her sweat, mingling with the sweat she was creating from her nerves.

He looked away first, yet nothing was still said between them.

Words teetered on the edge of her tongue, but she didn't know where to start. Sure, the truth. But what was the truth?

She had feelings for him. Strong, heady feelings that were hard to pin down. It was all so fast, like riding a rolling coaster. Short, sweet, and full of turbulence the entire way.

"I'm sorry."

Those two simple words hung in the air between them. She was surprised he spoke first. She figured with the way he looked away, he wouldn't say anything at all. Simply let her say her piece and let her walk away.

Yet, though they were simple, they were also heavy. Filled with so much anguish and pain.

"I am, too."

He tilted his head in her direction, his bright-blue eyes searing into her. All of his pain and rage hit her like a ton of bricks.

"You have nothing to apologize for. I said things at my house I shouldn't have, and I'm sorry for that. I didn't mean them. It was more than just sex." He looked at the ground, and she missed seeing his brilliant-blue depths, even if they were killing her. "I don't know what is going on between us, but I do know it was more than sex."

"What do you want to go on between us?"

Soft laughter fell out of his lips as his eyes met hers once again. "Is that a serious question?"

Perhaps dumb, but yes, completely serious.

"Why wouldn't it be?"

"Where do I start?"

She shrugged. "Wherever you think is best."

"Having a conversation with you is so exasperating."

"Yet I think you secretly adore it." She couldn't help but add a wily grin to that statement. She knew she enjoyed their conversations, as lively and frustrating as they could be.

He held up his pointer finger. "We live in different states." His middle finger went up. "I have a record. A pretty serious one." His ring finger followed. "You work for the FBI who puts bad guys like me away." His little pinky joined the fray. "You deserve someone with absolutely no baggage like I have. I have nothing to offer you." His thumb rounded it all out. "I think my feelings are so strong for you that even the thought of another guy looking at you has me thinking of murder. That'll send me right back where I came from. Because that's who I am."

Well, she could confirm they were on the same page with their feelings—whatever they were. Strong and heady. Yet neither of them was comfortable enough to say the 'L' word.

"All good points."

He shook his head, slouched in his chair, and stared off into the cornfield. "So we have nothing else to say to each other."

"I said they were good points, not that they were true."

His attention snapped back to her.

"The FBI doesn't handle cases like yours. It was an accident, Dare. A terrible tragedy. One you keep paying for over and over and over. With yourself. Could've you made better decisions that day? Sure, but you can't redo it, so why do you keep torturing yourself over it?"

"Do you honestly think I wouldn't pulverize some guy into the ground for looking at you the wrong way?"

"Yes, I don't think you would. You held your control with Rick when you told him to stop calling me love. It might piss you off, but you're not who you think you are. Stop trying to live up to this imaginary image you have of yourself."

He stretched his legs out, his eyes gravitating toward the group around the bonfire. "I'm not the only one who thinks of me that way."

"Ava isn't asking you to go undercover because she thinks you're a bad person. She's asking because she thinks you can handle it and put a bad person away."

Now was as good a time as any.

"And like your sister and Emmett think, I agree with them."

Dare was silent a moment before looking at her. "Now you think I shouldn't do it?"

"No, I don't."

"Because I can't handle it? Because I'll fall back into that life? Because it is who I am?"

"Because—" She paused, unable to articulate the reason why. It was so many reasons, yet to put them into words seemed impossible. "Because."

He laughed. "Oh, okay, that explains it all."

Yeah, well, she didn't have the correct words. At least, not yet. But she'd find them and then she'd tell him.

"I don't expect you to stay. I don't expect anything from you, Julie. As much as we both might want something to happen between us, we're both wise enough to know it'll never actually happen. Go home. Forget about me. We'll pretend it was only sex. No hurt feelings."

But her feelings were already hurt. Because he was saying what she knew to be true. How could it possibly work between them?

Yet she honed in on the one thing that didn't sound right.

"What do you mean you don't expect me to stay?"

"I had a long morning to contemplate about a lot of shit. I've decided I'm going to help Ava. Because I can." Then he stood up, steady on his feet and determination on his face. "I'm sorry if I ruined your vacation. It was never my intention to cross any lines."

He walked away.

Oh, lines were definitely crossed. She'd do everything in her power to uncross them.

12

He had nowhere to be, and yet he was wide awake. There was no sense lounging in bed and wasting the day away, not that he knew what the hell he was going to do, but still. Dare showered, dressed, made his bed, and started a pot of coffee. He was enjoying the first few sips of the delicious brew when the doorbell went off.

"Hey, Gabe." Dare opened the door wider and nodded for him to come in. "You look better today."

"Odd, because I don't feel better yet." Gabe chuckled.

Dare joined in because there wasn't anything to do but laugh at their antics from yesterday.

"Olivia pissed at me?"

Gabe frowned. "No. She's not even mad at me. I am the luckiest man alive to have found such an amazing woman. Some days I think it's all a dream, and then she reminds me it's all very real. We talked—and celebrated," he said with a hint of red appearing in his cheeks, "last night after I recovered from our fun time."

"Well, tell her I'm sorry anyway. So she knows."

Gabe frowned again. "She's not mad at you. You didn't

do anything wrong. I'm the one who wanted to go for drinks, so I'm not sure where you fall into being the bad guy here."

Dare shrugged. "Because I always am."

"I didn't come here to argue with you about something that doesn't need to be argued about. I stopped by to say thanks."

This time Dare frowned. "For what?"

"For being there for me. I needed a friend, and you..." Gabe blew out a breath. "Well, you were there for me like Jimmy would've been. I know you never met him and only know him through stories people tell, but you're like him in a lot of ways."

Dare busted out laughing. It came so sudden, it was impossible to stop. Though, as Gabe's frown deepened, it died quickly.

"I am nothing like Jimmy. He was a hero. He saved Ava's life. I *took* two lives. We are nowhere close to being the same."

"He was more than just the person who jumped in front of a bullet. He was my friend—my best friend. My confidant. If I had a problem, he was there for me. If I needed to vent, he was there for me. If I was feeling down, he was there for me. If I wanted to celebrate something, he was there for me. Maybe you don't realize it, but you've been there for me, too. In those same ways. In more ways than my brothers at times." Gabe's eyes widened. "And please don't tell them I said that. I don't mean it in a bad way, and they'll take it badly. They don't always understand me. For some reason, you do. I don't want to argue about this either. Just say..." Gabe shook his head. "You don't have to say anything if you don't want to."

"Anytime, Gabe. I'm here for you anytime."

Finally, Gabe smiled wide. "Same goes for me."

"So I told Ava I'd help her."

"You sure that's what you want?"

Dare wasn't sure about anything. But sitting on his ass thinking about it wasn't going to solve anything. Or help him decide what the right move was. Plus, he was still pissed at Rick and the way he called Julie love. He deserved everything he got for that reason alone. Not that he had any claim over Julie, but it was the principle of it. In that brief moment in time, she had been with *him*, and anyone stepping in thinking they could ignore him standing there was unacceptable.

"It'll pass the time for now."

"Well, good luck. And be safe."

The way Gabe frowned again, memories of Jimmy had surfaced. Dare had no plans of getting in any crossfire. Hell, he wasn't even going to touch a gun. He couldn't. Felons weren't allowed to. He didn't think Ava had that in her plans anyway.

"Always am."

"Julie sticking around?"

No, he made sure about that.

"Her flight leaves today. In the morning sometime. At least, that's what I heard all of them talk about before Deja brought me home last night. I don't expect to see her again. We talked yesterday. We said all we needed to say to each other."

"Sorry, man."

He was, too. But no use crying over something that would've never been forever anyway.

"Well, hey, let's go out again sometime soon. Let's not make it random anymore."

Gabe clapped him on the shoulder with a grin. "I'd like that. I have to get to work, so I'll see you later."

Dare nodded and waved as Gabe walked out, leaving him alone once more. The silence never used to bother him. Just a few mornings with Julie and already his life wasn't the same anymore.

He finished his coffee, put the cup in the sink, and decided for once in his life he wasn't going to wash the dirty dish right away. He usually liked everything neat and tidy. Nothing out of place. Like his cell used to be. Everything put together, not even his bed had been left unmade until it was time to go to sleep.

Times needed to change. He didn't have to be so rigid in his routine anymore. Because he wasn't in prison anymore. Who cared if he left a dirty cup in the sink? Who cared if he didn't make his bed right away? Who cared if he left a shirt on the floor because he could?

Well, that last one might be hard to fix. He hated seeing crap lying around the floor.

He was thinking about taking a walk when his doorbell went off again. No more than thirty minutes had passed since Gabe stopped by. It was still pretty early in the morning.

Although he had tried to hear everything when they talked about the flight information, he had never heard the exact time the flight was. Maybe Julie was stopping by before she left.

When he opened the door to see Ava standing there, he realized how naive it was of him to think he and Julie had anything left to say to each other.

"Can I come in?"

He left the door hanging open and walked toward the kitchen, deciding he needed another cup of coffee. Just to keep his hands busy and his nerves hidden away. There was only one reason Ava was here, and it wasn't to chit-chat.

The coffee pot was still half-full because he hadn't poured it out yet—that monumental decision not to do the dishes paid off.

He lifted it, asking with the simple gesture if she wanted a cup. She shook her head and got right down to business.

"We'd like you to wear a wire."

His hand wobbled as he set the pot down and he hoped like hell Ava didn't notice it. "I don't think so."

"I wouldn't ask you to do anything that I didn't think you could handle."

He turned around and leaned against the counter. "Rick isn't dumb. Even if we set this up as me running into him is a coincidence, he isn't going to trust me right off the bat. He'll know my sister married a guy whose family is in law enforcement."

Ava nodded, then she pulled a weird-looking leather bracelet out of her purse and set it on the counter. "It's a stylish leather cuff that some men wear. I think it'll look good on you. It also has a listening device embedded into it. It's not your typical wire you wear on your chest like they show on TV. He'll never know. You press this button that looks like a snap on the end." She pointed to one of the two snaps that did indeed look like it simply held the bracelet together. "It'll turn it on and off. This way you can wear it all the time, even when you're not with him, and it won't look suspicious."

Meaning if Rick had him followed.

Dare picked it up, eyeing it carefully. It was smooth all around, with two snaps on the end to hook it together. The deep-brown color of the leather said it wasn't a flashy piece. He tended to wear darker colors as well. Either black or brown shirts, sometimes white on occasion. He wasn't into bright colors much.

He set his mug down and snapped the cuff on, twisting his left wrist this way and that, feeling the light weight of it, getting a sense of the look.

"Yeah, okay, I'll wear it."

Ava grabbed a piece of paper from her purse and pushed it his way. "Here's a list of the people he works with. From the top to the bottom. Little pieces of information that I thought might be useful for you. So when he mentions one of them, you're prepared. Not all of them are going to be pleasant."

Dare took that to mean some of them had nasty records. Worse than his. While he had killed his parents, it hadn't been intentional. He imagined some of these guys on the list made it their business to hurt people.

He also noted how she seemed very sure that Rick would let him into his world and talk about these people. Maybe even let him meet them.

"How will you know when I turn it on?"

"We'll be notified. Technology these days is great. Don't worry. I'll be there with you every step of the way." Ava took a few steps closer as if she wanted to hug him or something.

Which was so odd. They didn't have that sort of relationship. Hell, he didn't like most people touching him in any way. He even got the heebie-jeebies sometimes when Deja hugged him.

"We have reason to believe he'll be at Haverty's Bar again tonight. Chatter has it that he's having another meeting with another local gang leader."

"Same people I saw the other day?"

"Possibly. I'm not sure who was there the other day."

He lifted his left wrist. "At least it doesn't look too dumb on me."

"It looks great on you." Ava adjusted her purse strap,

smiled, and half-turned like she was going to leave, but didn't move. "Thank you for doing this, Dare. I know everyone else isn't on board with it. Not even Julie anymore."

He didn't want to talk about Julie, especially with Ava.

"I got nothing better to do right now." He cracked another grin, hoping it would lighten the sudden tense mood.

Yet, Ava didn't match his grin.

"You know Emmett and Deja still want you to work with them."

"It's time I moved on. Mowing lawns for the rest of my life isn't a goal of mine."

Problem was he had no idea what his real goal was. What he was meant to do for the rest of his life. Until he figured that out, he'd be in a sad, dreary limbo. Going through the motions of life, yet not living it.

Ava turned, took a step, then stopped and twisted toward him. "I'm sorry things with Julie didn't work out."

She just had to push it. So like Ava to not let shit lie.

"Are you, though?"

"You can be a moody son of a bitch, but you're not a bad guy, Dare. I know with you living states apart it would've been difficult as hell to make things work, but I have never seen Julie smile like she did when she talked about you. She didn't say much about what you two talked about last night, but I know she wasn't happy leaving this morning. You don't look any better."

"It was a few days of fun. That's all."

Even if he wanted to admit it was way more than that, he wasn't going to tell Ava.

"All I'm saying—"

"Ava, it's none of your damn business. I was trying to be

nice, but now I'm just going to say shut the hell up. I don't want to talk about Julie."

Ava nodded once. "Well, I don't need to know any more anyway. That told me enough." She took two steps toward the exit. "You won't see me tonight, or Officer Marcos, but we'll be listening. I'll chat with you tomorrow."

Then she left.

He was alone again, and this time he welcomed the silence. Anything was better than listening to Ava talk like she knew what the hell he was feeling. *That told me enough.*

What the hell did it tell her?

He picked up his mug, squeezing the handle a little too hard, prompting him to set it down before he threw it clear across the room.

Him telling her to shut her mouth couldn't have told her everything.

Like that he might've fallen in love and lost the woman he loved in a few short days. And he had no one to blame but himself.

ONE OF THE only positive spots in this mission was he could drink a beer and watch the baseball game. Two things he enjoyed doing. As much as he wanted to keep on drinking, he was still nursing the first beer after being in the bar for over an hour. Rick hadn't made an appearance yet.

Since he hadn't gotten a call, text, or some sort of sign from Ava, Dare figured he was to keep his butt in the chair until she told him so or closing time came around. It's not like he had anything waiting for him at home anyway.

Ten minutes later, he was forced to order another beer.

One could only sip for so long before it was depleted. Just as the waitress delivered the bottle, Rick walked into the bar.

Dare noted his arrival, but put his attention to the TV. He wasn't about to make himself obvious. In order for this to work, Rick had to approach him.

And he did. Before sitting down himself.

"Hey, second time seeing you here. Is this your normal hangout?"

Generally, he stayed at home drinking his beer and watching the game, but on occasion, when he went out for drinks, this bar was the place he frequented. Which made it interesting that Rick kept showing up. Because it wasn't his normal place.

They shook hands and did a one-handed hug before Dare resumed his seat, answering, "Now and again. I like it here."

"Yeah, it's definitely low-key."

And if Rick was up to no good then that's what he needed. Off the radar kind of joint.

"Where's your woman?"

His stomach clenched, his jaw tightening a bit before he remembered he needed to keep his cool. Julie wasn't his woman anyhow. No matter how much he wished it were different.

"Not around."

He hadn't wanted to chat with Ava about Julie, and he sure in the hell didn't want to do it with Rick either. With anyone, really.

"You waiting for anyone?" Rick looked around the bar as if casing the joint and who was lingering about.

For a Friday, it wasn't as busy as it usually was. Not all the tables were taken, but it also wasn't empty. It was so-so for the start of the weekend. Of course, it was still early, too.

Only eight-thirty. Time for more people to show up and have a grand old time.

"Na, watching the game and having a few."

Rick clapped him on the back and smiled. "Join me. Let's catch up."

"Yeah, all right."

Dare stood up and followed Rick to a corner away from prying ears. Rick sat with his back to the wall and his eyes available to the room. Dare took a seat next to him. Rick introduced him to two guys who had taken a seat while they chatted.

Dwayne and Terry.

Two men on the list Ava had given him. Dwayne was Rick's right-hand man and followed his orders without blinking. Terry was just below Dwayne, although had the worst record of the two. More drug possessions than Dare could count, a few assaults, and one charge for murder that got dismissed. Dare didn't like knowing that, but he needed every spot of information if he was going to survive this.

Though this shouldn't be any different from prison. He'd sat next to his fair share of scary dudes. Guys that you didn't look in the eye if you wanted to keep breathing for the foreseeable future.

Rick asked questions, getting up to speed on Dare's life. He kept it simple. Minding his own business, working with his sister's husband until he decided he had enough of mowing lawns, breaking his back for such low pay. He tried to make it sound like shit work—not because it had been. He had never minded the way it made him feel. Exhausted, yet accomplished. There was never anything better than seeing the end result. A nice manicured lawn, knowing he was the one who had done that. He made it look good.

But no, he made it sound shitty because he wanted Rick to make an offer. Any offer.

Because that's what Ava wanted. An in with the organization.

"You still looking for work?"

Dare shrugged, took a pull of his beer, and glanced at the TV. He forced himself to do it occasionally because he didn't want to seem overly interested in Rick and what he was doing.

"I've looked around a bit. Nothing popped out at me. Tried applying at the garage down the street from my house, walking distance and all. Never heard back. They see felon and yeah." He shrugged again because it was the truth. Well, the felon part and trying to find a job. Not the part where he actually tried to apply to the garage. He didn't want to work on cars like he had when he was younger, but he knew that Rick knew he used to and it sounded like a plausible thing he'd do.

"They don't know what they're missing. You were always good under a hood."

"I ain't losing sleep over it."

"You don't drive?"

He fiddled with his beer bottle and stopped when he noticed the nervous gesture. It wasn't something he had to be ashamed of, but saying it to himself and believing it were two different things.

"I don't feel comfortable behind a wheel yet."

Rick nodded as if he understood. His eyes even held a slice of sympathy. That was the last thing Dare wanted from anyone, especially a jackass like Rick.

"I run a business of sorts."

Dare didn't perk up in his seat, though he almost did at the words. Back in the day, Rick sold pills, weed, and dabbled with cocaine. Not in large quantities, but he had regulars he sold to. Dare had been one of them. It would be stupid of him to pretend he had forgotten that.

"Same thing as before?"

Rick shook his head back and forth nonchalantly. "I expanded a bit."

"I might be off parole, but I ain't looking to go back to the slammer, man."

He wasn't sure if backing off from Rick's offer was the smart move, but he also didn't think jumping at the chance was right either.

Rick's lips curved up into a friendly smile that indicated he said the correct thing.

"Hey, I haven't been there like you, but I get it. Ten years was a long time. I wouldn't ask you to do anything big. Consider it more like being a mailman. Delivering a few packages here and there."

Well, shit. Way to make him face his fears.

"I don't drive. I don't even have a license."

No matter what Ava expected, he wasn't getting behind a wheel for anyone but himself—and when he was damn well ready. If he ever would be.

"You don't have to worry about that. I have a driver. You'd just need to drop off some packages for me. I pay well." Rick laughed, slapping his shoulder jovially. "And for an old friend, I don't mind helping out until you find something else you'd rather do."

"What's in the packages?"

Rick's smile fell.

Wrong question.

But he couldn't take back his words now.

"Nothing for you to worry about."

"Even if the cops would stop me and open them."

"Well, if they stop you, they'll need a warrant. You give me a quick call, and we'll make sure it doesn't get that far."

Dare wasn't dumb. He knew either drugs or money, maybe even weapons would be in the packages. He wasn't worried about getting arrested for having it in his possession because he was doing this for Ava. But he had to appear worried about it.

"I can't go back, man."

Rick held up his hands in surrender. "No sweat off my back if you can't. Like I said, helping out an old friend."

"How good a pay are we talking about?"

Rick slid his hand under the table and pulled it back out, showing a wad of cash clipped together. A hundred peeked from the outside of it. "Something along the lines of this. For each package."

Dare had to guess at least a thousand or more was in that wad. It was thick, but not overly so that it'd stick out if Rick was carrying it in his pocket. And if they were all hundred dollar bills, oh yeah, that was good pay.

"I was thinking about applying at another garage about a mile further from the other one. I guess I can help out until I hear back from them. Nothing permanent, deal?"

Dare held out his hand, hoping like hell all the nerves had gotten out of his system.

"Sounds like a solid plan to me. Welcome to the team, Dare."

Rick's hand slid into his, and Dare knew when his eyes didn't flash betrayal that he was in. Now all he had to do was get the evidence to take down his old friend. He had no idea how he would do that.

He was pretty sure he was in way over his head.

13

A chair scraped across the floor before a shadow loomed over her. Then two slender arms wrapped around her and she sighed.

"It's nice to see you, too, Brenda," Julie said sincerely, although she had to muster a smile when she didn't feel like displaying one.

Brenda leaned away, adjusted her chair, then pinned a hard stare at her. "So, what's wrong?"

Julie swiped a hand behind her ear to fix a loose strand in her way, her brows drawing low in fake confusion. "Everything's fine."

"Tom says you've been a crab since you got home from your vacation three weeks ago. Which is odd, since vacations shouldn't do that to a person. They relax you and re-center you. And you, my friend, are rarely crabby."

"Not all vacations. Sometimes you need a vacation from a vacation."

Brenda rolled her eyes in only the way she could do. With a mixture of irritation and laughter. "Way to dodge the original question."

"Why is your husband talking about me? He should be more worried about Louis starting football this year."

"Because he's worried about you." Brenda's hand touched hers softly before pulling away as if she knew Julie didn't want her to coddle her too much. "And Louis is only nine. His football career isn't that serious yet."

"It's such a brutal game. Baseball is way better."

Tsking sounds ventured between the small space. Brenda's finger even waggled in her face. "We are not deflecting this conversation. Nor am I getting into another useless argument about whether football or baseball is better. Clearly, it's football."

Julie laughed, feeling lighter than she had when she sat down at the tall bar table waiting for Brenda to arrive. After a grueling day at work, tracking down evidence on a disturbing sexual assault case, all she wanted to do was curl up under a blanket and watch a comedy or something. Maybe even take a bath and let all her worries wash away. Instead, Tom betrayed her by telling his worries to his wife, who then bugged her until she caved and agreed to meet for drinks.

"Spill. I promise not to tell Tom everything."

That garnered another chuckle out of her. She'd been partners with Tom for the past four years. He was older than her by fifteen years, but despite their age difference, they were best friends. She trusted him with her life and vice versa. She'd made friends with Brenda just as easily. Although they were partners and needed to trust each other, she didn't have to tell Tom everything all the time, yet she did. They didn't keep much from each other. When he was having issues with Brenda, he unloaded on her. Same with Brenda. At times, that could get awkward. When she was having problems, she usually shared them with Tom as well.

Except this time.

"Why do you say that?"

"Because there's obviously something weighing on your mind that you're not comfortable sharing with him. Otherwise, I wouldn't be here grilling you. We'd be enjoying our drinks talking about football being the elite sport over baseball."

Where did Julie start?

The last three weeks had been a combination of pain and worry. Hurting because she should've never left without seeing Dare one more time. Of course, what would she have said? He made it pretty clear he didn't want her to hang around. She wasn't going to push him away further. Besides, having a break wasn't a bad thing. The past few weeks had given her a clear sign: she missed Dare way too much.

Despite it being beyond crazy to fall for someone so fast, the reality was she had. She missed him so much, she wanted to catch a plane tomorrow—hell, tonight—and show up on his doorstep. Make him see how idiotic he was acting by pushing her way. Make them both see somehow, someway they could make their unlikely relationship work.

But she couldn't. Because that's where her worry came in. Three little weeks and he was already deep into Rick's organization. Ava didn't give her all the details, but enough to know he was hanging out with Rick almost every night, and during the day he was making deliveries for him. He hadn't had a chance to see what was in any package as he was always with another person from the organization, but it was one step closer to bringing Rick down.

The longer it went on, the more she worried about how

hard it might be for him to get out. To find the right path he was meant to be on.

That's another reason she should be there with him. To remind him he was more than what he thought of himself. He was more than just a felon.

Brenda snapped her fingers, bringing Julie out of the trance she always fell into when Dare crossed her mind for even a moment. Which was every single day.

"Talk to me. I hate seeing you like this. Like you're struggling."

Julie picked up her glass of wine and took a large gulp. "When you first met Tom, when did you know you loved him?"

Brenda's head tilted to the side as she contemplated the question for a moment. "Four months into dating. He met my mother—you've met her—for the first time. He survived without walking away with his tail between his legs. Every other guy never made it all the way through the meal."

That wasn't hard to imagine. Julie always kept her distance when Brenda's mother was in attendance at any event. She was worse than the worst mother-in-laws out there. Julie didn't even understand how Brenda came out so normal growing up with a witch like her.

"You fell in love," Brenda said with quiet awe.

Well, she wasn't sure she was ready to bring the 'L' word into it, but she felt like it was damn near close to it. Could she have fallen in love so fast? She'd never actually said the 'L' word to a guy before. This feeling was too new and in uncharted territory to really know.

"I fell. Let's say that. I don't know what to do about it."

"Because he lives in Minnesota. I mean, I'm assuming that's where you met this guy. I don't think you've dated in the past month or so here."

She nodded. "It's not that."

"Ah, so we're getting to the part that you didn't want to mention to Tom."

Julie hated to admit she was afraid to talk to Tom about it. Not that she didn't think he'd understand. But more so what his response would be. His advice, that even if she didn't ask for it, he'd give. She always did the same to him. Normally, she appreciated it even when it was unwanted, but this time...she just...didn't know.

"Come on. You can tell me anything." Brenda cocked a brow. "You can also tell Tom anything. Are you thinking about leaving?"

Julie started to protest that but stopped before any words left her mouth. Was she?

"I...don't think so."

"Hmm...girl, you need to sound more confident about that."

Julie let out a heavy sigh, running her finger along the rim of her glass. "He has a record. He spent ten years in prison for..." Another dejected sigh escaped. It sounded so terrible when said out loud. If she couldn't even tell one of her closest friends about it, how in the world did Dare live with what he had done every day?

Brenda reached out, touching her arm. "It's okay."

Julie looked up, unaware she had averted her eyes. Her entire body felt wired to the T like she had taken a shot of an energy drink and she was about to bounce off the walls until she collapsed from exhaustion.

"He was nineteen, high, it was raining out, and his dad was having a heart attack. He was trying to get him to the hospital. The car crashed and both his parents didn't survive the car accident. He was considered at fault and lost ten years of his life paying for his mistakes. He's still paying for them. With his own guilt. No matter how many times someone tells him he's more than that person, he doesn't see it."

"I can see why you've been struggling. Despite the circumstances, the FBI isn't going to look kindly on you dating someone with a record."

Julie nodded.

"You know Tom would never judge you for that."

"It's not that I thought he would." Julie shrugged. "I don't know what I thought. I wasn't ready to have the conversation with him."

Brenda fiddled with the napkin sitting under her wine glass. "You know, he's loved being partners with you. Especially after his last one almost got him killed."

Yeah, Julie had heard the story once—only once—from Tom. How they had been hunting down a man who had killed three women. When they arrived at the location, Tom had a bad feeling. That gut feeling one should never ignore. He suggested they call for backup and wait. His partner disagreed and wanted to knock on the door, arrest the guy, grab a beer at a pub, and call it day. Well, they didn't even get the chance to knock before the guy was shooting holes through the door. Tom was closest to the door, and luckily only walked away with scratches on his cheek from the wood splintering and flying in his face. He parted ways as soon as he could with the hothead, and then Julie came into the picture.

"Tom has been amazing. I feel the same way."

Julie sensed Brenda was trying to make a point and figured she'd let her get there in her own time.

"He'd miss you, but he'd also understand if you're ready to move on to something else."

Julie frowned. "I don't want to leave the FBI."

Did she?

For a guy?

For one that continuously pushed her away when even a tiny speck of difficulty popped up?

"I wasn't saying that. But you can't have a long-distance relationship forever. One of you would have to move." Brenda reached out again, touching her arm, her eyes softening with concern and love. "Life's too short to let others dictate your life. To let a job make decisions for you. I almost lost Tom that day. So I try to live every day like it's the last with him. His job says I need to. I hate that. So don't let the job do that to you, too. Don't let it control how you live your life. If you want it to work with this guy, then make it work. Who cares what happened in the past, as long as he's trying to work for a better future. Clearly, you feel something strong for him. What's stopping you from taking that next leap? Because the Julie I know doesn't let anything stand in her way."

What was stopping her?

Well, a combination of fear and Dare himself.

Of course, Brenda was right. When did she let anything stand in her way?

She didn't.

When she wanted something, she went after it with everything she had. Failure was not a word in her vocabulary. She wasn't about to let it start invading her now.

"On a scale of one to ten, how irritated will Tom be if I take another vacation so soon?"

Brenda chuckled, picking up her wine glass.

"A one after I have a chat with him."

Brenda held out her wine glass and waited for Julie to clink glasses with her.

"You let that man of yours know who the hell he's dealing with. No walking away this time until you're ready."

The soft clinking sound filled the air, and the confidence that had fled her returned with a vengeance.

"I won't. Thank you, Brenda. This is exactly what I needed."

"Yeah, well, don't tell Tom he was right on calling this get-together. He'll never let either of us live it down."

They cheered one more time as laughter filled the table. Her mind was more settled, yet her heart was still troubled.

Dare was about to get a rude awakening from her. She wasn't sure how he'd respond and how her heart would survive if he pushed her away once again.

THE DOOR SLAMMED HARDER than he intended, but he buckled up and pretended like he hadn't entered the car with irritation.

"Seat belt. We talked about this." Dare's voice was cool and even without a hint of teasing.

Because it wasn't funny. Not to him. Jayden learned that the first time he laughed when Dare told him to buckle up.

Jayden didn't say a word as he strapped the buckle on and then put the car in drive.

They drove in silence.

Which was odd for them.

Dare had been driving around with Jayden for the past three weeks delivering packages for Rick like he said he would. He met the kid the second day after the first meeting with Rick. Jayden was only seventeen, full of attitude, and smarter than he gave himself credit for. Dare almost laid into Rick for recruiting a juvenile into his dirty business, but he stopped himself at the last second. If he wanted to take Rick down, he had to do it the right way and not screw up by showing his hand already. Not that he had dealt drugs when he was younger, but he had started smoking weed and popping pills when he was sixteen. He had no right to tell Rick—or even Jayden, for that matter—that it was wrong.

At first, he hated the fact some punk kid had to drive him around. After a while, when Jayden never said anything about it and didn't act weird, he let it go. It wasn't so bad. The kid was a decent driver, always kept his hands on the wheel and his eyes on the road. He never even went over the speed limit. Though Dare figured that had more to do with the fact he didn't want to get pulled over and caught with a bunch of drugs in his possession. For a kid who was so conscious about the driving rules, Dare was surprised he had to remind him about his seatbelt all the time. Cops pulled people over for the simplest shit. The kid should know better.

"You apply for that college yet?"

Dare knew the answer he'd hear, but he had a small flicker of hope inside that he'd hear the opposite of what he expected.

"Na. I don't think it's for me."

He'd gotten to know Jayden pretty well in the last three weeks. They were stuck in a car driving around with nothing to do but talk. Plus, he hung around Rick too much and so did Jayden. The kid was in his senior year, had the grades to go further, and he was wasting his life doing shit that would land him in prison if he didn't stop. Dare didn't know how to get through to the kid other than suggesting other things than life on the wrong side.

"Why the hell not?"

Jayden shrugged, slowing down for a red light.

"You wanna end up like me? No degree, no chance at ever having a decent job because I'm a felon."

Jayden glanced at him. "You make good money with Rick."

And every dollar Rick gave him, he handed over to Ava. The kid had no idea how deep he was getting himself into this. Dare had already told Ava that whatever went down, Jayden wasn't a part of it. He refused to see the kid get locked up and his life ruined because he was too naive to see how wrong it was.

Ava didn't agree, which was why he was in a bad mood. Another argument with her about the kid not getting arrested when it came down to it. He was driving Dare around. He knew what he was doing was the argument she always gave him. He had no real stability in life. No parents, stuck in the foster system. No real role model to show him the right path was the counter-argument Dare always delivered right back.

So he had to get through to Jayden before it was too late. Or he had to walk away from helping Ava. Because while he wanted to take Rick down, he didn't want to take the kid down, too.

"Money ain't everything, kid. You're good with numbers. You should do something about that."

It was crazy how good with numbers Jayden was. Dare could throw out three hundred twenty-five times twenty-eight and the kid knew it was nine thousand one hundred. Dare always needed to grab his phone and double-check the answer. Every time a smirk would grace Jayden's face when Dare saw he was right. Every. Single. Time.

"Money is everything if you want to go to college. How the hell do you expect me to pay for it, Dare? My foster parents are useless. They're already getting pissy because they're going to be losing out on the money I make them."

Yeah, Dare knew how useless those people were. They didn't even wonder where Jayden was when he stayed out way past his bedtime. Getting home near midnight, sometimes even later. They never said a word to him.

"Is that why you work for Rick?"

Jayden sighed. "Do I have a choice?"

The car stopped in front of a warehouse that looked like it had seen better days. Some locations looked like legit businesses when he dropped off the mysterious packages. Other locations looked like they needed to have a 'condemned' sign hanging on the door.

"You always have a choice. I had a choice growing up. I made the wrong ones. I'm trying to help you see you don't have to make the wrong choices like I did."

Then he got out of the car and popped the trunk to grab the package he knew would be waiting for him. As far as he knew, they only had one package to deliver. Like every other one, it was packed with tape all around it, so it was impossible to sneak a peek without making it obvious he dared to try.

He knocked once on the door and didn't flinch when a suspect dude with soulless eyes opened it. The guy's hair looked like he had just rolled out of bed, and his breath didn't show signs he brushed his teeth yet either. His clothes were stained, and he didn't even pretend he was a good guy. The gun tucked in his waistband said he wasn't messing around. This was the first time showing up to this place and the first time witnessing a gun so blatantly. Dare didn't like it.

Dare held out the box and didn't say a word. The guy

eyed him before snatching it from his grip. Dare turned around and took one step before the guy spoke.

"You opened it."

He gradually turned around, and he wasn't sure why he took his time. Maybe part fear he would see the gun pointed at his face. Maybe part anger that this guy would call him on something he didn't do.

"No, I didn't."

The guy lifted the box, pointing at the bottom. "The piece of tape here is sliced. You did."

"I didn't."

"You're a damn liar. I see the evidence right here."

"Look, man, I'm here to drop that shit off and that's what I did. I didn't do anything else."

The menacing look on the guy's face intensified as his body went rigid.

"Hey, what's—"

"Get back in the car, Jayden." Dare cut him off, and with a voice that brooked no argument, he knew Jayden listened immediately when he heard the soft click of the door.

Dare scarcely had time to react when the guy pulled the gun from his waistband. Instead of retreating, he surged forward, grabbing at the gun as the guy tried to point it. He wasn't worried about himself as much as he was worried about Jayden. Any stray bullet could hit the kid, and his life would be over before he could even live it.

They struggled, fighting for the gun. The guy was strong, but Dare held his own. He walked everywhere, building his endurance. He liked to do different exercises at home and also had a bar hooked up to one of the doorframes to work on pull-ups. He had the strength. Right now he needed to prove he was stronger than this guy.

Sometimes, it wasn't always about being the strongest, it

was about being smarter. His knee connected with the guy's crotch. Not enough to sting him where it would hurt, but enough to make him lose balance. He could feel the guy's grip loosening, and the gun was nearly in his hands when he heard the last voice he wanted to hear behind him.

"Stop or I'll shoot you."

Damn kid just couldn't listen to him.

Shots rang out, stinging his ears.

14

S he stopped and inhaled the fresh air, letting the sun beat down on her. Julie hadn't realized how much she not only missed Dare, but also the small town. The hot, humid air. The beautiful breeze that swept through her hair. Even the stinky smells from Ava's farm were a welcome to breathe in again.

"I can't believe you're back already." Ava stepped off the porch with a wide smile and pulled her in for a hug. "You didn't call."

Because she didn't want to give anyone a heads up, especially Dare. While she trusted Ava, she also knew the bad habit Ava had of getting into other people's business and messing things up. She meant well, but it didn't always turn out in a good way.

"Impromptu vacation."

"Sure it is. You're back for Dare."

She rolled her eyes but didn't dispute it. "Can you believe that man has gotten under my skin?"

"Yeah, I can. Because you've totally gotten under his. He's been a bear." Ava chuckled as they walked up the steps and entered the cool house. "More so than usual. I'd like to chalk it up to what he's doing, but I know it's not that."

"Three weeks and still nothing."

Julie knew Ava wanted to see more progress as well. It wasn't a statement to garner answers she knew Ava didn't have, but she felt compelled to say it.

"He's gotten close with one of the guys. A kid, really. He's only seventeen. Dare is more concerned about the kid than finding the evidence we need."

That statement bristled Julie more than she cared to admit.

"Aren't you concerned about him? He's not even an adult."

"Well, of course, I am, but I want to take Rick down."

Julie set her purse down on the side table near the door and looked around, noting how quiet the house was. She sensed an underlying tension about the subject, so decided it was best to move on from it—for now.

"Shouldn't you be at work? I tried the precinct first, but they said you were off. Where is everyone?"

"Zane and Austin are outside working, as usual. Eleanor took Jimmy to the playground, and it's my rare time to myself. Officer Marcos is keeping an eye on Dare in case he's needed."

She decided to ignore the last statement. It only made her worry even more about Dare. "And I'm intruding on your time."

Ava batted her hand. "Of course not. You're always welcome, even without fair warning."

Now that tension was back, but this time a different kind.

"You're not happy I'm here."

Ava frowned. "I didn't say that."

"Just say what's on your mind."

"Are you sure it's best to jump back into Dare's life right now?"

Julie crossed her arms. "Because he's under your thumb and you want to take down Rick by any means necessary. Maybe it is a good thing I'm here. To save Dare."

"That's not fair."

"Well, I've never had my best friend jump down my throat about visiting."

Ava threw her arms out wide. "You've never visited so much within a short time span. All I'm saying is—"

"As people are so apt to tell you in this family, it's none of your business. I thought I'd do the courtesy of stopping by here first, but I think I should've gone straight to Dare like I wanted."

"That hurts," Ava said quietly, her entire body deflating.

"It does. Every time we talk about Dare, it hurts me."

Silence stretched between them as they stared at each other.

"I should've never left. He's stubborn, I'm stubborn. One of us needs to get past that. So here I am. I have no idea if what we have can work, but I've realized in the short time being away from him, I want to try. We might seem like an odd couple, but I don't care what others think. I only care what he thinks. I'm not here to mess up your case, but I'm not leaving."

She said her piece, and Ava could return her own savage words, but it wouldn't deter her decision.

Ava nodded. "I would never ask you to leave. I understand about the heart wanting what it wants. It's hard to ignore that. I almost did, and it hurt more than anything."

That, Julie knew, Ava understood very well.

Ava's phone rang, stopping Julie from whatever she

would've retorted with. She wasn't sure how to respond, so she was thankful to be saved by the phone.

Ava picked it up from the coffee table, answered it, and when her expression fell into horror, Julie's heart started to pound.

"I'll be right there." She hung up, saying no more and no less.

"What is it?"

Though she asked like she wanted to know, she dreaded what Ava would say. Julie could tell by her crestfallen expression it wouldn't be good news.

Ava wouldn't even look her in the eyes.

"Dare was shot."

In that precise moment, her heart stopped beating. Her lungs stopped working. Her entire brain shut off. Those three words reverberated around her, over and over, pounding into her system like a bad nightmare that wouldn't stop.

"Hey!" Ava shook her shoulders. "It's okay, Julie. He'll be okay."

"You just said he was shot," she whispered, surprised the words even left her mouth.

"Yeah, but it's always better to think positive."

Then Ava was pushing her out the door and into her vehicle, which was for the best. She could barely think; driving a vehicle was out of the question.

By the time they arrived at the hospital in St. Cloud, a drive that took longer than she cared for, her heart was beating so fast, she swore it was going to explode from the exertion.

They were directed to his room by a nurse who was calm and collected, despite the busyness of the emergency room. When she walked into the room and saw Dare sitting on the bed, alert, well, she nearly collapsed with relief. Only a hand to the wall saved her from embarrassing herself.

"What happened?" Ava went right into business mode instead of asking how he was doing.

Julie saw his left arm was wrapped with white gauze, but everything else looked okay. No other wounds that she could see.

Dare ignored Ava as he stared heavily at her. His bright-blue eyes bore into her so hard, she could feel the impact, the emotions he was trying to hold back.

Ava looked away from him to glance at her, then back at him. "I'm never going to get anywhere with you right now. Officer Marcos, join me in the hallway for a moment."

The officer nodded and followed Ava outside. Julie didn't even look at her in thanks or say a word as they walked past.

She approached the bed and took a seat next to him. Her butt grazed his thigh, and it was enough to calm part of her racing heart. Just that small amount of contact. Then she slid her hand through one of his, and the rest of the chaotic energy running rampant through her system quieted.

"What are you doing here?" Dare managed to speak first. His voice was low and she swore twinged with a bit of joy. Yet his expressionless face didn't portray any of that.

"I missed you." Her bottom lip wobbled. "And then Ava got that phone call, and I thought I'd be too late to say everything I wanted to say."

"Hey," he whispered, raising his good arm to brush a hand across her cheek. "I'm okay. Just a graze on the arm. Nothing too bad."

"Well, then whoever relayed the message to her should be fired. They said you were shot. Not cool."

He grinned, and she managed to match his with one of her own.

His grip on her hand tightened. "How long are you staying?"

"I didn't have a plan coming. But I'm not leaving until we talk. A serious talk. One where you don't run away from me again, or push me away."

Dare's eyes trailed behind her shoulder and he stiffened. She twisted to see a young kid standing there. She could only assume this was the kid Ava was talking about.

"I can leave."

She felt the tension leave Dare as fast as it built. "Come on in, Jayden. This is Julie. My—"

A slow, gradual smile grew as she waited for him to finish that sentence. She wasn't going to finish it for him. Curiosity was too much for her. She wanted to know what he thought they were before she said it.

Jayden approached the bed. "Your?" The kid laughed. "Your woman. She's hot."

Julie snickered, and then laughed at the way Dare scowled.

"Yeah, she's something like that, so watch what you say about her."

"Something like that?" She said the words herself, twisting them around in her mind, trying to decipher the meaning. It wasn't very clear to her.

Her hand slid out of his as she stood up. "You're going to have to do better than that."

Dare cleared his throat. "I was shot. I'm still in pain."

"You're an idiot at times, and I'll let it slide for now. But when we chat later, I expect more than 'she's something like that.' Got it?"

"Why do I get the sense you're about to walk away from

me right now? I can't walk away from you, but you can walk away from me?"

"You have things to deal with, so I'll let you deal with them. Then you can deal with me. This conversation is not over."

Whether he wanted it to or not. She wasn't letting him walk away this time. This was his chance to think things through. She had the last three weeks, and she knew what she wanted. She only hoped he did, too.

She looked at Jayden. "Nice to meet you. He's smarter than he looks. You'd do well to listen to him." Then she turned to leave.

"Hey, Julie."

She stopped in the doorway.

"I missed you, too."

She didn't turn around, but she smiled as she walked away.

———

"How come you've never mentioned her?"

Dare wasn't touching that topic, not when he didn't know what the hell just happened with her. What was she doing here? What would she have said if he had confirmed she was his woman? Because was she? Three long weeks of no communication had pretty much told him they were over. That nothing was ever going to happen. Yet here she was.

"You okay?" Dare swiveled his body so he could stand up. He was done sitting around, waiting for someone to discharge him. While he had needed five stitches, he hadn't been injured that badly. Thankfully. It could've been a lot worse.

Jayden had pulled a gun out of the car that Dare had no idea was even in there while he was fighting the guy. Jayden had threatened to shoot, and before he could do anything, the guy managed to get a shot off, hitting Dare in the arm. Instead of going down and writhing in pain, it fueled him. He cold-cocked the guy with a hard fist to the side of his head. He went down with a loud thud.

The cops showed up two minutes later, to which Dare thought the timeframe should've been a lot shorter. Like five seconds to show up, not two whole damn minutes. Jayden had been shocked—and scared shitless when they threw handcuffs on him. Dare hadn't been surprised at all. He knew whenever he went on the deliveries, one of the officers was listening, sometimes even Ava. He'd been cuffed, too, to make it look real.

Dare was surprised to see Jayden out of the cuffs and in his room. He hadn't seen him since they arrived at the hospital with Jayden sitting in the back of a cruiser.

"I'm good." Jayden frowned. "That chick told the cop to let me go. I guess we're not under arrest."

Dare chuckled, shaking his head. "I wouldn't let Ava hear you call her that. Best to address her as Mrs. McCord."

Jayden's frown deepened. "You know her?"

A large breath escaped. Then Dare rotated his arm, wincing from the pain. He wasn't ready to have this conversation. He wasn't ready to have any talks with anyone, especially the one with Julie.

"My sister's married to her husband's cousin. She's like family, I guess."

"I had a gun on me, Dare. The cops arrived pretty quickly."

Dare nodded. He knew Jayden understood the implications as the light dawned in his eyes.

"Rick gave me that gun. I didn't ask questions. I have no idea if..." Jayden's entire body went taut with tension. He kept fisting and unfisting his hands.

Dare wanted to give him reassurances, but he wasn't sure it was wise. He'd already argued with Ava multiple times about leaving Jayden alone, letting him have a second chance. Dare liked to think this was his second chance, but he couldn't be sure until he spoke to her.

"Rick's not a good guy, Jayden. I imagine that weapon is tied to other crimes."

"What are we going to tell Rick?"

Dare clenched his jaw and forced himself not to shout at the kid like he was his father. "You're going to stay away from him from now on. You're going to apply for college or some shit. You're going to do better than I ever did. You're going to stay away from prison. That's what you're going to do."

"Are we under arrest or not?"

"Did you hear what I said?"

Jayden scoffed. "You ain't my old man. I'll do whatever the hell I want."

"Well, I suggest you listen to Dare or I'll change my mind and tell Officer Marcos to put those handcuffs back on."

Dare tried to suppress the smile burning on his face when Ava walked into the room like she owned the place. Jayden visibly shuddered and was wise enough not to say anything. He stepped back, though, as if putting distance between them would stop Ava from putting the handcuffs on herself.

"Dare's had your back since the beginning. You're not an adult yet, but I could push to have you tried in an adult court rather than as a juvenile. Do you want to push your luck with me, Jayden?"

All Ava needed to do was put her hands on her hips to make her harsh words sound even more menacing.

"Do you?" Ava prodded when Jayden didn't respond.

"No, ma'am."

"You've been driving Dare around delivering those packages the last three weeks. Do you know what is in those packages?"

"No, ma'am."

Dare believed him. He'd asked the same thing, albeit a bit differently than Ava's biting question. He didn't think Jayden knew, but he figured he suspected. The kid wasn't dumb.

"Do you know Rick deals drugs? Do you know he's been connected to at least five murders in the past three years? One of those unofficially not labeled a murder, but a suspected overdose. Do you know how dangerous he is? I don't want to hear 'no, ma'am.' I want to hear a solid answer."

Jayden swallowed, the fear that had slowly been building as Ava grilled into him was a full-blown terror now glazing his eyes.

"I know he runs drugs. My dad used to work for him before he got sent to prison four years ago. He's doing twenty with no chance of parole. I know you don't mess with Rick or he'll make sure you know what happens when you do."

Ava's stern gaze softened. "Then why would you work for him?"

Jayden shrugged. "Because he asked me to. It wasn't so much phrased as a question, you know."

Dare wanted to hurt Rick even more in that moment.

Taking advantage of a young kid because he knew he could. Because Jayden knew the kind of guy he was from experience with his father. That no one said no to Rick.

"We have enough to arrest Rick for what happened today. We know the package came from him. It was full of drugs. Enough that you wouldn't see the outside of a prison for a long time." Ava looked at him briefly, then back to Jayden. "But we need more. We need to pin enough on him that *he* won't see the outside of a prison for an even longer time."

Dare didn't like where this conversation was headed.

"And I'll get it for you."

At his harsh retort, Ava tore her gaze from Jayden to him.

"If Jayden knows anything, we can use that, Dare."

"And have him as a witness? Not happening."

"Look—"

Dare took three sharp steps toward her, his expression hardening so fierce that Ava took a step back. "No, you look. I've told you from the beginning, he's just a kid. He doesn't know any better. He doesn't have anyone in his corner. Except he does now. He has me. I'm telling you he's not doing anything that puts him in any more danger. He's done. He's walking away from Rick and that's final." Dare looked at Jayden and pointed at him. "You hear me? That's final."

Jayden nodded, his eyes wide, swallowing hard once more.

Ava crossed her arms. "I need more than a small box of drugs to take him down, Dare."

"Then I'll get it for you."

15

S he paused at closing the rest of the newspaper over the mug. It was such a silly one, too. A big green frog with a loopy smile stared at her with a few ridiculous words underneath it. 'Ribbit, coffee. Ribbit, coffee.' Julie had seen it at a craft fair and for some reason thought of Ava. She bought it on a whim, and now it was Ava's favorite mug to use.

Her finger brushed over a small chip on the right side of the handle.

"Jimmy dropped it but had quick hands and managed to save it before it hit the floor. It still got nicked on the way down by the cabinet handle," Ava said as she moved in closer to the counter where Julie stood packing up the glasses and mugs.

"I remember." A wistful smile graced Julie's lips. "He felt so bad about it that he apologized to me, too. Remember that?"

A light chuckle floated between them as they shared in the memory, Ava nodding that she remembered.

"He was thoughtful like that. Always worried about making sure others were happy, and always forgetting to put himself first." Ava took the mug from her hand, rubbing a finger over the *goofy frog.* "Moments like this, remembering him so vividly, it hurts. It physically hurts my heart."

Julie inhaled a sharp breath to keep the tears she knew were pooling at the corner of her eyes. She could see Ava struggling to hold hers in as well.

"You're sure you want to move?"

The question came out before Julie could stop it. She knew without a doubt Ava had made up her mind. Even before Zane came rushing to New York to profess his love, and also getting shot in the process, she had known where she wanted to be. In Minnesota with Zane. Perhaps things had to go down the way they did because if Zane hadn't come to New York, he would've never been there to take the bullet for Ava. She would've been shot, and they would never know if it would've killed her or not. Best not to think about it, so Julie tried hard not to. She was still reeling over Jimmy's death a few months ago and Ava getting seriously hurt then.

Ava stared at Julie for the longest time before finding her voice. "I'm as sure as I have ever been. It's time for me to move on. I don't think I could go back to work in the crime lab here, even if I tried. I didn't make it up to my dad's office without shaking and sweating and losing my breath."

"I'm going to miss you so much."

"Oh, my gosh, same!"

They crashed into each other with a fierce hug. Those tears they had attempted to hold in came pouring down. They stood in Ava's half-packed up kitchen, holding each other, crying, and filling the space with so much grief and heartache it was hard for them to tear themselves away from each other.

Julie swiped at her eyes, shaking her head, a wisp of a smile emerging. "I have no idea what came over me. It's been—" She inhaled deeply to hold back more tears she felt teetering on the edge once again. "You know what it's been like. I don't have to try *to explain. I know losing Jimmy hurt you the most, but we almost lost you, too, and damn it, that hurt. That hurt the way you pulled away from everyone and everything. Now I feel like I'm losing you again."*

"You're not. I'm only a phone call away. You could always move with me." The goofy smile on Ava's face said she was only half-kidding.

The part that was half-serious, Julie was surprised by. Her, move to Minnesota? There was nothing there for her. Not like Ava. A man she loved, a new job, a new beginning. Julie wouldn't be anything but a third wheel. No, thanks.

"My life is in New York and always will be. I'll never move."

"In the wise words of Jimmy, never say never."

JULIE LOOKED over when the front door opened. Dare walked in, closed the door, looking at her the entire time with not much expression littering his face. No surprise or shock. No delight. No disgust. For now, she'd take it as a good thing. She didn't move from her spot on the couch. She had on the baseball game with a beer in her hand. Her spot was warm because she'd been waiting a long time. Though she would've kept waiting for as long as she needed to.

"I don't recall giving you a key."

A wily smirk smothered her lips as one graced his as well.

"Or giving you the code to the alarm."

This time she cocked a brow to add to the smirk. "One, you didn't set the alarm. Naughty, naughty. Two, you forgot to lock the door, too. Even naughtier. Didn't need a key. Didn't need a code. We should talk about your sense of security. It's not good. You're always forgetting to lock the door and set the alarm."

Dare frowned, silent for a beat as if running the morning through his head. Then he nodded as if it finally dawned on him that he forgot to lock the door and set the alarm.

"I was running late. My bad." He plopped down next to her and swiped the beer from her hand, taking a long swig. "And if it had been locked and set, what would you have done?"

His thigh grazed hers, and she had a hard time concentrating on the question. The heat between them—and not just his body heat—was building steadily...since the moment he opened the door. She sensed it was about to burn straight through her, especially if he didn't touch her in all the right places.

"Well, I've never broken into a house before, but I was once told to 'never say never.' I did come in uninvited. Are you mad?"

His bright-blue eyes seared into her as he said nothing at first, then he shook his head once.

"Did you get things settled with Ava and Jayden yet?"

Another tight shake of his head. "I don't want to talk about that right now."

"Then what do you want to talk about?"

"You."

One simple word, yet spoken so low and gruff it reached into her heart and twisted, like a tiny knife poking and prodding trying to find its mark.

"What are you doing here, Julie?"

She knew he didn't mean in his house. But why did she come back?

She was done hiding her feelings, from running away from a man who ran faster than her.

"I'm here for you."

He frowned, then took another swallow of the beer.

She knew this wouldn't be easy. Part of her didn't want it to be that easy. A challenge usually spurred her on, made her work harder for the finish line. It was such a gratifying feeling to hit that finish line with triumph and excitement. She would not lose this time.

"Should you be drinking after being shot? Did they give you any painkillers or anything? It's probably not wise."

She tried to take the bottle back from him, but he wouldn't budge. His fingers were curled tight around the bottle. So she curled hers around his, holding tight. He wanted to fight her every step of the way, so be it. She'd fight back. When it came to fighting, she would get down and dirty if she had to. Nothing was off-limits.

"It was a few stitches. I'm fine. The beer tastes good." His gaze glided from her eyes to her lips. "I want to kiss you."

She'd wanted a lot more from the moment he stepped through the threshold. All these little contacts, thigh against thigh, hand wrapped around hand, only made her want him more. It had been too long. Three weeks too long.

Of course, they had so much to talk about. It wasn't wise to jump right into the sexual part of their relationship. That wasn't the problem at all. It was everything else that stood on shaky ground.

But her body was feeling the same intense emotion his was. She couldn't ignore it, no matter how hard she tried to shove it out of her mind.

"I'm waiting. No one's stopping you from kissing me."

For that, she was so grateful. That Ava or Jayden, or his sister, or anyone else in the McCord family chose not to come home with him. Tonight was for them. Tomorrow could be for everyone else.

"I need to stop myself."

Her grip tightened around his, her nails digging into his skin. She saw him wince but say nothing.

"Why? Why would you need to stop yourself from kissing me?" She leaned closer, her lips getting near his, tempting him, prodding him to do something about his ache. "Why would you need to stop from touching me?"

He swallowed hard before closing the distance and pressing his lips hard against hers. The kiss was bruising, all his pent-up emotions escaping in one long breath.

He kept leaning into her until she was lying on the couch and his body was covering hers. The bottle found its way to the coffee table, nearly slipping from both their grip before plunking down with a soft thud.

Dare ground into her, sending electrifying sensations flying throughout her body. Yes! This was what she wanted. From the moment she decided she needed to see him. She wanted his arms around her, his body covering her, his lips devouring her. Him claiming her like no man ever had.

As quick and wanton as the kiss started, it slowed, turning leisurely with an aching gentleness, as if they had all the time in the world. Yet, she knew that was a lie. Because if he decided to run once more, it'd all be over again.

He broke the kiss and looked at her, his vivid-blue eyes blazing with so many emotions it hurt her. Hurt her that she couldn't stop the pain from touching him. Hurt her that she couldn't shield him from the harsh realities he lived with. Hurt her because she sensed he would continue to push her away, no matter how hard she tried to keep them together.

"I can't keep doing this with you. Every time makes it harder to walk away. I can't keep doing it."

She gripped the sides of his face. "I've never asked you to walk away. Not once. You chose to."

"We're worlds apart. It would never work. You deserve—"

Her hands grazed up and over his head, her nails dragging. The depth of which she pressed stopped him from finishing. His eyes closed at the movement, as if savoring the pain and pleasure mingled together in her touch.

"Don't tell me what I deserve. Don't tell me you know what's good for me. Don't tell me we can't work. Not until you at least try."

His eyes opened. "I don't know if I'm ready to try."

She could feel her heart shattering. She had known this would be hard. That he wouldn't make a moment of it easy on her. She didn't comprehend how much it would hurt.

"Damn it." He groaned, dropping his head to the crook of her neck. His hot breath hit her first, then his lips followed. "I need you. Even though I know I should stop. I need you, Julie."

She answered by smoothing her hands down his back and grabbing the edge of his shirt. Then she pulled it up and over his head, throwing it to the floor. That was enough for him to follow suit. Her shirt disappeared, her bra, and before she knew it they were both naked on the couch. After a bit of rustling, he had a condom and was rolling it on.

Then her world was back in its proper order when he slid inside. His low moan mingled with hers. Then their lips collided as the magic began. Hard, deep thrusts she met with the same ardor he delivered. Her hands grazed his back up and down, urging him on, telling him with every firm touch how strongly she was holding on. Not only to his body, but to him. To them.

Maybe that's why he broke the kiss and sat up, making

her let go of his back and the solid hold she had on him. He grabbed the side of her hips and kept on pumping deep and hard. As if he were trying to exorcise every tiny demon living inside him out.

That didn't stop her from finding a new spot to hang onto. Her hands grabbed the top of his thighs and sunk in like talons.

Their gazes met. She knew he wanted her to enjoy the ride, to loosen her grip. She could feel it to her very soul, the way his eyes bled with pain and heartache. Yet, they also held desire and longing. As if he were having an internal war with himself. *Hold me, don't hold me. Touch me, let go. Keep me, never come back.*

He let go of her right side and one of his fingers touched her where she needed to be touched, swirling and grinding, building her up until she couldn't hold it in. The desire hit her so quickly, she screamed his name, arching her back and closing her eyes to relish in the bliss spreading through her.

She opened her eyes as he tensed, groaning loudly, the same euphoric feeling hitting him. He lowered down on her, kissing her neck, whispering her name.

Her hands, once again, grabbed ahold of his back, latching on like a crab clamping onto its prey.

"I'm not going to make it easy on you this time. I'm not going to leave without a word. You can try your hardest to push me away, but I'm tougher than I look."

"You're the most stubborn woman I've ever met."

She smiled as his lips hit her neck again. Soft and sweet and filled with promises of more. "I dare you to push me away again. See how truly stubborn I can be."

THE SPOON HIT the side of the bowl, making a loud scraping noise as he slid it against it, trying to get as much of the ice cream as he could. Dare had one vice that he couldn't resist —chocolate ice cream smothered in fudge. He liked pie, but he wasn't like the McCords. He'd take ice cream over pie any day. What kind of pie went well with chocolate ice cream? Because whatever it was, that would be his favorite kind of pie.

"Mine's all gone. Share."

He glanced at Julie out of the corner of his eye, and pulled the bowl closer to his chest, shielding it.

"I don't think so. Plus, you didn't ask nicely." He cocked a silky brow as he grinned. "I didn't hear you ask at all. More like demanded. You're so damn bossy."

"You once said you could never deny me. You aren't going to start now, are you?"

Damn if her eyes rounded into those dreaded puppy dog eyes he could never resist. She wasn't wrong either. He couldn't deny her—anything.

The spoonful he had scraped would be the last bite of the ice cream, too. The things he did for—

He dropped the spoon when the nearly finished thought rushed through his mind. Julie frowned, catching his moment of shock. He smoothed his features out, trying to hide the chaos running rampant inside him, and picked up the spoon and brought it closer to her mouth. He shouldn't be thinking those thoughts. Nothing good would come from admitting his feelings. It could never work between them, no matter what she said.

Her frown vanished as quickly as it appeared. A beautiful smile twisted upon her lips as her tongue darted out, then her mouth closed over the spoon in the most erotic way. Forget the ice cream. He wanted to take her again. Love her body up and down until she couldn't speak, so exhausted from the exertion.

They had sex on the couch. Then in the shower, because she insisted he needed to take one, and he didn't argue. The time was well spent under the hot, steaming water. Afterward, she made him a sandwich, although he protested enough times that she finally shut him up by taking him once more in the kitchen. Now they were having a late-night snack in his bed, and he wasn't opposed to another round of sex. Each time made him ache for more. More of her. More of them. More of forever.

She let go of the spoon, and he dropped it in the bowl with a loud clang.

"All gone."

"And if I want more?"

The way her eyes sparkled with mischief with a hint of seriousness, he knew she wasn't talking about the ice cream.

Didn't he tell himself he wanted more, too? But could he give it to her? Hell, could he give it to himself? Did he deserve it?

Her eyes softened as she leaned closer and brushed her lips with his. "Stop thinking so much. So hard. Let it be. Let us be."

His heart pounded like he was about to board the craziest roller coaster on the planet. He'd only been to the amusement park once in his life, and once was all he needed. He hadn't been a fan of most of the rides, and the roller coaster had been the worst for him. He nearly threw up during the ride, it curdled his stomach so badly with the twists and turns, jerks and movements. That's how he felt right now. Sick to his stomach thinking he could actually keep her in his life.

"I wish I could."

She pursed her lips, shaking her head. "You can, dummy."

"I can—" He stopped himself from finishing the word 'can't' because one, the look on her face said he better shut up before she shut him up herself. Two, because she was right. He could if he put forth the effort. If he shoved his fear aside. Well, maybe not shoved it. Because then it would still remain. More like he needed to overcome it. Banish it and make sure it never came back again.

A very tall, tall order.

When he didn't say anything else, a smile appeared on her gorgeous face. A large beaming one that portrayed she was confident she was winning the war against him. Not that he wanted it to be a war between them. But he wasn't naive to think there wasn't a tiny battle going on, at least within himself.

He put the bowl on the nightstand, giving himself time to think of something to say. Anything. Even something stupid like what the weather was going to be like tomorrow. Thunderstorms if his memory hadn't failed him yet. Or how he and Ava had to convince Jayden walking away from Rick was the best thing. He'd gotten a text from Rick about the delivery going sideways and he hadn't responded. He wasn't sure what to say. He'd let Rick think he spent the night in the slammer and talk to him about it tomorrow. Maybe Ava would have a good plan of attack about it as well. As for Jayden, he was laying low for the evening until he came up with a good thing to tell Rick.

Of course, that wasn't a topic he wanted to talk about either. Bringing up the dumb weather would be better, even if he hated thunderstorms with a passion. They reminded him of things best forgotten. Was that a sign of something even more to come? The pinnacle of the conflict going on between them.

She laid her head on his chest, wrapping her arms tight around him. Though she didn't speak—even about the dumb weather like his bright idea to do—he felt her say so much in the gesture.

I'm here. I'm not going anywhere. Fight me all you want, it's going to take a lot for me to let go.

He wanted to squirm and finagle his way out of her embrace just because the longer she held on, the more he wanted her to never let go.

Perhaps that was her plan all along. Eventually, he'd cave and they could—what? Live happily ever after?

He couldn't foresee that future. Not even a blip of it.

But he also couldn't see her not in his life. She had to stay a part of his life or he'd never survive. That he knew. All it took to come to terms with that realization was her popping back into his life. The last three weeks he'd been kidding himself. He'd been lying to himself. That he didn't miss her. That he didn't need her in his life.

No more of that shit.

His arms circled her, squeezing just as tightly. Before he could put words with his strong gesture in return, he felt her entire body go rigid and tense.

His senses went on high alert as well.

Because the short creaking sound that echoed in the room was easy to decipher. Someone was in the hallway.

She sat up as Rick stepped into the doorframe.

"I'd say I'm disappointed in you, Dare, but oddly enough, I saw this coming. You didn't answer my text, and I knew something was up when I heard you weren't in lockup."

His jaw tightened and he forced way too many retorts

back down his throat. Keep calm and them getting the upper hand had to be the end goal. Although it didn't help he was only wearing boxers and Julie was only wearing his T-shirt—with nothing on underneath. Damn it!

It also sounded like Rick had a mole; otherwise, how did he know he wasn't sitting in a cell? Unless he had someone watching his every move. He wouldn't doubt that either.

Sometimes the best offense was playing ignorant.

"Saw what coming? That you'd walk into my place without knocking. It's rude as shit, and I'm only going to ask you once to get the hell out."

Rick leaned against the doorjamb and grinned. "Your little girlfriend there works for the FBI."

"So." Dare tried to remain relaxed, sitting against the headboard like he was bored with the conversation. He was pretty positive he was failing miserably at it. "My sister married into a family with people that work in law enforcement. I know you knew that. It shouldn't come as a damn surprise. What's your point?"

Rick stood up and stalked into the room. Two men walked in behind him—Dwayne and Terry. "Things went sideways today. The cops showed up and my shit was confiscated. Yet here you are, sitting in bed with your tramp and not sitting in jail on drug charges. Why is that?"

Dare ground his teeth together, holding in the rage he felt bubbling like a geyser at Rick calling Julie such a thing. But that was the point. Rick was looking for him to explode, for him to react so he could react in return.

"Because I didn't have any drugs on me. Neither did Jayden. I dropped off the package like you told me to, and the dude pulled a weapon. We fought, and I got the upper hand. Unfortunately, it went off and I got nicked a bit. The police were called. The guy got tagged with the box, not me. That's his problem. I told the cops Jayden and I were heading to the gym, which is in the area, when the dude stopped us and got in our face for no reason. They believed me over him. It does pay to have my sister married into the sort of family she did. They believed me. But they don't know the truth."

And where that story came from Dare wasn't sure, but he was damn proud of himself that it came out so smoothly and like it happened that way.

"You expect me to believe that?"

"You can believe whatever the hell you want to believe. You're going to do whatever you want anyway, Rick. Because that's what you do."

"What does that mean?"

He should shut up and try to talk his way out of this—calmly, with a cool head.

But it wasn't in his DNA to do that.

Dare swung his legs to the side and stood up before anyone could come closer and realize he was even making a move. Not a full move, but at least he had a better advantage now. On two solid feet and not sitting like a damn duck with a target on its head.

"I'm talking about Jayden. He's a good kid. Could go places, yet you reel him into your business because you're a greedy bastard."

Rick laughed. "You've gone soft, Dare. Prison should've hardened you a little more. Instead, it made you into a little bitch."

"Better than being a dickwad like yourself." Dare chuckled, crossing his arms, ignoring the pain in his left arm because he refused to show any weakness in front of Rick. "We do have one thing in common."

A slimy smile slid across Rick's face. "Oh, yeah? Like what?"

"Well, we're both a murderer. I killed my parents without a thought to the consequences. You killed a single mom trying to get by in life."

Rick's eyes narrowed. "You can't prove it."

But Dare just did. Sure, he didn't have actual physical evidence that Ava would need, but Rick confessed more or less. How did he know what single mom he was talking about for starters? Not to mention, it was in the way he said it. The way his eyes shimmered with knowledge and the corner of his lip curled up in cockiness. Dare would have to beat the confession out of him.

First, he had to get Julie away from these three guys. He had no idea how he was going to do that.

"Grab the bitch. Leave him for dead." Then Rick turned around at the same time the two men moved like lightning.

Of course, it wasn't like he was going down without a fight. He lunged forward toward the one guy coming at him, shoving the gun he pulled toward the ceiling.

Two shots rang out at the same time Julie screamed.

A terrifying scream that sent chills through his spine and more energy through his system.

Nobody hurt the woman he loved.

He'd had the 'L' word in his head long before tonight. He should've confessed. He should've told her how he felt. He loved Julie and he'd do anything to save her. Even if it meant dying himself.

16

She hadn't meant to scream, but the asshole coming her way stepped on her foot in just the right way it sent shooting pains up her body. Of course, before he could get a good grip on her—and he tried immediately, as soon as he was inches from her face—she fought back.

An elbow to the face, a knee to the groin. The guy blocked both blows, but that didn't stop her from continuing to fight. If they got her out of this room, there was a high chance they'd get her out of the house and away from Dare.

She had to protect him, too.

The two shots that rang out in concession had her wanting to turn, but the guy trying to grab her and throw her over his shoulder stopped her from doing so. She could hear grunts and groans coming from the other side of the bed, so she knew Dare hadn't been seriously hurt—or worse, killed. He was fighting back as hard as she was. It couldn't be easy, not with his left arm hurt from earlier today.

One fist managed to snag the guy in the chin, but not strong enough to make him go down. He grabbed for her hair that was slung up in a messy ponytail and yanked. Another cry tore from her lips, and so did another swing of her fist, this time connecting more firmly with his face. He grunted, lost hold of her hair, giving her enough momentum to step back and get a good kick in. Direct target to his crown jewels.

Foul words spilled from his lips as he howled in pain. She kept the attack on, throwing another kick directly into his face, knocking him down to the ground. When he didn't move or make a sound, she knew she had knocked him out cold. She'd have to thank Tom for teaching her some new moves when they became partners. They worked out together at least three times a week in the gym on the mat and lifting weights.

Turning toward Dare, she saw he was still struggling with the guy to get the gun, though he managed a side glance her way.

"Run, Julie!"

Not a chance.

She was the federal agent. He was the civilian. These were situations she had trained for. Though one wrong move and Dare could get shot—again, twice in one day. It would be tricky to intervene with both of them fighting for the upper hand.

Unless...

Doing a once-over of the unconscious man on the ground, she saw his gun peeking out from his waistband. She nabbed the gun, walked calmly around the bed, and pressed it firmly against the guy's head. The moment he felt the weapon, he froze. Dare snatched the gun and backed up.

"Hands up, put them against the wall, and don't move," Julie ordered, nudging the gun into his head. "Dare, call the police."

The man listened, raising his arms and laying them onto the wall. She looked at Dare when he swore.

"My phone's in the living room. I don't see yours on the other side of the bed."

Shit. Hers was in the living room as well. Or the kitchen. She couldn't remember where she put it. This night had been for them. Having her phone near her hadn't been a priority. She had even put it on silent.

"I'll go get it."

She nodded, her lips curling into a confident smile. By the hesitant look on his face, she knew he didn't want to leave her alone. But she didn't say anything. One, she didn't want to make the guy against the wall think she couldn't handle it by trying to console Dare. Two, she shouldn't have to say anything. This was like doing her job. Arresting the bad guys at the end of a long day. Of course, normally she was fully dressed, not in a T-shirt—and only a T-shirt. She would kill for a pair of underwear right now.

Dare's steps were slow as he walked by the guy. He even stopped a brief moment in front of her. Then he returned a nod and walked out of the room, the gun still in his hand. Good. They had no idea where Rick had disappeared. She had no doubt that asshole was lurking around.

"You know you're not getting out of here alive."

Julie grinned, although the douche who spoke couldn't see her with his back to her. She could appreciate confidence, but she also recognized stupidity at its finest. These three goons thought they'd walk into this house, kill Dare, take her, and they'd let them? Ha! They had no idea who they were dealing with.

"Did you hear me, bitch?"

"The only thing I hear is dumb shit spewing out of your mouth."

If she had handcuffs, she would've slapped them on him already. Of course, she didn't bring any with her on her second vacation—if that's what she wanted to call it— because she didn't expect to be thrown into this kind of mess. Not that she had brought any with her on her first vacation. Sure, she liked to bring work with her, but not to that extent.

A low moan behind her had her taking a step back so she had easy access to the bedroom exit and a good eye on both guys.

The guy against the wall chuckled. "You're in for it now, bitch."

Julie ignored him as the other guy slowly got to his feet. She kept the gun pointed at the guy plastered to the wall, although had more of her attention on the guy she had knocked out. Not good enough, apparently.

"I wouldn't try for round two. It's going to hurt a lot worse than round one," she said with a shit-eating grin, despite the fact her heart started to pound like an out of control jackhammer.

Two against one was never good odds, even if she did have a gun.

The guy laid a hand on the bed and delivered a smirk in return. "I'll take my chances."

If she had to, she'd put a bullet in both of them, though she didn't want to. She practiced at the range often as was required for her job. Keeping up with handling a weapon and making sure she was on target was a necessary component to being safe on the job. Not everyone they came across had good intentions. Like these two goons.

She swung the gun in his direction. "Are you sure?"

He had fully stood up, his eyes alert, his stance ready, yet didn't step forward in her direction. "You won't shoot me."

"What makes you so sure?"

"You don't have the balls to do it."

Julie chuckled. "I don't have balls, you're right. But neither will you when I'm done with you." She lowered the gun a fraction, lining her sights up. "I'm a good shot. Still wanna take the chance?"

The guy swallowed, darting his gaze to his partner, then back at her.

Her grip was tight. Her stance was steady. Her smile did not falter. But she was scared shitless. What the guy couldn't see was the pounding of her heart. The sweat gathering on her palms and under her armpits. The fear coiling deep inside her stomach. If she had to shoot, she would. And she'd make it count. Her gun was directed at his dick, and that's where she intended to hit. Why make herself a liar?

Her lips curled even higher.

The guy's eyebrow twitched.

Confidence—or faking it, at least—would get her through this.

She hoped, anyway.

Where was Dare? He'd been gone too long. The last thing she needed was Rick walking back into the room. She'd be a dead woman if that happened. She was already teetering toward that stuck in a room with these two goons.

Because she sensed they were dumb enough to test her skills.

DARE HATED walking out of the room and leaving Julie alone with those men, but he had no choice. He knew by the determined look in her eyes, she wouldn't have given him a choice either. Knowing she was capable of handling herself and letting her show him were two separate things. He didn't want to see her in that kind of position. He knew what kind of job she had, but he had ignored what that entailed. Seeing it firsthand was not something he enjoyed.

All he had to do was get to a phone, call the cops, and this would all be over. They'd have enough to nail Rick now. Breaking and entering, threatening and trying to kidnap a federal agent wouldn't go over well for him at all. Dare didn't have an ounce of remorse for him. Nobody threatened his woman and got away with it.

Yeah.

His woman.

He liked the sound of that. Nothing like a dose of reality and something to scare him shitless to drive home the point he couldn't live without her.

Hopefully, Julie felt the same way after this was all said and done.

The living room was empty when he finally hit the threshold, having tiptoed toward it not sure where Rick had disappeared to.

His hand was inches away from grabbing his phone from the coffee table when he heard the soft click of a gun.

"I wouldn't do that if I were you."

Dare straightened and turned toward Rick's voice. He stood near the entrance to the kitchen. The couch was the only thing separating them. The gun in Rick's hand was steady, not a tremble in sight as he held it up in front of him, pointing it directly at Dare's chest.

"It's over, man. You're not going to get away with this. Even if you do manage to kill me and hurt Julie somehow, Ava and the cops will know who did this."

Dare had to believe that. He also had to believe despite what he said, they'd both walk away from this unharmed.

"Knowing and proving are two completely different things." The evil grin that morphed onto Rick's face told Dare everything he already knew.

He killed that single mom. For whatever reason, he killed an innocent woman and made it look like an overdose. Left a child motherless. Parentless. What an asshole. A despicable, vile asshole.

"Put the gun down gently," Rick ordered, his eyes flashing to the gun dangling in Dare's hand.

If he let go of the one weapon at his disposal, he was truly and utterly a deadman. Nothing would stop Rick from putting a bullet between his eyes. Dare had no doubt he had good aim. Someone like Rick wouldn't let things like that go to chance. He'd practice and hone his skills, wanting to be the best. Never wanting to let anyone get the better of him.

"Or what? You'll shoot me?" Dare laughed, despite it not being a laughing matter. "You're gonna kill me anyway. Why make it easier for you? I make mistakes, but I'm not an idiot."

"I never wanted it to go this way. You should've been on my side."

"I'm on no one's side but my own. I could've said no. I could've walked the other way. But in the end, I wanted to be able to sleep at night without worrying I made the wrong decision."

He already did that enough with other past mistakes. Like if he had demanded his mother drive instead of him. Sure, she had been distraught and overwhelmed thinking her husband was dying, but she had been more levelheaded than he had been. Not high as a kite. Or if he had pulled over when it started to rain so heavily he could barely see, let it pass for a minute or two. Or better yet, knocked on one of his lame neighbors' doors until he found someone to help him and call an ambulance.

So many different choices he could've made that fateful day, and he picked the wrong one.

Now was the time to start living his life, not regretting the choices he made. Not second-guessing and wondering if he was making another mistake.

"Let's not kid each other either, Rick. We were friends back in the day, but you would've kicked me under the bus at the first hint of trouble. You've always been about yourself and nobody else."

Rick's grin widened. "You know me so well. That should've been enough of a clue that trying to double-cross me wouldn't work out."

"I try to tell myself I'm not a bad guy. But I know one when I see one." Dare's hand tightened around the gun. "I would do everything the same all over again. I'll see you go down if it's the last thing I ever do."

"Well, it's going to be the last thing you ever do."

Dare didn't even have time to think. As soon as the last word left Rick's mouth, he fired. But instinctively he knew Rick would strike, so he dove as he raised his hand and fired.

No doubt he missed, but whatever. It wasn't about hitting Rick, but more about defending himself until help arrived. Someone had to have called in the shots heard a few minutes ago when he fought with the other guy trying to get the gun. Of course, it felt like that had been ages ago. Someone should've arrived by now if that were the case.

He couldn't stay hidden behind the couch. Rick wouldn't stand around waiting for him to pop his head up; he'd attack immediately. Dare half crawled, half ran crouched around the coffee table and to the recliner in the corner. Not the best place to hide, but it meant Rick couldn't get to him from behind. There was no way he could get to the hallway that led back to the bedroom or to the front door to escape.

He flinched and automatically put his hands over his head when bullets rained down on the recliner.

Shit, shit, shit.

He was going to die.

That would leave Julie all alone with three dangerous men.

He could not let that happen.

If he was going to die, he'd at least take one of them out first.

Inhaling a deep breath, hoping to find some strength and courage, he gripped the gun even tighter. Then stood up when the bullets stopped flying and aimed his gun at where he assumed Rick would be. Directly in front of the recliner.

A shaky breath escaped, his lips trembling when he saw the last person he expected to see standing there instead —Ava.

Shit. He could've shot her. What was she doing here? And why was she standing where Rick should've been?

She looked just as shaken as he did. Her arms were outstretched, a gun gripped tightly in her hands. Rick was lying on the floor, a pool of blood already forming on the carpet from the bullet wound Ava hit him with.

He lowered his weapon.

She did as well.

"Julie..." he whispered, looking at the hallway.

Ava nodded. "I'm not alone."

"Good. That's good."

His arm suddenly felt heavy. Not his left arm that he'd hurt earlier today, though it was stinging from fighting for his life. The gun was simply too much weight. His vision started to blur as the room started to spin.

"Dare!"

Everything came back into focus. Julie's beautiful face was coming his way down the hallway. She looked a mixture of tired, scared, and relieved. He understood how she was feeling perfectly.

But tired most of all.

Ava put her arm around Julie in a half-hug when she made it to her. Julie stared at him with the relief shining through more prominently.

His vision started going wonky again. Pain radiating up his body and pulsating through his head. Why did everything hurt so much? They were safe. Rick was dead. It was all over.

"I swear when I heard all those shots, my heart fell out of my chest. I'm so glad to see you're okay," Julie said, maintaining eye contact with him. Then squeezed Ava's side harder. "I'm so glad to see you, too."

"The neighbors called it in. Thank goodness for that."

The longer he stared at them, the more the room spun.

"Dare?" Julie let go of Ava, frowning.

Though he looked straight at her, she was nothing more than a blurred image, reminding him of the time he'd been so high, he couldn't see straight.

The gun slid from his hand, tumbling onto the seat of the recliner. He gripped the back of the recliner and tried to step around it, but he lost his balance. He hit the ground hard, pain screaming up and down his body, especially in his back, despite the fact he fell on his face.

The last thing he heard before darkness took over was Julie screaming his name.

17

"Dare!" Julie rushed forward, dropping to her knees, and shoved her hands over one of the wounds leaking blood profusely.

He'd taken two bullets to the back.

"Ava! I need something to stop the bleeding. I need anything."

Julie pressed harder, yet Dare made no sound or indication he even felt her pressing on his back. She heard Ava dash out of the room, shouting orders to someone—she didn't bother to turn around to find out who. No doubt one of the two officers that had rushed into the house with her.

Thick, crimson liquid seeped through her fingers as she applied as much pressure as she could. It didn't seem to matter how hard she pushed, it kept coming, like an unstoppable river. The two wounds were so far apart, she couldn't keep pressure on both of them at the same time. Not with two hands over one wound, anyway. She needed as much pressure as she could, and it aggravated her she couldn't use two hands on both of them at the same time.

"Don't do this to me, Dare. I won't stand for it. Wake up right this instant."

Not even using her stern, slightly shrill tone of voice had him listening to her.

She hiccuped, trying to keep a sob inside. Her bottom lip wobbled, but she held it in. All the torrential emotions bubbling to the surface stayed suppressed. They had to. Dare needed her to stay calm and in control. His life depended upon it.

Ava was suddenly by her side, shoving a bright-blue cotton towel over his back. This time a cry erupted from her throat.

The sharp color reminded her of his eyes. His vibrant eyes that always had a way of looking at her with such intensity, such desire.

"An ambulance is almost here. He's going to make it," Ava said as they both pushed hard on his back.

It didn't seem to make a difference yet, even with the heavy towel. Blood soaked through, coating her fingers with ease.

Her gaze lifted to Ava's, hating the terror she saw in Ava's eyes.

"You thought the same thing when Jimmy took a bullet, too, and look how that went."

Ava's lips curled into a nasty sneer. "Don't say that. Don't even go there." Ava glanced down at Dare, no doubt noticing how much the towel was getting saturated with blood. "He was talking. He was alert and aware of his surroundings. Jimmy died instantly. There's a big difference here."

That was a good point. It didn't make Julie feel any better, though. All her mind could conjure were images of that fateful day. Not that she had seen firsthand Jimmy dead on the pavement. But talk had ensued while they waited in the hospital waiting room for Ava to make it out of surgery. The dirty details. The mayhem. The screams of Ava's pleas for Jimmy to hang on, help was on the way.

"Julie, don't go there. You have to stay positive."

Easier said than done. How could she remain positive when the man she loved lay bleeding on the floor? Not only bleeding but unconscious as well.

She didn't know how much time had passed before she was being shoved out of the way by paramedics and Dare was being carried out of the house. Blood covered her from head to toe. Her hands were soaked, her arms coated with his blood. Streaks and smears covered her shirt. Even her legs and knees were covered in blood. It didn't even matter she had no panties on. Nothing registered other than the fact she could lose Dare. That in any moment his heart would stop and he'd leave this world.

"Come on. You need to wash up and change, and then I'll bring you to the hospital."

Ava held out her hand and Julie wanted to ignore it. She wanted to slap her friend's hand away, curl up in a ball, and cry.

"Now. Dare needs you."

She wasn't given a choice to wallow in her self-pity. Ava grabbed her arm and pulled her to her feet. Despite her mind wanting to protest, her body followed orders and walked out of the room with Ava by her side. She wiped a washcloth over her legs and arms to get most of the blood off, while Ava grabbed her new clothes. Julie was semi-clean and dressed within five minutes.

Less than twenty minutes later, they were walking through the white corridor of the hospital to the emergency room where a nurse directed them to wait. Julie didn't have a chance to contemplate Dare's odds when the room became loud in an instant.

"Where is he? Where's my brother? What the hell happened? I knew he should've never helped you. I told you this was a bad idea," Deja hollered as she advanced at Ava.

Before Deja could take a swing at Ava, Emmett was wrapping his arms around her and swinging her entire body in another direction.

"Let me go, Emmett. I swear I'll hurt you. I'll drop you to your knees," Deja shrieked, as she fought with him.

Julie looked at Ava, feeling Deja's pain as if it were her own. Not that she blamed Ava as Deja did, but part of her felt a rage simmering as well. "You should leave the room right now. I'll talk to her."

"I'm not..." Ava sighed, her words dying. "You're right. I'm sorry, Julie. I hope you don't hate me, too."

Ava didn't give her a chance to dispute that. She left with Deja still ranting and raging toward her, wanting to follow to enact her vengeance.

Emmett held his wife until her anger lessened and her energy dwindled. She went from fighting him to almost going dead-weight in his arms. He steered her carefully to a chair and sat down with her in his lap.

Julie wasn't sure whether she should engage with Deja yet, but she knew she couldn't stay in her own corner, wallowing in her sorrow. She took a seat next to them.

"I know you don't want to hear it, but it's not Ava's fault."

Deja's eyes narrowed at her. Emmett's muscles contracted in his arms, indicating he had tightened his hold.

"Nobody can tell Dare what to do. That man is the most stubborn, obstinate man I've ever met. He didn't do anything he didn't want to do. If it's anyone's fault, it's mine."

Julie hung her head, hating the guilt that swam through

her veins, yet at the same time knowing it was ridiculous to blame herself. She didn't lock the door before going to bed. Knowing Dare was terrible at it meant she had to be the responsible one. That was their first mistake of the night. Not locking the door. And not setting the alarm.

The second mistake had been not realizing Rick would've retaliated for the botched delivery job. Just because he and Dare were old friends didn't mean Dare was immune to his wrath. Well, at least Rick wouldn't be a problem any longer. So much had happened in such a short time span she didn't ask who had killed Rick. All she had seen was his dead body and that's all that had mattered to her.

"Why do you think it's your fault?" Deja asked. For the first time since arriving, she spoke in a calm, quiet voice.

Julie shrugged. "I'm a trained FBI agent. I should've been able to protect him. Instead, he got shot."

Deja sat up straighter but didn't get off Emmett's lap. "Tell me everything that happened tonight. From the very first moment. I need to know everything."

Julie gulped in a large breath and let it out with a pained release. If only that was the most pain she'd feel tonight, but she knew it was just beginning.

She opened her mouth and it all poured out—words and tears.

SITTING in an uncomfortable hospital chair wasn't as terrible as being in a room filled with extreme tension. Julie wanted to leave the room, but if she did, she might miss any news concerning Dare. Since she wasn't family, she had to stick close by Deja to hear any information when the doctor came out. It wasn't that she planned it out or anything, but somehow she found herself sitting next to Deja.

They'd been sitting for a few hours already with no good updates. Dare was in surgery and fighting for his life. He lost too much blood from the house to the hospital. Two bullets lodged in his back with no exit wound, one close to his spine. When she heard that part, she nearly broke down in sobs but managed to control her emotions. Deja was hanging on by a thread, and she didn't want to add any stress to her already strung emotions.

The entire McCord family was in attendance. Despite the obvious devilish glares sent Ava's way by Deja, Ava remained with everyone. No one spoke, and on the rare occasion they did, it wasn't anything to keep a conversation going.

A loud, energetic song broke through the icy atmosphere. Julie startled, then felt her cheeks flame when she realized it was her phone breaking the silence.

She pulled the phone out of her purse, something she would've forgotten if not for Ava guiding her out of the house in one piece. She cleared her throat and answered Tom's call. Trying to talk quietly in an already silent room was difficult. Every word she spoke sounded like she was shouting into the phone. Tom wanted an update, and sobs coated her throat when she had to relay she had none. Though she didn't want to hurt his feelings because she appreciated he reached out, she told him she'd call him next time when she had something to report. But Tom wasn't offended easily, and he understood her short words weren't meant with malice.

Before she slid her phone back into her purse, she clicked the silence button on the side so it wouldn't be her again to break the eery silence.

A few minutes passed before the quietness was broken once again.

"You never told me why you're back here."

Julie looked at Deja, unsure of how to answer that. She was here for Dare. Yet there were things she wanted to say to him before anyone else heard. That wouldn't be fair to him to have his sister hear her feelings before he even did.

"I missed your brother."

That said enough, but not all of it.

Deja nodded. "He didn't say so, but I know he missed you, too. He was such a bear these last few weeks."

Ava had said the same thing.

"Grizzly or black bear?"

Julie didn't know why she decided to try a little light teasing, but she was glad when Deja's lips curled into a short grin.

"I'd say more like a polar bear."

A giggle escaped. "Polar bears are cute and look so fluffy. I can't imagine he was acting like that."

"You'd be surprised." They shared a look before giggling together this time. Deja's smile dimmed but didn't fully dissipate. "I gave my brother a hard time about a lot of things, especially about moving. If he wants to move near you, I'm not going to argue with him anymore."

If he survives...

Those dreaded unspoken words.

"And if I want to move here?"

Ugh. What happened to waiting for Dare to have this conversation? So much for telling him first how she felt.

"Then even better for me because my brother will still be here and I'll have a new friend around."

Julie's eyes wandered toward Ava without realizing, then back to Deja who had noticed the short gesture.

"I'll forgive Ava. That's what we do in the McCord family. It's so annoying sometimes because I want to hold a grudge and they won't let me."

Emmett drew his arm around Deja and kissed the side of her head, yet didn't say anything to her bold words.

"Do you love my brother?"

Some things were better left unsaid—and to the right person.

"When he recovers, he'll be the first to know the answer to that question."

Deja smiled, knowing the answer anyway.

From there, the talk between them fizzled and the room was silent once more. Emmett sat with his arm around Deja with Julie on her other side. Ethan and Penelope sat on Emmett's side. On the other side of the room, Ava sat with Zane, Austin, and Sophie. Gabe and Olivia had the seats bunched in the middle of them. Even Jayden had heard what happened—Julie wasn't sure how—and sat in his corner, never making eye contact with any of them.

Minutes passed, turning into hours. Night fell and dawn came, and her eyes ached to close, to rest, knowing she was in for a long day, but she held off. No one else had closed their eyes, and she wouldn't either. She'd never sleep again if Dare didn't make it.

The doors swung open—finally.

A tired-looking doctor stepped in, and Julie breathed out a sigh of relief before he even spoke. She knew by the sparkle in his eyes that Dare had made it through surgery. What his prognosis was would be another story, but he had survived. Anything else could be dealt with as long as he was alive.

Deja stood, Emmett right by her side, and listened with rapt attention as the doctor informed her Dare made it out of surgery with flying colors. The bullets didn't hit any vital organs and they were able to remove the one close to his spine without too much trouble. With recuperation and rest, he'd be back to normal in a few weeks.

Music to her ears.

He told them he'd be wheeled to his room and could have visitors in a few hours when visiting hours started. Julie wouldn't argue with that, even though she wanted to lay eyes on him right this instant. She could tell by the way Deja stiffened she also wanted to see him.

Without any prompting, the doctor offered a gentle smile. "I'll talk to the nurses. A short visit right now, and only one or two people. He won't be awake yet anyway, so it won't do much good, but if you want to peek in on him, you can."

Another grateful sigh released, yet Julie knew she wouldn't insist on seeing him before Deja, even if part of her wanted to fight about it.

When the doctor left, whoops of relief and congratulations circled the room with everyone hugging Deja.

"We'll check in on him later and let you see him," Ethan said first, saying what everyone was thinking.

Deja nodded, tears brimming in her eyes. "Yeah, okay." Then she grabbed Julie's hand. "You can come with me. He'd want you there."

Her eyes filled with tears. As full as Deja's. Then she was swinging her arms around Deja and squeezing her tight.

"Thank you. You have no idea what that means to me."

Deja's arms strengthened as well. "Well, we're gonna be sisters soon."

She started to laugh at the same time a sob wanted to escape, making it sound like a funny hiccup. "I don't know about that."

Because Dare was a difficult man. Trying to convince him they were meant to be together had already proven to be the hardest thing she'd ever done in her life to date.

"I do. Two against one. My brother doesn't stand a chance."

Julie wasn't going to say no to that kind of help.

In a weird, roundabout way, she was going to become a part of the McCord family, and she found she couldn't wait for it to happen.

18

The first two things to puncture his senses was the excruciating pain slicing up and down his back and the beautiful sound of an angel's voice.

Dare opened his eyes, twisting his head in the direction he heard Julie's voice, and met her gaze.

"I gotta go. Bye." She lowered her phone and stood, sliding onto his bed, and grabbed his hand. "You're awake. It took forever."

A laugh escaped, which turned into a groan when the movement from laughing hurt. "You're always on my case about...everything."

She smoothed a hand across his cheek. "Someone has to be."

His eyes closed as she caressed his cheek once more.

"You had us all worried."

He opened his eyes again, realizing for the first time it was only Julie in the room. Besides his sister—he wondered where she was—she was the only one he was glad sat next to him.

It must've been written on his face or he said the last

thought out loud because Julie responded, "Your sister went home to freshen up. She sat all day yesterday and through the night with you. You've been out for almost two days. The doctor said your body was healing and it was all good. I was about to call him out on it."

He grinned. "I'm glad you're here."

"You're stuck with me."

He liked the sound of that. But right now wasn't the time for that kind of conversation, especially with the pain attacking his back. When he grimaced with barely the slightest movement, Julie understood his discomfort.

"I'll go get a nurse."

Dare didn't even nod, knowing that would hurt, but he offered a short grin to show his appreciation.

The nurse came in, asked him a few questions, gave him some medication to block out the pain, and he felt better within a few minutes. He could still feel a dull pain in his back, but it was tolerable.

Despite wanting to talk with Julie and just look at her beautiful face, knowing she was alive and well, he couldn't. His body refused to cooperate with his mind. But of course, Julie knew. She held his hand while he rested. When his sister finally returned, he chatted with her a few minutes before he had to stop and relax again.

The doctor visited as well, giving him an update on everything that occurred, which was silly in his mind. Julie and Deja had told him everything. He'd been shot twice in the back, from hiding behind the dumb recliner. He was lucky he didn't get hit more than twice. One bullet missed his spine by a fraction, for which he was extremely grateful. A few more days of observation and rest and he'd be free to go home. He had to take it easy and not overdo anything.

Not a problem. He didn't have a job. He didn't have anywhere to be.

The only thing he knew for certain was he didn't want to lose Julie. No matter what happened, he wasn't going to let her walk away this time. If he had to move, then so be it. He could learn to like New York. Hell, he'd never been there before. He might love the place. Though he suspected he wouldn't. Big crowds made him itch, and loud noises were annoying. Small-town life might have its problems, but he liked it over a big city. For Julie, he'd have to deal with it.

Four days later, he was released and on his way home. His back still hurt and required aftercare that would be impossible for him to do himself. Cleaning and tending to the wounds where he couldn't reach. Julie assured him she'd help with everything. It made him wonder how long she was staying, yet they hadn't touched that conversation yet. Nothing about where they stood with each other. Part of him wanted to do it, and the other part was scared shitless of what she might say.

How could a felon and an FBI agent make it work? It didn't sound possible.

Ethan, Emmett, and Gabe were waiting outside the house when Julie pulled into the driveway. He almost shook her hand off when she helped him out of the car, but decided against it. Having help wasn't a terrible thing, and he sort of liked how much she was babying him. He'd never had a woman do that for him. While he still had some discomfort in his back, it wasn't enough to immobilize him or make it hard to walk without help.

"Welcome home, man!" Ethan said and started to reach forward as if to hug him and paused. "How's the back feeling?"

"Better, but still shitty at the same time." Then Dare took

the option away from him and hugged him. He didn't want to be coddled by everyone, just Julie.

Emmett and Gabe also gave him a half-hearted hug, and he didn't complain about it. Did it tweak his back a little? Yeah. Would he say so? Hell, no.

When he walked inside, he noticed the new recliner and couch right away. It was impossible to ignore because they were tan suede compared to the black leather from before. Even the carpet looked new. Dare figured it was easier to replace it all instead of trying to get blood out of it.

Ethan cleared his throat. "Don't even think about arguing about the new furniture. The house is still mine, so consider it me replacing my shit."

Dare had no intention of arguing with him about it. It had been a nice gesture. He wasn't having nightmares over what happened, but it was great to come home and not have the reminders about what happened so blatantly in his face.

"It looks nice."

Julie set the bag his sister had packed for his hospital stay next to the front door and headed toward the kitchen. "I'll make us something for lunch."

He wasn't sure why Julie escaped the room, but he wasn't going to follow her and start an argument when they had just arrived home.

"So?" Emmett asked as he plopped down on the couch. Gabe took a seat next to him. He and Ethan remained standing, though his back screamed at him to relax.

Dare decided to try out the new recliner, sighing in bliss when the comfort level surprised him.

"It's got a built-in massager, too." Ethan lifted the control sitting on the armrest and grinned like a jester. "I couldn't help myself."

"I guess you're going to say I can't argue about that

either."

"Nope," Ethan said, popping the 'p' with emphasis.

Arguing wasn't worth it. Not when he hit the gentle massage button on the controller and it started working the kinks in his back. It was soothing rather than jolting his back with more pain. He still had to be gentle about putting on shirts and how he sat or slept on it, but massaging it now and again wouldn't hurt him.

Ethan snagged a spot next to Gabe and eyed him critically. "You didn't answer Emmett's question. You can't ignore us."

Dare chuckled. "He didn't ask a damn question. All he said was so. I don't know what the hell that means."

"They're wondering about Julie. Tell them to mind their own business," Gabe said in his usual quiet way. Yet with more firmness than was normal for him. Obviously, Olivia was helping his confidence to speak out more.

"She and Deja are like best buddies now," Emmett replied. "Even Deja doesn't know how long she's staying."

Neither did Dare because they didn't talk about it.

But it didn't matter. When she left—if she did—so would he.

Since when were his sister and Julie best buddies? Sure, he noticed them laughing and talking in the hospital room, but he hadn't realized they'd gotten closer.

"I don't know either."

Ethan sat up, resting his elbows on his knees. "Whatever you decide, I got your back one hundred percent."

A simple saying and it made him laugh. Ethan joined in when it dawned on him what he said. *I got your back.* Something so silly, yet now held more meaning than ever. Damn, he never wanted to get shot in the back again. That shit hurt.

"All I know is I need her in my life. If she'll have me."

Emmett grinned. "Oh, she'll have you. I have no doubt about that. If not, your sister will change her mind. You know how Deja gets when she gets something in her mind."

That garnered more laughter from him. His sister was a force to be reckoned with. So was Julie, though.

It was time for reckoning. To find out if she loved him as much as he loved her. That scared him more than anything in his life ever did.

JULIE SNUGGLED AGAINST DARE, although didn't put her full weight on him like she wanted to. The less pain in his back, the better. She wasn't going to be the cause of any pain.

He had other plans. His arm snaked around her body and pulled her more firmly against him, her head now on his chest. Right where she wanted to be.

"Do you want more popcorn?"

She was full. While she wanted to be pressed up against him like this, her worries that she was hurting him were escalating like an earthquake going haywire on the Richter scale. So any excuse to get up was all she needed.

Dare's arm tightened around her and then a kiss hit the top of her head. "I want to watch baseball with my girl sitting next to me."

That had her head popping up.

"Your girl?"

Dare always looked either aloof and like nothing mattered to him or intense as if he were ready to go to battle about something. There usually no in-between with him. Right now he looked a mixture of apprehensive and very, very afraid. His bright-blue eyes shimmered with a fear she had only seen once. When Rick and his goons walked into the bedroom and they were exposed without any weapons to protect them.

"Yeah, my girl. You got a problem with that?"

She pursed her lips in a way to hide the smile she wanted to display. "That sounds like you want me to fight about it."

"I want to hear you say it."

"That I'm your girl?" She tilted her head and couldn't help a small part of her smile to escape. "You didn't even ask me."

"Do I have to? Why can't it just be?" He frowned, his brows drawing low. "Why do you always have to argue with me about stuff?"

"Because then our conversations wouldn't be as fun." Without giving him time to counteract that statement, she leaned forward and brushed his soft lips with hers, lingering and savoring the kiss. "Well, as *your girl*, I insist we move in together as soon as possible. You need someone to take care of you, and it makes sense."

This time he shifted away, his brows dropping even lower. "I don't need someone to take care of me. Sure, clean my wounds every now and again."

"Oh my gosh. You're going to get an infection or something with an attitude like that." She rolled her eyes for added effect to his ridiculousness. The man just couldn't take her words for what they were. She wanted to be with him. To make a go of this abnormal, completely off-the-wall relationship.

Did she have to spell out for him word-for-word?

"I love you, you big dummy. I almost lost you. You almost bled out right in front of me." Her eyes filled with water, and she had to rapidly blink to keep the tears at bay.

Crying wasn't something she wanted to do—ever—in front of him. "So, yeah, I want to move in together and make a life together. Get married and talk about kids. I don't know. I'm not sure I want any, but if you do, you can try and convince me. We can argue about who's cooking supper because I hate cooking. And you hog the bed. I look forward to shoving you back on your side and then it turning into something more. What do you have to say about that? What's your counter-argument?"

He stared at her for the longest time, until it started to make her nervous that she put her heart on the line and he was about to stomp all over it with a rejection. Push her away and keep running like he always did.

"I don't have anything to dispute there other than I don't hog the bed. You steal the damn covers like a klepto."

"Out of all of that, *that's* what you focus on? I do not steal the covers either. Men and their ridiculous—"

His lips slammed down on hers, stopping her tirade on her feelings toward the other species with finesse. His tongue dove in, surging her desires that were simmering all evening snuggling on the couch to a full-blown roar ready to go to battle. While she wanted to get it on and show him with her body how much she loved him, since the words didn't seem to be enough, she knew they shouldn't. Not with him still recovering from two gunshot wounds. He should know better. One of them had to be the sane party here, and she figured it had to be her.

Yet, when she tried to break the kiss, he didn't let her. His hold on her strengthened as did the kiss. His lips burning, searing his touch directly upon hers. So not only would she know the touch of his lips, everyone else would know as well.

She was his.

From that knowledge, letting it really sink in what he was trying to tell her without words, she let it go. She surrendered to the kiss, pouring her heart and soul into it. The kiss went from manic and frenzied to slow and tender within seconds as if her yielding to him was all he had wanted.

"I love you, too," he whispered against her lips. "So much it scares the shit out of me. I want this to work, but I don't—"

Arguing by silencing the other with a deep, intense kiss could be a new way to fight with each other. She could get down with that strategy. If he could interrupt her that way, then reciprocating was fair play, blocking out his idiotic words. They could make this work if they made the effort. That's all they needed. The willingness to put forth the effort.

"Say you love me again and leave it at that." She had moved her hands from lightly holding his sides to cupping his cheeks. His lips weren't going to escape if she needed to silence him once more.

"I love you."

For once, he didn't argue with her. He followed her directions to the T. She'd take the win.

"To make things easier, I've decided I'm moving to MN. I'm ready for a change."

She let her hands fall when he leaned away. His forlorn expression foretold he was most likely going to try and talk her out of that.

"I was the one who originally said I wanted to move. Wouldn't it make more sense for me to move to New York?"

Maybe, but she was deliriously excited that they were arguing about something so monumental.

"Do you want to live in New York City? Can you handle

the city life?"

Because she couldn't picture him enjoying it. At all. He didn't even like small parties, keeping to himself, sitting in his own little corner. New York City would be in his face all day, every day.

He shrugged, looking apprehensive about it.

"I can handle anything as long as I have you."

His words speared her heart with such love she almost couldn't handle it. Hearing him say something like that felt so surreal. She hadn't been sure he'd express his true feelings, and for him to continue to do so was everything.

The tears she had wanted to hold back let loose. Silently and slowly, but down nonetheless.

"Why are you crying? Please don't cry," Dare whispered as his thumbs brushed the tears away. "I'll agree to anything if you stop."

"You already can't say no to me. Tears shouldn't make a difference."

"Well, they do. So knock it off." He said it with such a firm tone and stern look it only made her giggle. It also helped to clear them away.

"I wasn't sure how this conversation would go, and it's been better than anything I imagined. I know you said you wanted to move, but do you?"

"I don't know. I honestly don't know anymore."

"Well, nothing has to be decided right this second."

Then his lips were covering hers, and if things progressed further than that, she wasn't going to complain. The man she loved was holding onto her as if he never wanted to let go, and she couldn't be happier. As he had told her he couldn't say no to her, she was learning she couldn't say no to him either.

Love was the most finicky thing.

19

Sweat rolled down his back, coating his armpits. His heart rate was beating like crazy, his breathing erratic. His legs were sore—a good kind of sore. And his back, for the first time in weeks, didn't hurt. Maybe a small ache lingered if he moved or twisted a certain way, but nothing where he'd have to take some pain medication. Though he was tired as shit, he felt great.

He caught the basketball and dribbled it, deciding what his next move would be.

"Come on, old man. You ready to give up?"

Dare eyed Nicholas with his *signature glare* as most of the boys at the center liked to call it. In reality, he wasn't annoyed or mad or whatever the hell they thought. It was simply the expression he used when contemplating something. He couldn't help it that it looked like he was ready to bite someone's head off. But the nice thing about his facial expressions was it helped the boys warm up to him a lot faster than they did for any other counselor at the place.

Not that he'd call himself a counselor. Nor did the community center where he started working three short weeks ago. He was considered a 'peer advocate.' He didn't like the title, but he wasn't going to argue with it because it was a paying job and something he was passionate about. He hadn't realized how passionate until Jayden came into his life.

This was the same center Jayden came to on occasion. Since Dare had started, he came every day. Played with the other kids and stayed out of trouble. He had even chatted with one of the counselors a few times, trying to sort out his feelings and get him started on the right path to finishing high school. Maybe even trying out college, but Jayden was still not on board with the idea. Dare was proud of Jayden for taking that first step into a good future. Dare knew it scared the shit out of Jayden to even think about it. He had never thought he'd do anything but work for Rick and slum his way through life on the wrong side of the tracks.

They had kids of all ages show up for support or a safe place to be for a short time. Dare tried to engage with the older ones—fourteen to eighteen—most of the time. Considering that was a pivotal moment in his life when he needed someone to help him out, he thought it was the best fit for him. He wished he'd had something like this to keep him on the straight and narrow. To show him that his life didn't have to be shitty. That he had a support system when he should've had one with his parents. Maybe if he had had something like this in his life, he wouldn't have messed around with drugs. Maybe he would've never been high and driving in a rainstorm. Maybe he wouldn't have crashed the car and killed his parents.

So many maybes he couldn't find the answer to—for him, anyway. But he was here to change that for other kids that might pave the same path.

He darted right, dribbling the ball hard. Instead of

taking a shot, he passed the ball to Darnel, who stood wide open and shot the ball with a wonderful swish through the net for three points.

"I never give up, Nicholas. And when I know I don't have a good shot, I rely on my teammate." Dare winked, which garnered an eye roll from Nicholas.

The kid had been a tough one to crack. He didn't give in easily about anything, had a bad attitude most of the time, and could get down and dirty when they played basketball. But Dare wasn't giving up on him. He might've been talking about the game, but he had meant in general. Nicholas knew it.

"We won!" Darnel high-fived Dare, smiling and whooping loudly. Nicholas scowled, grabbed his water bottle, and stalked off the court. Nicholas generally didn't lose, and he wasn't a graceful loser either, not if the expletives that came out of his mouth were any indication.

Darnel was fourteen, young and naive about most things, but smart enough to know when to leave his house when his dad drank. His mom worked two jobs to make ends meet, and all his dad did was drink, smoke, and gamble the money away. When he really got on a bender, it was better not to be around the guy. Dare had given Darnel his number, telling him to never hesitate to call him if he needed anything. Dare wouldn't hesitate to show his asshole dad a little of his own medicine. Not that he wanted to resort to that. It would most likely send his ass back to prison, but if it came down to it, defending a little boy who couldn't defend himself, he'd do it. He'd knock the guy on his ass so fast, he wouldn't see it coming.

Nicholas was seventeen, failing school, and getting into trouble more often than not. He only showed up at the center because his latest arrest put him in front of a judge that said he had to for therapy sessions if he didn't want to see the inside of a jail cell. While Nicholas hadn't been too cooperative with the therapist yet, he was here. He played basketball. For those brief moments in time, he wasn't getting into trouble. Dare knew he wasn't the therapist, wasn't even close to being qualified to give advice like one, but he liked the progress he was seeing with Nicholas. It was tiny—very tiny—progress, but there, nonetheless.

He shared in Darnel's excitement about winning and then grabbed the towel he brought and wiped the sweat off his face and neck. Once finished, he took a long drink of water. Another twenty minutes or so and it'd be time to clock out and head home. While he enjoyed his days at the center hanging out with the kids, he enjoyed his evenings even more spending the nights with the woman he loved.

After much deliberation, making a pros and cons list—insisted by Julie—they had decided she'd move to MN. She put in a transfer to the Minneapolis office within the FBI and was approved a week later. Dare had been shocked, even more surprised when she told him they were aware she was dating him—and didn't appear to have a problem with it. Or so she said. He didn't press the matter because, in the end, he didn't give a shit what they thought. He wasn't a bad guy, and he'd prove it to her for the rest of his life.

The past month had been busy with helping Julie pack, move, unpack, get settled in the house, and start a new job. That didn't count healing from his wounds, seeing the doctor a few times, and his sister getting on his last nerve that he needed to take things slowly. He didn't know how many times she hollered at him for lifting boxes. His woman was moving in and he was going to help with that, damn it.

Sure, everyone else had been there, too, and he didn't need to lift anything, but he had wanted to. Feeling helpless was not something he enjoyed, especially when it came to Julie.

The end of his shift went quickly, and he was packing up the backpack he carried with him every day. He liked to be prepared to play basketball or any other games some of the boys liked to do, and of course, Julie packed him a lunch for work every day. Something she didn't have to do, but he liked the gesture so much he couldn't find it in him to tell her he could handle it himself. Having someone else take care of him was foreign. It felt odd at times, like he didn't deserve it. But he was coming to realize he did deserve it, and letting someone else take control over some things was nice.

He threw the backpack strap over his shoulder, said good-bye to a few co-workers, and headed out the door. Unfortunately, the community center was in St. Cloud, a little too far for him to walk to and from every day. Driving still made him nervous, and he didn't foresee that changing any time soon. He was making progress with some things in his life, but not all. So he was forced to take the bus, which wasn't terrible. Some days Deja drove him, but most of the time, he declined because his sister shouldn't have to go out of her way for him. Not that she would complain about it.

Nicholas was sitting on a ledge around the corner from the center, smoking a cigarette, looking bored. As Dare strolled past him, he swiped the cigarette from his mouth, threw it to the ground, and snuffed it out.

"What the hell, dude!"

"Have a good night, Nicholas." Dare kept walking toward the bus stop that was still a block away.

Nicholas knew he wasn't supposed to be smoking, not until he was eighteen, so Dare didn't find it necessary to explain why he did what he did. A few weeks ago, he wouldn't have cared what any kid did because he wasn't the kid's dad. But someone had to care. Nicholas's mom was sitting on drug charges, and his dad didn't give him the time of day. Dare wouldn't be surprised if his dad got locked up for drugs soon, too, since he dealt them. So Nicholas's parents weren't doing any caring. They definitely weren't doing the parenting thing right either. Just like his parents failed him. Maybe he'd never get through to Nicholas. Maybe he'd only antagonize the kid until he retaliated in the wrong way.

"Whatever, old man. I'm gonna school you tomorrow in basketball! Get your beauty sleep!"

Dare turned around, walking backward, and grinned. "Can't wait. You're gonna be wearing the loser sign again tomorrow." Dare winked and formed his fingers into an 'L' against his forehead. Then turned back around, smiling even wider.

And maybe he was making a small, tiny difference with the kid. He'd never shown up to the center two days in a row. That was progress.

While the bus route in St. Cloud didn't take him all the way to St. Joe, it got him close enough where it wasn't as long of a drive for someone to pick him up. Sometimes Deja or Sophie picked him up, Jayden on occasion when he insisted he didn't have anything else to do. The kid hung around him a lot, and Dare wasn't going to complain. It meant he was staying out of trouble. Some days, Jayden even brought him straight home from the Center. While he hated relying on others to get him home, there wasn't anything he could do about it. Nothing except try to get his license, and he was not ready for that.

Today, Gabe met him at the bus stop, which surprised Dare, because he thought it was going to be his sister.

"How's it going? Thanks for the ride, man," Dare said as he slid into the passenger seat.

"Good. Happy to be off work and relax. Olivia wants to do some baby shopping this weekend. I'm a mixture of terrified and excited. How am I supposed to know the right crib to buy and what diapers are good enough?"

Dare chuckled. "That's why Olivia is going with you. You guys can muddle through it together." Then his brows drew low, eyeing Gabe critically. "We're not making a pit stop to chat about this more, are we?"

Like the last time they had one little drink that turned into way too many, so many his head hurt for days after.

Laughter floated between them. "I'm not that terrified of it, but one drink couldn't hurt. Olivia won't be home for a while. Want to swing by my place for one?"

Dare thought about it for a moment. It was his turn to start supper so it'd be ready when Julie got home from the Cities. Her days were much longer than his, having to drive an hour and a half to the Cities there and back every day. There wasn't much she could do about it since that's where the FBI field office was, unless she wanted to find a new job. In the few short weeks she'd been here, it had crossed her mind a few times. That maybe she was ready for more change than a simple move. A new career, too. Which also made him think her job was making waves because she was with him, though she swore that wasn't the case. They had only talked—argued, more like it—about it once. Once had been plenty for him. If she insisted it wasn't a big deal, he'd stop making it into a big deal.

"Yeah, a drink sounds nice."

He and Julie took turns every week making dinner, but it wouldn't hurt if he took the easy way out tonight and ordered pizza in lieu of cooking. That woman could eat, and he loved that she wasn't shy about food. Pizza was one of her favorites, though she said nothing beat a good New York slice.

Gabe pulled into his driveway a few minutes later, and Dare realized he didn't ask an important question. He followed Gabe up the walkway to the front door.

"Hey, how come Deja didn't pick me up? She didn't tell me you were."

Gabe's cheeks flushed red, and Dare knew right away something was up. "Umm...you know, she had a thing come up."

"Dude, you are a terrible liar. What's going on?"

A large breath released by Gabe, yet his cheeks were still tinted a vibrant red. "It wasn't my idea. I do as I'm told."

Then he swung open the door and walked inside. Dare was forced to follow and groaned when everyone yelled, "Happy Birthday!"

Ugh.

He hated celebrating his birthday. His sister would pay for this.

JULIE'S SMILE stayed plastered on her face, but her heart beat wildly when she saw the panic and horror on Dare's face. Deja had warned her Dare wouldn't be a fan of a birthday party, but she couldn't ignore the fact they had never celebrated their birthday with a party. Things like that didn't happen in their childhood, and the thought made Julie sad and determined to rectify it.

Dare accepted personal 'happy birthdays' from everyone as he walked farther into the room. While he wasn't unpleasant with anyone, she could tell it was taking a lot of effort on his part to keep his anger in check.

When he finally got to her, there was no smile detected and his vivid-blue eyes blazed with irritation.

"My sister is in so much trouble. I should've told Gabe no to the drink and went home to cook us supper." He leaned in and kissed her.

The simple touch relieved her that he wasn't upset at her —but only because he thought it was his sister's idea. She hated to turn that anger at herself, but she couldn't let Deja take the blame.

"Gabe would've gotten you here no matter what. It was his job to do so."

Dare wrapped his arms around her and stole another kiss. "What do you think about slipping out the back door?"

She caressed his cheek. "We can't and you know it. You didn't even tell me it was your birthday today."

Because she knew he had a rough childhood and some things were hard to talk about, she didn't take it personally that he hadn't told her.

"It's not a big deal. It's another day. Another year older. So what?"

"How much do you love me?"

Dare frowned, his brows puckering. "Why?"

"Answer the question."

"Why should I? That was a serious conversation switch."

"A little, a lot, so-so? It's important to know."

"Since when are you so damn insecure about how I feel about you?" Dare's fingers tightened on her back, which gave her hope. He wasn't pushing her away, and perhaps he wouldn't when she confessed.

"Sometimes a woman likes to hear it."

"So does a guy." She didn't think it was possible, but his

expression fell even further into melancholy. "This was your idea, not Deja's."

He hadn't let go of her yet, but to prevent him from pulling away if he decided to do so, she strengthened the hold on his shirt. "She warned me, but I wanted to do something special for you. You deserve it." She inhaled deeply and released it before continuing. "Because I love you so much. I want to show you in as many ways as I can. Now, how much do you love me?"

He remained silent for a beat, his expression not changing an inch. "I love you." Then his lips curved into a devious grin. "So much that I'm only going to spank you a few times instead of so many you'd lose count."

Her erratic heartbeat calmed down to a slow gallop. "That's my punishment? A spanking?"

"That's just the tip of the iceberg. You're in serious trouble when we get home."

She leaned in closer, brushing her body as close to his as she could get, then pressed her lips to his. "I'll take the punishment...as long as you open your presents with a tiny smile on your face. Pretend you're enjoying the party."

"For each smile, I get to spank you."

Julie giggled, loving the playful part of him coming out instead of rage. Each new day was a new experience for them, learning things about each other. She loved every moment.

"Deal." Then her lips split into their own devilish smile. "For each spank you deliver, I get to moan so loudly the neighbors hear."

Dare rolled his eyes, chuckling. "You're going to give the old guy next to us a heart attack. He can't handle things like that."

"It also embarrasses you. I love how your cheeks get red

when we chat with him and he insinuates he can hear our extracurricular activities sometimes."

"I do not blush. Or get embarrassed."

Julie brushed her lips with his. "Keep telling yourself that. But it's so adorable." Then her tone turned serious. "I'm sorry. I should've heeded Deja's warnings. I didn't mean to upset you. I wanted you to have what you should've had growing up."

Dare was silent again. She had come to find he did that when he was trying to find the right words, not wanting to say the wrong thing.

"I made progress with Nicholas today. Schooled him finally in a game of basketball with Darnel's help. He insists on a rematch tomorrow. He's never come two days in a row."

"That's wonderful news. I'm so happy for you. I know you've been wanting to get through to him. Keep at it. You'll get all the way there with him."

Dare nodded. "I want to help in a way I never got. I get why you threw me a birthday party. While it makes me uncomfortable, I get it. I can't be mad at the why of it. But don't do it next year."

"Let's worry about next year later."

"Julie..." he said in a warning tone.

"Baby steps, Dare Bear. Baby steps."

"I don't know about that nickname."

She smiled. "Pick your battle. Birthday party talk or Dare Bear. Gonna only win one."

Dare sighed, then twisted his head toward Emmett and Austin, who were chatting. Then he looked at her. "So more than just family was invited. They set up a blowup pool in the backyard for the kids."

"Yes," she said hesitantly, not liking the sly twinkling in his eyes. Despite it being early August, some nights could get cooler than others. Tonight happened to be a cooler night, but little Jimmy enjoyed the water.

"Well, sweetheart, it's time for you to pick your battle."

"What are my options? Because mine we're clear."

Dare made the buzzer sound indicating she picked the wrong answer. "I love you." Then he picked her up and slung her over his shoulder.

"Dare! Put me down. Your back can't handle it."

He walked through the living room toward the kitchen, smiling and saying hi to people as he passed them.

"Dare! Seriously, this isn't good for your back."

He swatted her ass. "I can handle it. It barely hurts anymore."

"Which means it still does hurt. Put me down."

"You wanted to argue. I'm arguing back."

"This is not arguing." Julie's eyes widened when they walked through the sliding doors to the backyard. "Don't you dare. Don't do it!"

"You wanted to know how much I love you. So, so much, sweetheart."

Then he dropped her into the pool, soaking her to the bone. Little Jimmy was sitting in the pool splashing, getting her even wetter.

Dare stood to the side laughing, the joy prominent on his face. Julie couldn't find an ounce of anger at being thrown in the pool because he was enjoying himself instead of sulking in his own little corner.

That was progress.

EPILOGUE

9 MONTHS LATER

He slid a finger between the tight collar of his shirt and neck, groaning when nothing moved an inch. Ethan swiped at his hand, wiggling a finger in his face.

"You can't mess with the bow. If Ava has to come in here again to fix it," Ethan cocked a brow, "for the fourth time, she will not be happy."

Dare scowled at him. "So? It's making me itch."

Laughter coated the air. "Literally or figuratively? You're not even the one getting married today. I am." Ethan blew out a breath and his finger started to rise as if he were about to try and adjust his bowtie. But he stopped, grinning. "I can't wait."

"You sure?"

Ethan rolled his eyes. "Yes, dude, I'm sure. What is this nervousness? Do you really hate it that much you have to stand as my best man? You did so well planning the bachelor party and everything else."

Only because Emmett and Gabe helped. He would've never been able to do that on his own. He knew those two enjoyed helping as well.

"No. Hell, no." The last thing Dare wanted was Ethan thinking that kind of shit. He was honored that Ethan asked him to be his best man. He hadn't expressed it correctly nine months ago. Okay, he didn't jump for joy back then. He even told him no because he thought running away from everything that mattered was better than meeting it all head-on.

He knew better now.

Julie helped him see the beauty in life every single day. Waking up next to her kept him sane when on some days he felt like he was losing his mind. From guilt. From regret. From anger. Without her, he'd still be moping and feeling sorry for himself.

"Well, what is it then? You can tell me."

And ruin his day. Well, not ruin his day, but take some of the shine off it? No. Dare wasn't that kind of best man—or friend. The engagement ring burning a hole in his pocket would stay where it was—a secret. What was one more day when it had been in his pocket for the past month. One of these days he'd get the nerve to ask Julie to marry him.

"It's nothing. I'm happy for you, you know that. I hate eyes on me. It's all good. The ceremony will fly by, and you'll be a married man."

Ethan released another breath and nodded, taking his words as the truth. They were, but not the whole truth. Some things were better left unsaid.

"Yo, you ready, bro?" Emmett asked, popping his head in through the doorway. "It's about that time."

"Yep. Let's do this." Ethan clapped him on the back and headed out of the room first.

Dare followed, sweating the moment they peered at the congregation waiting patiently in their seats.

"That's a lot of people."

Ethan chuckled. "You're going to do fine. Now knock it off. You're supposed to be giving me courage, not the other way around."

This was true. Talk about failing at his best man duties.

"You look great and Penelope is a lucky lady. You got this. There. How was that?"

"Better, but it needs some work." Ethan blew out another breath. "I'll see you at the altar." Then Ethan walked down the aisle, taking his position at the front of the church.

Dare waited with Emmett and Gabe for the ladies to arrive so they could get this show on the road. When Penelope finally walked into the area dressed in a white wedding dress that hugged her curves, his heart settled down. This wasn't about him. Nobody would be staring at him, not when Penelope looked downright gorgeous and Ethan looked like a prince in his suit. This was their day and they would shine.

Penelope had asked three of her friends from high school who she was still close with to be in her wedding party. Gabe walked down first, followed by Emmett, and Dare went next, holding onto the arm of Bethany, the maid of honor. He could feel her shaking as they made the trek down the aisle. He squeezed her arm and whispered, "I got you. This is a piece of cake."

That garnered a tiny chuckle, and after two more steps, the shakes were gone. He might not be a big talker, especially at big gatherings, but he could find the words when they were most needed.

When it was Penelope's turn to walk down the aisle, he

had to step in again and whisper words of encouragement—real ones this time—to Ethan whose hands were trembling. Again, he found the right words, and the trembling disappeared.

The ceremony passed in a blur. Besides watching Ethan profess his love to Penelope, Dare's eyes sought out Julie a few times, to calm himself from the nerves. Every time he made eye contact, it did the trick. He couldn't have been happier once the ceremony finished and they had finally arrived at the reception hall.

Everything was wonderful, from the twinkling lights and garland hanging from the ceiling to the open bar that called his name. He took a seat next to Julie after delivering her a drink and, for the first time that day, relaxed.

"You look so handsome. I can't wait to get you home and do very dirty, naughty things with you," Julie whispered in his ear. She was leaning to the side as she spoke, making him instantly hard. His woman should know better than to say such things. It didn't take much for him to get hot for her, and she knew it. They were not shy about touching each other, and definitely not shy about where they might happen to be either. That was something that surprised him the first time they had quick, dirty sex behind the barn at Ava's house. Julie had initiated it, and he couldn't say no to her—ever.

He twirled a strand of hair that hung near her cheek. "You know I can—and will—find a closet or something in this joint. I'm not waiting until home. Not after that statement."

The devilish twinkle in her eyes said she wasn't opposed to that idea and it was her intent all along. The woman knew how to play him.

He stood up and grabbed her hand. "Why wait? Come on."

Julie gasped, surprised. "Dare, we should wait until after the meal and speeches and everyone is very, very drunk."

"Where's the fun in that?"

She looked terrified at the prospect, but she also didn't fight him as he weaved them through the crowd and out of the ballroom.

That was the thing about her. She constantly surprised him. Like when she told him right before Christmas she wanted a change. To quit the FBI. The drive sucked and she hated being away from home as much as she was. Yes, the drive was long and terrible, but it was the cases that pulled her away days at a time that was even worse. There was a two-week stretch in October he didn't see her at all. So she quit, just like that. Of course, she'd had a backup plan before doing the deed, and two days later, she became a detective at the same police department Ava worked at. It wasn't a large department, and it also wasn't a large town, she didn't get near as many cases as she did working for the FBI. The drive was short, and she was home every night with him now. The best part, she seemed happier. More carefree and less stressed. Though she never admitted it, he thought one of the main reasons she quit the FBI was because they didn't approve of her being with him. The police department she worked at now didn't mind. He knew because the chief of police was an honorary uncle to the McCords and he'd never been anything but nice and friendly with him.

After walking down a short hall and opening and closing a few doors, he found a small room with a table and a few chairs. Most likely a conference room of some kind.

He shut the door, clicked the lock, and pushed her

against the wall, kissing her as if his life depended upon it. She dove in, tangling tongues, grabbing his ass, and pulling him closer. Light moans filled the room.

"You gotta be quiet, sweetheart. No need to alert everyone," he whispered against her lips.

"I can't help it. I thought you were crazy to do this, and now all I want is you inside me." Her hands ran across his ass to his hips and to the front of his pants, but then she paused and swiped a hand across his right side again. "What is in your pocket?"

"It's nothing." He gripped her wrist, holding tight before she could slide her hand inside. Of all the days for him to put the ring in his pocket, he had to pick today. There were a few other times he had it on him, thinking he'd pop the question, but then ultimately chickened out. He wasn't sure why he grabbed it today other than it was an impulse. Nothing but wedding crap had been on his mind and his hand just reached for it.

She leaned away, as best as she could trapped between him and the door. "Seriously, what is it? You wouldn't be gripping my wrist in a death grip if it wasn't something."

His heart started to hammer, to the point it felt like it'd jump right out of his chest. "Tomorrow. I'll tell you tomorrow what it is."

"You'll tell me now."

"Or what?" he asked with a sly grin, grinding into her. "You know how hot and bothered I get when we argue."

Her free hand reached between them and pressed against his chest, right over his heart. "I can feel how nervous you are about whatever is in your pocket. It's okay. Tell me."

Then it hit him.

"You already know what it is."

She bit her bottom lip, the truth shimmering in her eyes. "I might've seen you put a box of some sort in your pocket this morning. Is it what I think it is?"

"And if it is, what do you think about it?"

"Nope, mister, that's not how it works. You want to know, you have to do it the right way."

Of course he did. When did she ever make anything easy on him?

He let go of her wrist, and she moved her hand away, putting the situation entirely into his hands. His heart still pounded erratically, but the quiet calm in her eyes helped to settle some of his nerves.

His hand slid inside his pocket and then drew out the black velvet box. The lid opened and a one-carat, princess-cut diamond stared back at her.

A low gasp left her lips as her eyes shimmered with unshed tears.

"When I got out of prison, I didn't expect much. I didn't even expect to be in my sister's life. I thought it'd be better if I wasn't around."

"Oh, Dare..." Julie reached up and caressed his cheek.

"I'm glad she didn't give up on me. I'm even more glad I didn't give up on myself. I'm pretty sure I would've if you hadn't walked into my life. You make everything so much better, so much brighter. I know I don't deserve you, and nothing you say will change my mind about that. But I want to be deserving of you. I will spend the rest of my life trying to do that. If you'll have me. Julie, will you be my wife?"

She opened her mouth to speak and nothing came out. A lone tear sliding down her cheek spoke first. "You would've had me at a simple 'will you marry me' but this version is way better. Yes, of course, I will. I look forward to arguing with you all the time about how much you deserve everything and more."

"You'll never win," he countered because he couldn't help himself. She giggled with him, then he closed the box and put it back into his pocket.

"Hey!" Her mouth dropped open. "You're supposed to put it on my finger, not back in your pocket."

"And tomorrow I will. Like I said before, today is Ethan's day, and I don't want to take that away from him."

She nodded, not arguing about that. "First thing tomorrow. Ring on my finger."

"So demanding...but anything for you."

Then he sealed his words with a kiss and proceeded to love his woman against the door, moans and all filling the air.

Don't miss the rest of the books in this sweet, heartwarming series!

PROTECTING YOU
TRUST IN LOVE
DESERVING YOU
ALWAYS KIND OF LOVE
FINDING YOU

FOR ZANE & AVA'S STORY
PROTECTING YOU
A MCCORD FAMILY NOVEL - BOOK 1

He wanted to hate her. He just might fall in love instead.

Zane McCord might not say it often, but he loves his brothers no matter what, even when he's acting like a jerk, and he knows it. When his brother Jimmy dies with tension hanging between them, he turns all his hatred to the woman who deserves it—Ava Rainer, the one responsible for his death. He refuses to like her. He won't help her. He wants her nowhere near him. Except she's suddenly on his farm and sneaking her way into his heart with her own pain. The guilt is eating him alive, but maybe...just maybe...they can heal together.

For Austin & Sophie's Story
Trust in Love
A McCord Family Novel - Book 2

He didn't want to fall in love. And then he met her.

Austin McCord has always enjoyed women...to an extent. He's all about the fun. Anything beyond that, not so much. Until he meets his neighbor Sophie. He knows he can't touch her—she has marriage written all over. Except temptation overwhelms him every time he sees her beautiful angelic face. It doesn't matter. Because whenever he tries to take two steps toward her, she keeps taking three steps back. Someone hurt her, that's obvious. For the first time, he's thinking a happily ever after sounds nice. Now his only obstacle is convincing her of the same thing, and keeping her safe before her past tears her apart.

FOR EMMETT & DEJA'S STORY
DESERVING YOU
A MCCORD FAMILY NOVEL - BOOK 3

She doesn't think she's worthy of his love. He'll prove her wrong.

Emmett McCord has wanted Deja since the moment he met her, despite how she came into their lives. It didn't take long for him, and the family, to forgive her and see just what kind of woman she is. Strong. Determined. Remorseful. Faithful to a fault. He wants to declare his feelings, but he knows she'll resist him. He can't risk losing her friendship. When her brother walks back into her life, causing her pain, he's done keeping his feelings to himself. He wants her, and she'll just have to get used to it.

For Ethan & Penelope's Story
ALWAYS KIND OF LOVE
A McCORD FAMILY NOVEL - BOOK 4

He wanted to forget her. But he can't deny his love.

The last thing Ethan McCord wants to deal with is his old high school flame, even though his desire for her hasn't diminished. Battling the burning blazes and an arsonist bent on destruction is nothing compared to fighting the temptation to rekindle the love he always wanted.

NOTE: THIS STORY WAS PREVIOUSLY A PART OF THE RISKING EVERYTHING CHARITY ANTHOLOGY.

FOR GABE & OLIVIA'S STORY
FINDING YOU
A McCORD FAMILY NOVEL - BOOK 5

What happens in Vegas doesn't always stay in Vegas. One wild mishap could be the best thing that ever happened to him.

Being shy makes it hard for Gabe McCord to talk to women, but throw in a fun, wild night of drinking and it's not so hard. Until he learns he didn't just wake up next to a gorgeous woman—he married her. Nine months later and he's still trying to find her...when she accidentally finds him.

Olivia Brenson is the new arson investigator in town trying to find the person responsible for multiple fires, the latest one which almost took a life. When she learns married—because neither remembered their nuptials—Gabe finds himself on another fun adventure. She wants to stay married for a short time to keep her overprotective, demanding father off her back. He doesn't protest as it gives him a chance to prove he isn't always the shy guy. But if he's not careful, he might lose more than just his reserved tendencies. He'll lose his heart along the way. Because he's finding Olivia is the woman he never knew he needed in his life.

ABOUT THE AUTHOR

I'm a *USA Today* Bestselling Author that loves to write sweet contemporary romance and romantic suspense novels, although I am partial to romantic suspense. Honestly, I love anything that has to do with romance. As long as there's a happy ending, I'm a happy camper. And insta-love...yes, please! I love baseball (Go Twins!) and creating awesome crafts. I graduated with a Bachelor's Degree in Criminal Justice, working in that field for several years before I became a stay-at-home mom. I have a few more amazing stories in the works. If you would like to connect with me or see important news, head to my website at http://www.a-mandasiegrist.com. Thanks for reading!

Lightning Source UK Ltd.
Milton Keynes UK
UKHW020941020922
408232UK00001B/150

9 781955 886321